SCENES FROM A POISONER'S LIFE

Nigel Williams was born in Cheshire in 1948, educated at Highgate School and Oriel College, Oxford, and is married with three children. He is the author of TV and stage plays and of several novels, including the bestselling Wimbledon trilogy: *The Wimbledon Poisoner*, *They Came From SW19* and *East of Wimbledon*.

Scenes from a Poisoner's Life

NIGEL WILLIAMS

faber and faber

LONDON · BOSTON

for Suzan

First published in 1994
by Faber and Faber Limited
3 Queen Square London WC1N 3AU
This paperback edition first published 1995

Phototypeset by Intype, London
Printed in England by Clays Ltd, St Ives plc

© Nigel Williams, 1994

Nigel Williams is hereby identified as author of this work
in accordance with Section 77 of the Copyright,
Designs and Patents Act 1988

'Ring Out the Old, Ring In the Bastards' (under the title
'I Will Be Nicer') and 'The Right Set' were first
commissioned for Radio 4's *Short Stories* programme

A CIP record for this book is available
from the British Library

ISBN 0-571-17498-1

2 4 6 8 10 9 7 5 3 1

Contents

Ring Out the Old, Ring In the Bastards

1   I WILL BE NICER TO MY WIFE.

HENRY FARR drew a line under the first of his resolutions. Then, after some thought, he drew another line straight through the middle of it.

He stared out at the bleak, winter garden. One of the reasons he had taken two weeks away from the solicitors for whom he worked had been, ostensibly, 'so that he could get the garden into shape'. Elinor was always talking about getting the garden into shape. Henry had, it is true, spent a lot more time looking at it than he usually did. But so far, at any rate, he had resisted the temptation to get out there with the Roxburgh fork and spade that his wife and daughter had bought him for Christmas.

Oh well. Maybe just looking at the uneven grass, the long-dead roses and the gnarled apple tree was having some effect on them.

His eye wandered further down the page.

2   I WILL BE NICER TO MY DAUGHTER.

This too was clearly not going to be possible. After the way Maisie Farr had behaved on Boxing Night, there was a strong case for chaining her up in the garden shed for the next twelve months. Henry could still not believe his daughter had reached the age of fifteen. Neither could he recall doing anything to prepare her for reaching such an advanced age.

He thought about his daughter. Why was her face the shape of a ripe pear? Why did her mousy hair hang down around her cheeks in greasy curls? Why was she beginning to look like her father, a man who, in his schooldays, was known as the Bad-Tempered Blob? He crossed out the second of his pledges and then inked out the words carefully so that not a trace of the sentence should be visible. It was only four or five days since he had made his New Year resolutions. As he forgot almost everything these days, he had decided to keep them in his desk

1

drawer. But, already, they seemed more like a list of lost causes than anything else. The second sheet of paper was no better.

3   I WILL NOT BE SO FAT.
4   I WILL CURB MY ANGER.
5   I WILL NOT DRINK BEFORE 7.30 P.M.
6   I WILL NOT SHOUT AT THE TELEVISION.
7   I WILL NOT SHOUT AT OTHER ROAD USERS.

Henry picked up the sheet of paper, screwed it into a small ball and hurled it in the direction of the waste-paper basket. There seemed little point in bothering to live through 1994 if one was not going to be allowed to do any of these things. In the middle of the next sheet of paper were the words:

8   I WILL

Even the crazily optimistic swine he had been last week had not been able to complete this one. Before he dared look at sheet three he had better get some more plausible, enforceable resolutions into draft form. Something so bland and vague that even Henry Farr could live up to it. The sort of thing they churned out by the yard at the UN.

He grabbed a piece of scrap paper and scribbled:

1   I WILL GIVE AN UNSPECIFIED AMOUNT TO CHARITY.

He looked at this. It seemed to suggest that he was about to sell the house and donate the proceeds to Greenpeace. He scratched out the word *unspecified* and put *reasonable* in its place. Then he crossed out *reasonable* and put *small*. Charities were all overstaffed, corrupt, inefficient companies designed only to advance the careers of their employees. He crossed out *small* and inserted the word *perhaps* at the start of the sentence. Then he took a new sheet of paper and wrote:

NEW YEAR RESOLUTIONS

1   I WILL TRY TO BE BETTER.

That left him enough scope. Henry got up and walked to the lavatory. These days it was the only place he felt safe.

He seemed to be spending his holiday shuffling between his study and the lavatory. The last time he had been ordered out into the garden, he had told Elinor that he was writing a novel. If things got any worse he might actually start one.

He really ought to get on with the *Complete History of Wimbledon*. He needed an alibi. Elinor would be back soon from Sainsbury's, saying things like 'I need a strong pair of hands.'

Once inside the lavatory he lost enthusiasm for the project. It seemed, suddenly, as colossal an undertaking as any of his New Year resolutions. This did not stop him from removing his trousers and sitting, for several moments, with his head in his hands. He looked around for the *Good Hotel Guide*, but it was not in its usual position. Anyway, today he did not feel like looking at what was available, in the bed-and-breakfast line, in eastern Turkey. He hoisted his trousers past his knees and, holding them up by the belt, crept back up to the small room overlooking the garden.

When he turned over the final sheet of his resolutions he remembered that that was when he had given up. It was blank. Apart, that is, from nine words, scrawled across the middle of the page in capital letters. He did not recognize the handwriting but was immediately sure that it was not his. And he certainly had no recollection of writing it or anything like it. It read:

I WILL TRY NOT TO KILL ANY MORE PEOPLE.

If he was looking for a resolution, mind you, this wouldn't be a bad one. Some six or seven years ago, while trying, unsuccessfully, to murder his wife, he had very nearly poisoned one of his closest friends. It wasn't something he had ever discussed with anyone. As far as he was aware, he was the only living person who knew. It was not the kind of thing he wished to become public knowledge.

Was someone trying to tell him something?

He crept out on to the landing and looked down the stairs.

Maisie came out of the kitchen, carrying a plate of digestive biscuits, a bowl of scrambled eggs and two cans of Strongbow cider. Maisie ate more or less continuously. She would occasionally show signs of flagging during Sunday lunch, but, after a choc bar or two, she would pick herself up off the floor and get right back into the roast beef.

It couldn't be Maisie. She was too young to have suspected anything. Unless it was a confession. Maisie was quite capable of killing someone (all the Farr family were, in Henry's view, more or less permanently on the verge of homicide), but even if she had, she would never tell him. She never told him where she was going for the evening, what class she was in or why she was expected to get a D in GCSE maths.

As usual she was wearing green Doc Marten boots, ripped jeans and the kind of shirt usually seen on lumberjacks or American construction workers used to sub-zero temperatures.

She went through to the television room. Henry heard a familiar signature tune. His daughter watched most episodes of *Neighbours* six or seven times, cheering, insulting and offering advice to the principal characters each time she watched it. As she left the hall there was a thump and a clatter from the front room. Then the angry, tireless sound of a Hoover started.

Sheila. It was Sheila. Sheila was on to him.

Sheila had only been cleaning for them for about six months but, as she spent most of her time cross-questioning Elinor and Henry about their private lives, and as she also worked for at least six more people in the street, she was very well placed to piece together an alarmingly accurate biography of Henry. If she *had* uncovered his secret, she would certainly not go to the police. She would try to make some money out of it. If she charged as much for blackmail as she did for cleaning, it was going to be a tough New Year.

Henry ducked down behind the bannister as Sheila emerged from the front room. She sniffed the air cautiously, like a small animal preparing to cross a dangerous stretch of open ground. Sheila had waist-length, mouse-coloured hair, huge buck teeth and a thin, worried-looking face. She was wearing a T-shirt which read I CAN PUT ON A CONDOM. CAN YOU?

Henry had not really had a chance to observe the way she worked before. Elinor had said to him, in a grim voice, just before she left for the supermarket, 'Watch her timekeeping!' He checked his watch. Sheila was paid for two hours but, during the period she had been working for the Farrs, she had never stayed longer than an hour and fifteen minutes. Yesterday, after her first hour was up, Henry had seen her in the hall, pacing about restlessly like a trapped animal. When she saw him watching her she had called, in a plaintive voice, 'I'm off now!' Which seemed to be the signal for Henry to rush down and shower her with five-pound notes. She wasn't the only cleaner for whom he was responsible. When he thought about it, life at 54 Maple Drive was quite as exhausting as life at the Blackfriars firm of Harris, Harris and Overdene.

He still did not understand why they had two cleaners. But, last September, in addition to Sheila, Elinor had hired a Guatemalan woman called Angelica, who spoke no English but was, apparently, 'brilliant on surfaces'.

Once upon a time Elinor had had a timorous, vaguely liberal attitude to the women who came in to clean her house. These days she was a kind of brutal connoisseur of their best and worst qualities.

'Sheila gets around,' she had said one day, with savage contempt, 'but does she ever do paintwork? Is she scared to go into the lavatory or what? She is *on probation!*'

But she had still not fired the woman. She was still paying the Guatemalan to come in and supplement Sheila's deficiencies. Even though Angelica, too, after a few months had been found guilty of 'half-hearted' polishing and 'a lack of interest in the kitchen floor'. She also threw away almost everything that was not locked away in a cupboard or desk. In November she had thrown away Henry's Access card, a cheque from the Inland Revenue for £25 and a complete set of the works of Virginia Woolf.

'Why don't you get rid of both of them?' Henry had said, just before Christmas.

'And who polishes then?' his wife had snapped. 'Who scrubs and cleans and gets down on her hands and knees and tries to keep all this in order? Eh?'

It was only during his holiday that Henry had discovered that neither woman was supposed to know about the other. Elinor seemed to think that either one might leave if she knew about her opposite number. It was Henry's job to keep them apart.

'I'm off, Mr Farr!'

Pretty soon, thought Henry, as he clumped down the stairs, Elinor would start recruiting more and more cleaners to do more and more specific jobs. There would be a Filipino to do the floors, an Irishwoman to get to work on the windows, a –

'I'm off then, Mr Farr!'

It must be Sheila. She was grinning up at him from the front door. She liked Henry. And yet weren't blackmailers, like poisoners, supposed to have a rapport with what, nowadays, might be termed their clients? There was something leeringly complicit about her smile.

'All right, then?' He tried to make this sound more hearty than usual.

'Not so bad!' Another leer. Was it her? How could you tell such things? She pushed her face into his. 'We're being re-housed!'

'Good!' said Henry, wondering whether Merton Council had any properties abroad. 'Good!'

She leered again as he handed her three five-pound notes. Her manner certainly suggested that she had something on him. Not least the fact that he paid her fifteen pounds for doing absolutely nothing. He opened the door for her.

'I'll see you tomorrow, Mr Farr!'

'Yes indeed, Sheila!'

She was counting the notes carefully. She was, admittedly, shaky on integers above two but, even so, there was something definitely suspicious about the way she was looking through her profits. *Cross my palm with silver*, her manner seemed to suggest, *and you might not find yourself banged up in the Isle of Wight for the next fifteen years!* Henry decided to flush her out into the open.

'And . . . er . . . here's a little something extra for . . .' He winked in a conniving manner. 'You know what!'

She certainly did not raise any objections as he pushed another fiver at her. She probably did this sort of thing regularly. There can't, thought Henry, be many houses in Maple Drive without some kind of sordid secret.

'Thank you, Mr Farr!'

This time her smile was wide enough to be an open challenge to dentistry. Her eyes, wide with something that might have been greed, stayed on his face. 'Goodbye, Mr Farr!'

When she had gone, Henry slammed the door. Then he kicked the wall. After he had kicked the wall, he spat on the floor. He had taken to doing this quite frequently these days. The other day when travelling alone in a lift between the third and fourth floors of the National Car Park in Kingston, he had committed the same offence. It was important to let the swine know you were there.

Just after he had spat on the floor, he heard the squeak of the brakes on the Farr family Volvo. Then there were heavy footsteps outside, an ominous key in the lock and into the hall came his wife carrying three plastic bags and a garden trowel.

'It's in the car!' she said in the grim, determined manner she always affected when speaking of shopping.

'I'll go,' said Henry. Then he doubled up and, at the kind of pitch and volume employed by a lifeboat skipper when issuing commands in a force eight gale, screamed at the closed door of the television room, 'Maisie! Shopping in! We have to get the shopping in!'

Elinor was looking at the floor suspiciously. 'What have you been doing while I was out?'

Henry coughed. 'Nothing my love,' he said. 'I was . . . er . . . thinking of getting out into the garden.'

Elinor snorted. 'What have you been up to, Henry?'

'Nothing,' said Henry, placing his foot on the saliva. She looked at him.

'I've asked Angelica to come in tomorrow as well,' she said. 'It's very important you get Sheila out before eleven. There'll be hell to pay if they become aware of each other!'

'I thought you might be around tomorrow,' said Henry. 'I thought we might do something. Together.'

Elinor snorted again. She was going to see Tabitha Greenwood, she said, and she thought Henry was going to make a start on the topsoil.

'And,' she added, 'keep those two useless creatures apart!'

Henry pointed out that there would be little danger of their meeting. It was difficult, he said, to stop Sheila walking in the front door, collecting fifteen pounds and climbing out of the kitchen window. Elinor looked at him impatiently.

'You should go back to work,' she said. 'The holiday is making you irritable. Anyway, you're under my feet!'

She marched off through to the kitchen, running her hand along the surface of the bannister. Halfway there she stopped, and, almost to herself, said, 'We need someone else anyway. Julie Plough-Denewood has a Belgian girl apparently.'

Then she went into the kitchen, whistling to herself. Maybe it was her. Maybe she had known all along that Henry had once tried to kill her. Maybe that was why she treated him with such breezy contempt. Maybe that was why she seemed determined to make him spend his holiday caring for the house, while she spent as much time out of it as possible.

Henry went to the door of the television room and started to limber up for his next scream. He was in the middle of allowing the word 'shopping' to be ripped out of his chest with the kind of attack usually only seen in persons who are being flayed alive, when the door opened and his daughter looked at him, levelly. 'Keep your hair on, fatso!' she said.

As he was trying to think of an adequate reply to this remark the bell rang. Henry did not move at first. Then, very slowly, he turned from his daughter and tiptoed towards the front door. He lowered his eyes to the letterbox and peered through the slit. He found himself looking at a rectangular section of Angelica's broad, tanned face. She, like all the other women around 54 Maple Drive, seemed remarkably pleased with herself.

'Meestair!' she said.

Perhaps it was Angelica. Perhaps Angelica was on to him.

Henry straightened up. It seemed unlikely that Angelica had enough English to blackmail anyone. The only English words she knew were 'Persil', 'Jif' and 'Flash'. He opened the door, wearily.

Angelica was a small but powerfully built woman of about thirty whose normal stance was to crouch like a boxer, arms swinging loosely at her sides. She gave the impression of immense, contained energy. As if she were only waiting for one word of command before tearing towards the Persil, the Jif and the Flash with the speed of an Olympic hurdler getting away from the blocks. She had been supplied to the Farrs by a local convent, whose only comment on her had been that she was 'hoping to get back to Guatemala' but was 'first class for heavy-duty domestic work'. Henry still had no idea where she lived, whether she had a family or how she had got here all the way from Guatemala.

She liked Henry. 'Hullo, Meestair!' she said.

'Hullo!' said Henry.

Then, leering in a manner that reminded him strongly of Sheila, she pointed over Henry's shoulder. 'Furry liquid!' she said.

Her English was improving. Maybe the two cleaners were in it together. As Angelica shouldered her way into the broom cupboard, singing some Spanish folk song, Henry made his way to the bottom of the stairs. He sat on the lowest stair and put his head in his hands.

'You've got to help too!' said Maisie. 'I'm not doing it all on my own. So don't think I am.'

He looked at his daughter blearily. The year was only about a week old. But it already showed signs of being even more of a stinker than the last one.

Henry had never blackmailed anyone. The only damaging information he possessed was on the subject of his own private life. But, he decided over the next few days, if he had ever set about extorting money from a close acquaintance, he would have done it just the way Sheila did.

Nothing explicit was said. She never pounced on him as he came out of the lavatory, or waved her open palm at him as she was hoovering the front room. But her manner did seem extraordinarily provocative. It was as if she was daring him to accuse her of doing too little. Her method of work seemed, as far as Henry could gather, to be to arrive about an hour late, sit in the kitchen talking about her marital problems, and then leave. While she was in the kitchen she did, admittedly, pick up a dirty plate from time to time and look at it in a resigned manner. But at no time did she approach any household implement, even for purposes of research. At first Henry thought this was how she normally carried on, but, after a few days thought, he decided her behaviour could only amount to a deliberate insult.

If he had known he was going to spend his days being blackmailed by his cleaning lady, he would never have taken a holiday. Going in to work was less stressful. And, when the end of the week came, he found he was once again the only member of the Farr family in the house. Elinor went off, at eight-thirty, to something called the Wimbledon Recorder Group.

'When will you be back?' said Henry in a pathetic voice.

'It depends on Esmond,' said Elinor mysteriously. 'He's having terrible trouble with the *tempi*!'

Maisie left at nine-thirty, and when he asked her what time she would be back, said, 'I'll be back by midnight!'

Maisie, Henry reflected, as the front door slammed and he stooped to pick up one of her crisp packets from the floor, only came home to sleep these days. She had struck up a friendship with an even fatter girl called Erica and the two of them spent their time combing the district for what they called 'possibles'.

He was alone.

He would have to perform most of Sheila's duties, he decided, when at ten-thirty she still had not appeared. He hadn't dared tell Elinor how little the woman was doing. At ten-forty-five he started to clean the stairs. Nearly an hour later he started on the hall floor. Perhaps if she came in to find him on his hands and knees, scrubbing, she might start to have pity upon him. Yesterday, she had said, after a long pause in the conversation, the edge of her lips curved up in the beginnings of a sneer, 'Shall I unload the dishwasher, Mr Farr?'

Shall I unload the dishwasher? Even this casual remark seemed loaded with unpleasant significance. Henry, who could already see her photograph on the front page of the *Daily Mail* under a headline that read, I TELL OF WIMBLEDON SOLICITOR'S MURDER PLANS SAYS SHEILA, had clambered to his feet and scurried towards the sink, muttering, 'Let me do that! Leave it to me!' Sheila had smiled, silently, to herself.

Her hours were now little more than a carefully judged insult. If she arrived at this very moment, thought Henry, as he ground his J-cloth into the hall floor, she would already be so late that, even if she were to turn round and walk straight back out again, she was in serious danger of running into Angelica. If Elinor should get to hear about *that*, she would want to know why Henry had been allowing her such latitude, and once he told her why, it was heigh-ho for the Old Bailey, the expensive barrister, the psychiatric tests and the unflattering artist's impressions of him on *News at Ten*.

Perhaps he should confront the woman. Perhaps Elinor would understand. He had tried to murder her. Was that *so* bad? Surely they were grown up enough to understand such things now. He would take her out to a meal and tell her himself. He would lead up to it gradually and then, when they were on the brandy and the coffee, tell her the whole story. 'You'll never believe this. But a few years back I actually . . .' – incredulous little laugh here – '. . . tried to murder you!'

Henry tried to imagine his wife raising her face from the plate and saying, in a considered tone, 'I don't have a problem with that, Henry!' Somehow the image just wouldn't come. These days if he did so much as disagree with her, or try to watch a television programme he wanted to watch, or made some minor domestic blunder, she came at him like a hungry tiger. If she could make so much fuss about the two cleaners she had hired running into each other then . . .

'Oh my God,' Henry found he was saying out loud, 'it's twelve o'clock. They're going to arrive at the same time!' Just as he was trying to comprehend the full horror of two cleaning women, one of whom was blackmailing him, standing together on his doorstep, the bell went. Henry froze. If he stayed very quiet they might both go away. He had tried this technique when the MP for Wimbledon had arrived to canvass his vote. The bell went again.

He had better not move. Ever since Elinor had torn up the carpet and sanded the front hall, the most cautious footstep was audible from across the street. He would remain motionless. The bell went again. He heard Angelica's voice.

'Meestair!'

Suppose she should look through the letterbox? He was directly in her line of vision. Better get face down on the floor. But quietly. He would lower himself from the crouching position then ease forward on to his hands then, very slowly and carefully, slide on to his stomach. Would he still be visible through the letterbox?

'Meestair?'

He was now face down on the floorboards. With infinite caution, straining to keep the toecaps of his shoes off the wooden surface, he started to wriggle towards the front room. He was about halfway there when he heard the letter-flap go up and heard Sheila's voice, 'You all right, Mr Farr?'

Or are you gearing up for another attempted murder? Henry looked up and saw Sheila's piggy little eyes peering at him.

'Exercise!' he said, with as much brightness as he could muster. Then, trying to look as if this were part of a carefully rehearsed programme of movements, he leaned on his palms, and, landing both feet on the boards, tried to get vertical with a gymnastic flourish. Sheila, who was looking at him suspiciously, slammed the letterbox shut. Henry ran for the door.

The two cleaning women were standing side by side. They looked, thought Henry, a little like Jehovah's Witnesses. It was one of the few moments in his life when a Witness would have been an attractive alternative to what was on offer.

'Hi!' he said. It was probably best to keep things informal. If he played this carefully, there was no reason for either woman to suspect that the other was a cleaner.

To try to loosen things up even more he leaned forward and gave Sheila a peck on the cheek. 'Great to see you!' he said.

She looked up, warily, through her fringe.

'It happens!' said Henry lightly.

Angelica was looking at Sheila with open hostility. Sheila was squinting suspiciously at the Guatemalan woman. Drastic action was required. Henry crooked his arm through Angelica's and swept her into the hall with what he hoped was a flamenco-like stomp.

'Hola!' he said. This was obviously a mode of address he should have tried on her earlier.

'Hola!' said Angelica.

He did some more stomping on the floorboards. 'Hola!' he said, again.

'Hola! said Angelica.

Henry snapped his fingers and stomped again. If he had a distant Spanish relative, he thought, this might well be how he would greet her. If it wasn't, tough. The main thing was to create a diversion. In a minute he could drop his trousers or start to yodel. Sheila, who was goggling at him from the front door, looked as if she expected him to do either or both of these things at any moment.

'Angelica! Sheila!' he said. 'Sheila! Angelica!'

'Hola!' said Angelica.

Sheila said nothing. Henry grabbed Angelica by the shoulders, propelled her towards the kitchen, shoved her in and closed the door behind her. Then he ran back to Sheila.

'All right,' he said, 'how much do you want?'

Sheila did a devastatingly good impression of dumb ignorance. 'How do you mean?' she said.

'It's OK,' said Henry, through his teeth. 'I'm not *taping* you! This conversation isn't being *recorded*! I'm not *wired*! How much do you want?'

Sheila made a grimace of bewilderment. 'Five pounds an hour,' she said.

Henry had never heard of blackmail being charged by the hour. And he had always assumed it would work out more expensive than domestic cleaning. It shouldn't, however, he told himself, be that surprising that she charged the same for both. In his opinion the two were closely related activities.

'Are you thinking of giving me a rise?' said Sheila.

Henry looked at her with open contempt. 'I suppose,' he said, 'you think the sky's the limit, don't you? You can ask what you like, really, can't you?'

Sheila made a face at him. 'I try to give satisfaction,' she said.

'What you're doing,' said Henry, 'is one of the most despicable things one human being can do to another!'

Sheila tossed her head. 'Not all of us can be brain surgeons,' she said. 'Someone has to do it!'

This seemed, to Henry, to be a desperately cynical attitude to the taking up of a criminal career. *Someone has to do it!* Henry felt his shoulders sag. 'There's no need to stay and *pretend* to clean!' he said. 'Just take the money and go. Let me know when you want more.'

Sheila was doing a very good impression of someone who had not the faintest idea what he was talking about. Presumably, your average blackmailer got rather good at acting. Henry started to push her towards the front door when he became aware that Angelica was watching them. She did not look pleased.

'She cleaner?' she said.

It was her most sustained attempt at the English language so far. To judge from her expression – her mouth was working furiously and her eyes were bright with anger – if the pressure of market forces did as much for her cleaning as it did for her language she was going to be an asset. 'I no clean no more?'

Henry rounded on her. 'I don't know!' he said. 'Maybe we all clean, you know? Maybe we all ponce around the house like land girls while Mrs Farr sits on her fat arse up in Wimbledon playing Telemann!'

Angelica was looking sullen. 'You no like my clean?' she said.

'I love your clean!' said Henry. 'I adore your clean! I can't get enough of your clean!' He strode to the front door and flung it open. 'If you don't like it,' he said, 'leave! There is a world elsewhere! I will clean! I will crawl on my hands and knees through the remains of last night's dinner! I will personally supervise the sterilization of the toilet bowl! I will get down and – '

He became aware that he was screaming. With one last furtive glance, Sheila scurried out into the road, and Angelica, her face dark with fury, followed her. Henry watched the two of them. The Guatemalan woman shambled just behind Sheila, her hands loose at her sides. From time to time, Sheila would turn and shake her head at her as one might try to warn off an importunate dog. Henry watched them both until they were out of sight, and then, with the weary consciousness that he was going to have to explain all this to Elinor, went to look for the Hoover.

He couldn't find it. He wondered whether to clean the bathroom floor. Then he thought about the bucket – how he would have to fill it with hot water, carry it upstairs, then find the mop, then . . . He went into the bedroom. He would make the beds. While he was thinking about how he would do this he lay down on one of them. He closed his eyes. Sleep. If only he could sleep.

But he couldn't sleep. Between him and oblivion came an image of the white sheet of paper, even now lying safe in his desk drawer under his other, unachieved New Year's resolutions.

I WILL TRY NOT TO KILL ANY MORE PEOPLE.

It wasn't a wildly ambitious bid for moral self-improvement. But if things went on like this, he was not going to be able to keep to it. He could see himself taking a steamhammer to Sheila in the very near future. And if Elinor reacted, as he feared, to the news that both her cleaners had left, she too was probably going to have to undergo some form of termination in order to shut her up.

Henry turned over on his side and thought seriously about how he might end Sheila's life. No self-respecting judge would convict him for the murder of a home help who was not only incompetent but also blackmailing her employer. Down below he heard the front door open.

'Anybody there?' called Maisie's voice.

Henry did not reply. He heard another voice, male, say, 'He's gone out. Let's have a party!'

Maisie laughed. Henry thought he recognized the male voice as belonging to James Seebohm, a bat-eared youth from Cranborne School with whom she seemed infatuated. He heard Erica's voice muttering something and then the two girls giggling.

'Are you there?' called Maisie again. Henry did not reply. He closed his eyes once more and tried to sleep.

It was the last day of Henry's holiday.

'I'm off!' called Elinor from the front hall. 'I have to teach Lin Po piano.'

Henry, who was still in bed, did not answer this. He was not sure whether Lin Po was a pupil or a method. Once again he was alone in the house. Maisie had spent the night with Erica's cousin in South-fields. She wasn't expected back until midnight. Henry didn't want to be alone. He wouldn't have minded going to the cinema, and would have even been prepared to have Elinor accompany him.

'I'm going on to Vera Patel's. To play some two part canzonetti with Esmond.'

Who was this Esmond? Some charismatic swine in green cords and brown brogues who probably knew how to get his lips round rather more than a front-action flute. Why did she have such a busy social life? Did people in Wimbledon *like* her?

Elinor was still talking. 'So you'll let in Sheila and Angelica won't you?'

Henry made no response. There was a muttered curse from down below and then the crash of the front door. A minute later, Henry heard the Volvo's engine start, followed by the sound of metal colliding with metal as Mrs Farr bounced their new car off the adjacent vehicles.

Where *was* Sheila? What was she planning? He hadn't yet dared to tell Elinor that the woman hadn't turned up since the confrontation with Angelica. As, somewhat to his surprise, on the next day Angelica had arrived on time, he had offered her an extra five pounds to do whatever Sheila did.

She was probably preparing some new demand. Blackmailers liked to play with their victims, didn't they? She was probably tormenting him with a little taste of freedom before she got round to demanding 350 pounds for washing the kitchen floor. He shuddered to himself, as he dressed, recalling the woman's terrible grin as she sidled up to him and whispered, 'Shall I clean the fridge?'

Unless she had decided to get out while she was still ahead. Maybe she sensed that even Harry Farr had a breaking point. He had continued to think, quite seriously, about killing her. Once or twice last week, when she was pretending to clean the kitchen sink, he had come up behind her and found himself wondering what would happen if he fastened his fingers around her throat and squeezed and squeezed and squeezed! People could tell when you were thinking things like that. Thompson at the office had refused to share with Henry for precisely that reason.

Maybe she was gathering fresh evidence. Not that she had, so far, *produced* any evidence.

They wouldn't need evidence, thought Henry as he struggled into his trousers. The whispering campaign would be enough. He could hear them now as he stood at the gates of the Mary Louisa Haddock School for Girls, waiting for Maisie to lumber out with her violin. *'That's Farr. The one who tried to murder his wife. Couldn't even manage that, from what I hear.'* He would be a laughing stock.

If he had done a decent job of murdering the old bat in the first place he would not now be cowering in 54 Maple Drive waiting for a cleaning woman to come and blackmail him.

The front doorbell rang. Henry tiptoed to the window overlooking the street and peered down. It was possible that there were two of them out there. If that was the case, he was in for a taxing morning. Judging from their previous encounter he was going to find himself refereeing a fifteen-round contest round the furniture.

There was no sign of Sheila. Only Angelica, her square shoulders poised for action, waited by the door for him. She looked up, saw him and gave a broken grin. 'Jeef,' she said. 'Jeef!'

'Yes!' said Henry.

Since her encounter with Sheila she had lapsed back into brand names as a form of communication. 'Flash!' she went on. 'Persil!'

'Yes,' said Henry wearily. 'That's right. Persil.' And he went down and let her into the house. Outside the January street, grey, cold and empty of people, mirrored and mocked his mood. Not for the first time since his fortieth birthday, he found himself thinking, *where has it all gone? Is this all there is?*

Since he had offered her an extra hour, Angelica had shown signs that her enthusiasm for domestic work threatened to disturb the balance of her mind. She had scrubbed and polished and hoovered and swept and washed, and now, unasked, was rearranging the contents of the lounge. As far as Henry could make out, she was grouping books and compact discs by colour and trying to get everything on the mantelpiece to face north.

'Blich!' she said, as she shambled past him. 'Wundolene!'

He would go back to bed. It was either that or driving up to the Roehampton Estate to see if he could catch sight of and/or run down Sheila. Being blackmailed was an exhausting business. He went into the bedroom and, fully clothed, lay down on the duvet. Down below Angelica started to sing in Spanish. As far as Henry could make out, the words of the song began 'Hola! Hola! Hola!' He hummed the tune to himself quietly, pulled the duvet round him, and let the world slip away.

He awoke with the certain knowledge that something was wrong. Someone had got into the house. Something was on fire or missing or leaking. There had been some noise that broke through his dreams. Had Sheila, perhaps, come back? Had she brought a list of new demands? Perhaps Henry was going to be required to employ her whole family? Her brother even!

The thought of Sheila's brother, a small, heavily tattooed man with pretensions to window cleaning, made Henry swing his feet to the floor, tip-toe to the landing and listen.

No noise. Silence in the house. No sound, even from the front room downstairs. Perhaps she was doing something in the garden. Perhaps she had taken to reading the books as well as tidying them. Henry thought back to those first moments of wakefulness. Where had the noise come from? It was close. From somewhere up here. *It had come from his study.* Perhaps Sheila had come back and was going through the things in his desk!

When he went next door he saw at once that someone had been moving things. The Sellotape, which was always next to the card index file, was no longer there. Mr Greenbaum's will, which had been on top of the *Yellow Pages*, was now peeping out from under an old copy of *Vogue*. The plastic container of deodorant was now on top of the word processor whereas previously it had been –

Oh my God, thought Henry, *what's she on to now? The VAT returns? The hideously self-pitying diary he had begun in the winter of 1991?*

The top drawer, where he had kept his resolutions, was open. He was sure he had closed it. He half ran across the floor and found he was looking at the blank sheet of paper, despoiled with those fateful words:

I WILL TRY NOT TO KILL ANY MORE PEOPLE

Underneath it, was a new message. In the same, shaky capitals, someone had written –

BUT IT IS SO HARD! OH JESUS IT IS SO HARD!

This struck Henry, forcibly, as the kind of statement with which he could identify. There were usually at least three or four moments in each day when he got the urge to lay someone out on the grass and set about them with a pickaxe.

He looked up. There was someone on the landing. He was halfway to his feet when Angelica came round the open door.

'Hola!' said Henry.

'Hola!' said Angelica. There was a long pause. 'I write on your pad!' she said, eventually.

Henry did not respond.

'I see what you write and I too write. I make resolve.'

There was total silence in the room.

'I try not to kill more people,' said Angelica, 'but it is hard!'

Her English, thought Henry, was really remarkably good. It was a relief that he had only just discovered the fact. Think of all the amazingly boring conversations they would have been forced to have!

'I kill in Guatemala City,' said Angelica in measured tones, 'I kill when my brother is attacked. Also soldiers of the Government I kill.'

'Yes,' said Henry in what he hoped was a non-judgemental voice. It was important not to offend her. If she could perform this well against the average Latin American soldier, there seemed no reason why she should stop at the chance of stiffing a middle-aged Wimbledon solicitor.

'In my country,' she went on, 'you must kill to survive. It is like animal. He also kill. The fox, for example, he kill the rabbit!'

'He does!' said Henry with some emotion. 'He does!'

Angelica shambled into the room. Henry noticed once again how large her hands were, how broad and muscular her shoulders.

'I kill this woman,' she said, 'who makes your clean! She wishes I not clean! But I must clean! I clean all the time so as I can go once more to Guatemala.'

And kill a few more people, presumably, thought Henry.

'We argue in park,' Angelica went on, 'and in trees I strangle her. Then I find a big stone . . . '

'Yes,' said Henry thoughtfully, 'you might as well do the job properly I suppose.'

Angelica sat, heavily, on Henry's black and white sofa. 'She try stop me clean. So I kill. I dig hole in earth and bury her. It will be many month before they find I think.'

She really was an amazingly resourceful woman, thought Henry. And, somehow, he couldn't bring himself to feel anything at all about Sheila's rapid and undignified exit from South West London. He couldn't help thinking how much easier this was going to make his life. Even Elinor might consider a cleaning woman's sudden death as a reasonable excuse for giving in notice.

'Naturally,' said Henry, 'as the . . . er . . . fox kill the rabbit!'

She looked up at him. Her big, black eyes pleaded with his. 'You not tell police,' she said. 'I clean for nothing. You not tell police.'

Henry sat next to her. 'I not tell police,' he said. Now he was close to her, he could smell her perfume. She smelt of sweat and musk and mingled in seductively with these scents was the acrid tang of bleach, the purity of Jif, Persil and Flash. 'And you must not clean for nothing,' said Henry. 'That would be a kind of blackmail.'

This was, clearly, not an English word in her vocabulary. It had not been in Henry's a week or so ago. Now he seemed to be using it almost all the time. He put his arms round her shoulders. Under her blouse he could feel her heavy breasts.

'Let's say,' said Henry, 'fifty pee an hour. Is that fair, do you think?'

14 February or Near Offer

HENRY FELL IN LOVE while he was buying Valentine cards for his wife.

It was his custom to buy her eleven or twelve Valentines, although most of them were not Valentines at all. This year he started with one which read THINKING OF YOU WITH DEEPEST SYMPATHY, and followed it with a large colour picture of a labrador, under which was written TO THE BEST SON IN THE WORLD. After that he bought a picture of a kitten. There was a balloon coming out of the kitten's mouth which read WELCOME ON YOUR FIRST DAY IN YOUR NEW HOME. He rounded his purchases off with three GET WELL SOON cards and a few of the most insulting birthday cards he could find.

He looked up at the shop assistant as he fumbled in his pockets for change.

'That'll be four twenty,' she said.

It was at that moment precisely that he realized he was hopelessly in love with her.

Henry had never been in love before, although he had been married for twenty-five years. He had never had any feelings for a woman that were not, in some degree, bestial. There was absolutely nothing bestial about what he felt for this woman, which was perhaps why, had he not hit on the word 'love', he would have been unable to find words to describe it.

All he could say, at first, to try to explain in more detail what he felt about her were the words 'Margaret de Courcelles'. At first he couldn't think why this name had occurred to him. Was she, perhaps, a fashion designer? And then he remembered. Years ago he had been taken to a church in Norfolk and, in one of the side chapels, had seen a woman with a helmet of blonde hair and a perfect oval face. She was the centrepiece of a stained-glass window.

Stained-glass window. He didn't even *like* stained-glass windows. As a child his mother had taken him to Chartres cathedral and pointed out the sequence of brightly coloured panels depicting the medieval guilds of the town. He had described both windows and cathedral as 'boring' – a word he later used to sum up the Sistine Chapel, Brahms and nearly all the work of Saul Bellow.

'Margaret de Courcelles!' he muttered to himself, as he carried the cards back along Maple Drive. 'Stained-glass window!'

He was not even very sure what she looked like. She had tight blonde curls, a heart-shaped face and he was fairly certain she had brown eyes. She was wearing a blue overall. Or maybe the overall was brown and her eyes were blue. Or maybe – 'Margaret de Courcelles!' he said out loud, as he passed number 36. 'Stained-glass window!'

Elinor was waiting for him. She was still occupied, as she had been last month, with plans for redesigning the garden. She had already read *Italian Formal Gardens, Composing Your Secret Garden* and *Sunken Water Gardens of the Late Eighteenth Century*, a book which, Henry had reminded her, had cost about as much as hiring six landscape gardeners for a week.

'I don't see,' he had said, 'what any of this has to do with forty foot of scrubby English suburb!'

She had not even bothered to reply. She had only recently appeared to notice that she was sharing the house with a forty-seven-year-old man called Henry. To judge from the expression on her face as he came into the hall, she did not like what she saw.

'You're late!' she snapped, as he closed the door behind him.

Margaret de Courcelles! Stained-glass window! thought Henry. *Stained-glass window!*

With elaborate and not entirely unfeigned courtesy he said, 'I'm sorry, darling! You know you're the one I hurry home for!'

'Hurry home for my arse!' said Elinor.

Henry did a brief, balletic movement around the hall. 'Indeed,' he said, giving her a friendly grin. 'Hurry home for your arse!'

Watching him suspiciously, Elinor backed down the hall. 'You're up to something!' she said. 'God knows what it is! I have to go to Marie Helene's.'

When she had closed the door after her, Henry did another, slightly more complicated dance around the polished wooden floor. 'Stained-glass window!' he said to himself as he danced. 'Stained-glass window! Oh my God! Stained-glass window!'

*

She was not as amused as usual by the Valentine cards. She said she found the one inscribed THINKING OF YOU WITH DEEPEST SYMPATHY in poor taste. Inside it read:

> When loved ones are beyond our reach
> We cannot touch or feel.
> And yet we have kind thoughts of them
> That mend and soothe and heal!
>
> For too much closeness mars all joy
> Makes feelings workaday.
> The ones we love can be more dear
> When they are far away!

'I think that's a rather good description of our relationship,' said Henry.

Margaret de Courcelles! Stained-glass window!

Elinor snorted and went off to run her bath. Downstairs, Henry could hear Maisie turning over the hall carpet, up-ending chairs and ransacking the small wooden cupboard next to the front door.

'She's convinced someone's sent her a Valentine!' said Elinor when Henry went in to brush his teeth.

If they had, thought Henry, they were keeping fairly quiet about it. Mind you, if he had been sending Maisie a Valentine card, he would have buried it several feet in the earth. You didn't want to risk giving a girl like her too much encouragement.

'Bastard!' she was growling to herself downstairs. 'Bloody, bloody bastard!'

Perhaps, thought Henry, someone had marked 14 February by sending her a dead dog or a defaced photograph of herself.

'I think James Seebohm said he was going to,' whispered Elinor loudly, 'but I'm not sure he has!'

Henry started to dress. Seebohm, from what he had seen of the youth, was incapable of writing his own name on an envelope, let alone anyone else's. Henry sang to himself as he climbed into his boxer shorts. While he was knotting his tie he went up to the mirror to inspect his skin. It was a little blotchy, but there wasn't much light in the newsagent's. He would call in on his way to work and buy a Valentine. A proper Valentine. Something tasteful and romantic. A picture of Derwentwater or a reproduction of a Matisse. On the back he would write the kind of thing he had never, in forty-seven years on the planet, felt able to write before:

My darling,
I have never felt what I feel for you. Have you ever seen the rain clear off a mountain top and the peaks glisten in the morning sun? Have you ever caught sight of the sea from a distant hill and felt your heart tremble on the edge of the discovery of distant continents?
What I feel for you is all of those things. It is the hunger and the thirst. It is the journey and the journey's end. It is the *spirit* that for years I have buried in my narrow little English soul. I have started to feel, my darling!
One who wishes you well . . .

If he could fit all that on a postcard it would do the job nicely. It would certainly awake her interest. Unless, of course, she was the kind of girl who automatically sent all anonymous letters straight round to the local police station.

He decided, after thought, that the last line of the letter could have suggestive overtones. He would write it again. He wanted this letter to express something fine. He knew, for once, that a woman in his life had nothing to fear from him. For once in his life he was feeling something pure. Something pure and good and true.

My darling, darling girl,
What I feel for you is sudden and total and almost horribly *real*. Have you ever seen a river wind its way across the valley floor under sweet willows and the wise oak trees? Have you ever seen the spring rain wake the blackened earth from its winter sleep?
What I feel for you is like that. And more. I have never really felt loved, my darling . . .

Elinor put her face round the door. 'What are you grinning about?' she said.
'I'm happy!' said Henry. 'I'm terribly, terribly happy!'
'Why?' said Elinor.
Henry did not feel able to tell her. Glaring at him suspiciously, she came into the room. She was wearing a white towel round her head, and, as usual after her bath, was a light pink in colour. She rolled her enormous bulk on to the bed and, from the table on her side of the bed,

she took a gigantic hardback novel. It was, Henry knew without having to look at it, about India. Elinor was only reading books about India at the moment. In January she had only read books written by women, and February was India Month. To judge from the size of the book, March might turn out to be India Month as well. She looked at him as she dragged it on to her upper legs and geared herself up for the massive task of lifting it to a reading position.

'What we did in India,' she said, 'was appalling.'

'What are we doing there now?' said Henry.

Elinor guffawed. 'Not a lot!' she said.

He suddenly felt sympathetic towards her. She wasn't a bad woman really. If she lost about four stone she could be almost attractive. She had probably never been in love. Never known what was now happening to Henry. Never known that sudden, irrational feeling that individual objects had a kind of . . . what was the phrase? . . . a kind of . . . *luminous grace!* Yes! That was the phrase! *Luminous grace.* Never known what it was to see a waterfall cascading down a rugged mountainside in a rush of pure water or a lark swoop down through the pure night air.

Did larks swoop? And weren't they all in bed by six?

Henry didn't care. He was in love.

'Goodbye, my darling girl!' he said, pecking Elinor on the cheek. 'I shall see you tonight, sweet thing!'

Elinor flinched, and, as he made for the door, she clutched his hand, hard. 'What is the matter with you?' she said.

Henry pecked her once again on the forehead. 'Don't let's fight, tootums!' he said. And skipped, lightly, from the room. He could hear her snorting to herself as he went down the stairs and out through the hall to the street. He didn't mind. The newsagent's was on the way to the station.

When he walked in the first thing he saw was the girl. She was standing over by the window, looking out at the February rain. He could see now, quite clearly, that it was her overall that was blue and her eyes that were brown. It was good to get that out of the way. He could see, too, that she had a determined little chin and that her nose (dear, dear nose!) swooped up from her upper lip like a . . . like a . . . like a lark!

Love, Henry reflected glumly, was not doing anything for his powers of self-expression. Not that he had many. Some other people might have been inspired to poetry by emotions such as the ones that were now rooting him to the spot by a shelf full of DIY manuals. All love did for him was to remind him of the poverty of his vocabulary.

He moved, with assumed casualness, along the lines of magazines until he came to the greetings cards. When he was sure he was unobserved he stole a glance across at the girl.

She was serving someone. Not a man. An elderly lady. The elderly lady was counting out coins, one by one, from a leather purse. The girl in the blue overall was watching her with total calm, total concentration. *She is good*, thought Henry, *she is good and sweet and kind!* She was saying something. Henry edged a little closer so that he might catch what it was.

'We need rain,' she was saying, 'for the gardens!'

It was, on the face of it, a commonplace remark. But, like a folk tune reworked by a musical master, the words, in her mouth, acquired a delicacy and a subtlety which no one else alive could have given them. *We need rain for the gardens!* thought Henry. *We need rain for the gardens!* Of course! Why hadn't he thought of that?

Henry had never before looked for a card that expressed his feelings. He had thought, up to now, that it was down to him to express his own feelings. Why leave it to some jerk from Hallmark cards? His own feelings, or so he had imagined, were far too subtle and clever to be summed up in a few halting quatrains by some low-rent version of John Betjeman.

This, he realized as he scanned the Valentines on offer, was simply an indication of the shallow, sneering sort of chap he had been up until this moment. Great thoughts and great feelings were always simple. As simple as larks and waterfalls and stained-glass windows and luminous grace!

He hadn't really felt anything up to now. As he browsed through the cards, pulling out each one to study its message, moving on from Valentines through To My Loving Brother, For a Sister, My Son's Birthday, and on through Anniversaries Silver, Gold and Diamond, Hospital Visits, On Your Engagement and all of the other lovingly marked stages on the way to the tomb, he found there were tears in his eyes. He was bursting with sympathy for the clumsy sentiments and the clumsier verses in which they were expressed.

I'm thinking of you very much
And wishing you were here
How much more sweet our life can be
When one we love is near!

This struck Henry as being absolutely brilliant. It was *exactly* how he felt. It did not matter that, outside, rain was falling on the grey streets of Wimbledon. It didn't matter that, in a little while he was going to have to stand on the platform waiting for the train to rattle in and take him to an office he did not like. He was fifteen feet away from someone so beautiful, so pure, so calm, so –

He looked at the front of the card. It said: YOU'RE MY FURRY PURRY VALENTINE. Underneath it was a picture of a kitten in a pink bow tie.

Who needs Matisse? thought Henry. *Doesn't that say it all?* Simple, direct emotion – that was what it was all about. That, at the end of the day, was worth any number of weirdly triangulated versions of the Mont St Victoire or whatever lump of rock it was on which Matisse had wasted so much of his time.

He picked up the card. The girl was alone now. She smoothed down the newspapers in front of her. She looked, suddenly, lost and vulnerable. Henry wanted to go over to her, hold her in his arms, smooth down those tight little curls and say, 'It's all right, my darling! It's all right!'

She was not, he decided, quite ready for this yet. He would have to exchange a few words with her first. Maybe even find out her name. And yet, all of the mundane questions that would have to be asked in order to get this information seemed somehow hollow and pointless. Worse than that, they might be misinterpreted. What did her name matter? He didn't want to know her name or her address or her hobbies or what she was doing tonight. Because, Henry felt, he *knew* her. He knew what the heart of her was. For the moment it was enough to be standing in the shop, a Valentine card in his hand, feasting his eyes on her face.

'Do you want that?' the girl was saying. *Do you want that?*

'Er . . .' Henry found he was blushing. 'I think I do.'

She smiled.

When she smiled Henry saw her teeth for the first time. They were, on the face of it, just teeth. She seemed to have the full complement. They were white. They were, on the whole, fairly well matched as far as size and appearance were concerned. There were no stray bits of parsley attached to them, no yellow stains of the kind that Henry noticed, every morning, on his own gnashers.

But, he found himself thinking, they were *her* teeth. That was the thing about them. They were sunk deep in her own red, vibrant gums. They chewed, nibbled and ground only when she gave the orders. They were, like her elbows and her (yes) breasts and her shoulders, inexpressibly precious to him.

'That'll be sixty-five pee.'

Sixty-five pee!

Henry held out a five-pound note. He realized he was smiling foolishly.

'Who's it for?'

'It's for you.'

He had not planned on saying this. But he did not regret saying it. Every remark exchanged with this girl seemed somehow strange and unexpected. It was as if the normal rules of conversation had been suspended. And he had no idea (he was thinking extraordinarily quickly) what *his* response would be to the laugh or the slap or the gasp of horror with which she might greet his suggestion.

'I should be so lucky!' she was saying. She was smiling. 'It's for that lady you were buying for the other day, isn't it?' she went on. 'It's your wife, isn't it? I've seen you in the village.'

She gave him a rather maternal smile. Then she wagged her finger. 'You had your little joke with her yesterday and she said, *You go out and get me something nice,* didn't she?'

This speech seemed to Henry so complex and filled with meaning that all he really wanted to do was to rush away to some quiet place, transcribe it and spend a few hours studying it until each delicate shade of meaning should emerge.

She thinks of me as a father or an uncle. That's OK. If that's what she wants I'm happy to be that for her. I don't want anything that she doesn't want. This is love, thought Henry, *this is a pure, altruistic feeling, a passion as pure, as pure as . . . as . . . Evian water.*

'There we are!'

That maternal smile again. Henry took his change. 'Thanks!' he said.

When he got to the door of the shop he waited a moment at the door, the coins in his hand. 'Thanks . . . *darling!*' he said to himself.

Outside, the rain had got harder. It was lashing into Mr Pritchett's privet hedge, bubbling and boiling in the gutters, stinging Henry's face as, scarcely aware of where he was going, he moved through the morning crowd in the forecourt of Wimbledon Station.

Where was he going?

It was not until he saw the sign on the townbound train that he remembered. He was a forty-seven-year-old man. He was going in to Blackfriars. He was going to sit in an office and talk to Mr Greenbaum about his divorce. He was –

He suddenly realized that he was going to do no such thing. Not today. Not maybe any other day. He was going to stand in the rain. For hours.

He lifted his face up to the grey suburban sky. The rain trickled through what was left of his hair, down on to his neck. He held out both his arms. The water was soaking his shirt. Someone, hurrying for their train, pushed him roughly to one side. Henry opened his mouth and let the raindrops spit into it.

'I'm not going anywhere!' he said, out loud. 'I'm in love! I'm in love!'

'Well, get out of the way then!' said an elderly lady in a headscarf. Henry, grinning to himself, turned and started to walk back up the hill.

He would stand outside the newsagent's. He needed one more glimpse of the girl. Once he had seen her again, he would be able to face the day. As he wandered away from the station, he looked into the faces of the commuters, hurrying for the morning train.

Don't you understand? he wanted to shout to them. *Don't you realize? There isn't any point in any of this. Stained-glass window! Luminous grace!* And, as he turned off the hill into the street where the girl in the blue overall waited, looking out at the same rain that was soaking him, he flung his arms wide once more and yelled up at the sky, 'Luminous grace! Stained-glass window! Luminous grace!'

'Why don't you have a paper delivered, Mr Farr?' said the girl.

Henry gave a rueful smile. 'Who needs it?' he said. 'I only come in here to talk to you!'

The girl laughed.

It was a Saturday at the end of February. A whole day in which he could find endless excuses to visit the newsagent's. Recently he had spent, on average, about fifteen minutes a day in the shop. He had bought chocolates. He had bought copies of *GQ, Vogue, Cosmopolitan, Good Housekeeping, What Car?* and many other publications which he had no intention of reading. On one occasion he had even bought a copy of the *Guardian*. He had bought almost every flavour of crisp, Maltesers, Wispas, Mars bars, lemonade, sliced bread and tin after tin of cat and dog food, even though his cat had died three years ago and he had never had, would never have, a dog anywhere near the house. Although he threw most of them away, one or two ended up on the floor of the car.

'Why,' Elinor had said, 'have you got these cans of pet food?'

'They're for Maisie!' Henry had replied.

He had joined the video club. He had taken out *Heartburn*, *Indiana Jones* and a film called *Raw Love*. Although Maisie had watched *Raw Love* eight times, Henry had not bothered to see any of them. It was enough to watch Her hands delicately wrap the black, rectangular cassettes, slip them across the counter and hear her voice, light and slightly tremulous, whisper, 'Back by Tuesday night!'

When he wasn't in the newsagent's he was hanging around outside it. Three or four times he had followed the girl home.

She hadn't seen him. He had kept about a hundred yards away. He had lost her near Leopold Road, picked her up on Arthur Road, trailed her through the village, only to discover, after ten minutes of diving into front gardens and crouching behind trees, that he was following a long-haired youth of about her age.

He still had no idea of where she lived. He didn't really want to know. Sometimes he found himself wondering whether he had fallen in love with a shadow, a trick of the light.

'Well,' he said finally, 'better get off to household chores!'

'How's the dog?'

Henry blinked hard but recovered well. 'He's been a bit peaky!' he said. 'He didn't want his Chum this morning. But Alsatians can be choosy.'

The girl smiled. 'It's wonderful you call him Frank!' she said.

It's wonderful you call him Frank. He hugged this sentence to himself as he went out on to the pavement. Like many of the things she said – *it's all swings and roundabouts, really* or *start bad, come good* – it had the mature calm of a folk saying, but this time she had managed something wittier, more dense than he had thought possible.

It's wonderful you call him Frank.

He found he was walking into the butcher's opposite her shop. Why was he doing this? He didn't know. A small, weasely man in a white coat was grinning at him. He was holding a tray of pork chops. There was blood on his hands. He was nodding over towards the newsagent's. Henry saw that the girl was letting herself out of the shop. Still in her overall (dear, dear overall!) she ran, splay-footed, down the road.

'I could give that a right poking!' said the man.

'I'm sorry?' said Henry.

The man pushed his face at Henry's. 'I could give it a right seeing to!' he said, in the tones in which one might explain a simple point to a foreigner. 'I could go a few rounds of rumpy pumpy with it!'

For a moment Henry genuinely had no idea what the man might be talking about. 'Rumpy pumpy?' he said.

'Doo da!' said the man. 'Humperdincke! Porking!' He put the tray of pork chops down and started to lick his lips. 'Lovely little arse on that!' he said.

He could, of course, thought Henry, be referring to the pig. It was hard to believe, really, that a man like *this* and a girl like *that* could co-exist on the same planet, let alone the same road. He must, Henry decided, be talking about the pig.

'I'd like to get its head face down in the pillow and spank its little white bum!' crooned the butcher. 'I bet it gives the best gobble in South West London.'

Henry found he was blushing with shame. How could men talk like this about women? Why did they do it? Didn't they realize how pathetic they sounded?

'I'll have a pork chop,' said Henry, in what he hoped was a quiet, dignified voice.

While he was serving, the man kept peering out through the shop window. Henry followed the direction of his gaze. The girl came running back down the road. Her elbows were drawn into her sides and her hands bounced helplessly, like flowers too heavy for their stalks. When she reached the newsagent's she stopped, smoothed down her overall and pushed open the door of the shop.

'Bit of parleroony,' said the weasely man. 'Bit of the old chat. What-are-you-doing-tonight-darling? sort of thing. And then it's down with the tights and *spear the bearded*, as our Australian friends say!'

He leered, openly, at Henry. 'Or go for a stroll down the Bournville Boulevard!' he added, brightly.

Henry goggled at him. 'I don't know what you're talking about . . .' he said, although he had a horrible suspicion that he did.

The man seemed glad of the chance to enlighten him. 'The Bourn-ville Boulevard,' he said. 'You know. Sneaking a chocolate biscuit. Going round the dark side of the moon.'

Henry's mouth was wide open. The pork chop was swinging to and fro in its plastic bag.

'Up the back way,' said the man, clearly losing patience. 'Into the fudge. Sticking your naughty up her naughty! You must have heard of it!'

Henry could not believe what he was hearing. The man, really, should not be allowed near food. He was probably, thought Henry, mentally ill. As he got out on to the pavement, he passed an elderly woman dragging a basket on wheels up the steps of the shop. He wanted to seize her by the arm and warn her of what lay ahead. But, as he looked behind him, he saw that she was nodding and smiling at him. Presumably he reserved his filth for other men.

The newsagent's door opened once again. There, in the pale Febru-ary sunshine, was the girl. Not only that. She was waving and smiling at him. Henry waved back. He felt, suddenly, as he had felt as a child, waving to his mother from the school gates. He flung his right arm backwards and forwards in a kind of hectic semaphore. He found he was grinning, foolishly, the way he often did when she was near.

'Hi!'

'Hi!'

She was crossing the road. She was smiling and she was waving and she was crossing the road. For a moment Henry wondered whether she might, perhaps, have been thinking and feeling some of the things he had been thinking and feeling for the last three weeks. It wasn't impossible. Girls sometimes fell for older men. His passion for her was so clear and strong that it would not surprise him to learn it had infected her as well. Was his longing knocking at her own heart as well as his?

'Tell me,' the girl was saying, 'are you going my way?'

Henry swallowed vigorously. 'It depends,' he said. 'Which way are you going?'

'Home!' said the girl, and smiled, coyly.

This was too good to be true. Perhaps he was going to be able to meet her mother! Dear, dear mother! Like everything about the girl she was bound to be sweet and kind and gentle and good. He would be able to meet her father and sisters and brothers too. Give them money possibly. The brothers he imagined as salt-of-the-earths types. He could go to the pub with them!

Maybe she had pets. A dog. He didn't usually like dogs but *her* dog – he knew this instinctively – would be different. Maybe she would have a kitten, like the one on the card he had wanted to give her, or one of those delightful caged birds that could be taught to say things like 'Drop your knickers!' whenever anyone entered the room.

Henry wasn't really very fond of animals apart from the ones that sat there and shut up. He was capable of feeling tolerant towards lizards. Or rather – he wanted to put this in the past tense – he had *only* been capable of feeling tolerant towards lizards. His love for her had made him realize that he could start to love things. Things that were even harder to love than cats or dogs or parrots or lizards. People, for example. He could love people. People were beautiful. He smiled at her. She smiled back.

Oh, even that ghastly little creature in the shop was worth loving. Without love, how would his stunted soul develop? How would he ever see that women were not *objects*, not collections of . . . Henry could not bear to think about the intimate things of which the girl from the newsagent's was composed, especially as she was now about three yards away from him, smiling up into his face . . . Not collections of things but people. And people were beautiful.

'Of course I'll take you home,' said Henry in a measured voice. 'I'll take you anywhere you want to go!'

The girl smiled. As they went off down the street she linked her left arm into his. She did this quite unselfconsciously. It was as if Henry and she were indulging in one of those friendships found among women in closed communities, where the men are away about their greedy, cruel business.

'Where do you live?' said Henry.

'Wimbledon,' said the girl.

He smiled down at her. 'That's funny,' he said. 'I live in Wimbledon too!'

They both laughed. Then the girl said: 'The thing is . . . I don't want to trouble you or anything like that. But . . .' She looked up and down the street nervously. 'I think there's someone following me.'

Henry gulped. 'No,' he said, 'surely not . . .'

The girl was speaking in a whisper. 'Three or four times,' she said, 'I've been sort of aware of a . . . bloke. You know? Too far away to sort of . . . *see* . . . but a bloke. Sort of shadowing me . . .'

She shuddered. ''Orrible!'

'Really?' said Henry. 'You actually feel he's . . . a nasty character?'

'Well,' said the girl, 'anyone who follows a girl around the place must be pretty kinky.'

Henry coughed. 'I don't know,' he said. 'He might be quite a nice person.'

The girl let out a peal of laughter. 'You're so sweet,' she said, 'and *funny*!' She lifted her face up to his. 'Your wife,' she said, 'is a very lucky lady.'

Henry's feelings of love towards the world had not extended quite as far as Elinor. He did feel much more able to bear her than usual. Once or twice he had risked a kiss dangerously near her lips. But when he was close to this . . . this *vision* in an overall, he became uncomfortably aware of what his wife was. How loud her voice was! How enormous her behind!

The girl was speaking again. 'There are some creepy men about!' she said.

Henry nodded sadly. 'There are,' he said. 'But there are some fine, decent ones left. There are some of us who look at the rest of us – if you see what I mean – and say, *My God what have you done?* You know? You treat women as objects. You have no respect for them. You think they're stupid. My God! You only gave them the vote about fifty years ago!'

The girl's eyes widened. 'Is that right?' she said. 'I thought women had always been able to vote!'

They turned up Leopold Road, past a shop decorated with wicker baskets, and then right into a long suburban street. The houses here were smaller than in Henry's road, although almost every one seemed to have a garage. In some cases the garage seemed a more imposing building than the house next to it. About a hundred yards down the road the girl stopped.

'I'm all right now,' she said.

'I'm sure it was just your imagination.'

She bit her lower lip. 'If there is some creep following me, I'll do . . .'

Henry put a fatherly hand on her arm. 'You won't need to do anything,' he said. 'I'll knock his block off for him!'

He really felt he could fight for this girl. What he felt for her was so pure and strong that he could imagine himself squaring up to the little bastard who had frightened her and smashing his fist, hard, into his face.

''Bye,' said Henry. He watched her skip off down the street.

If he was going to follow her again, he would need a disguise of some sort. Something he could carry in his briefcase. A hat. A wig perhaps. A beard. A hat, a wig *and* a beard. And dark glasses. He would also have to make absolutely sure he was not seen. He didn't want to upset her. Maybe he should stop following her.

Somehow the idea of following her was now even more attractive. It wasn't that he wanted to frighten her. The thought of her looking over her left shoulder to see some swine in a hat, a wig, a beard and dark glasses pained him inexpressibly. He would give everything to rescue her from such a sight.

Give everything, luminous grace, stained-glass window. All these things that up till now he had dismissed as cliché or recherché, were now part of his armoury. *Armoury.* He was engaged in a war. A war with any thought or feeling that didn't dignify things. A war with nasty little perverts in hats, wigs, glasses and beards who had nothing better to do than skulk around Wimbledon after innocent girls.

Where did one buy a false beard?

When he was child he and his brother Nigel had had one. Henry had often put it on late at night, when they were in bed, in order to scare the living daylights out of the little rat. Nigel had always been easy to frighten. It was a spade-shaped affair with two rudimentary hooks – rather like crude spectacle frames – that fitted over each ear. They had bought it a shop in Holborn called Ellisdons. Ellisdons was now, almost certainly, no more. In fact, you hardly ever saw joke shops these days – places where you could buy plastic fried eggs, rubber reproductions of dog faeces and imitation Dracula fangs.

It was the fangs that made him remember. There was a shop near the station where, years ago, he and Elinor had bought Maisie a pair of fangs. She was always, Henry recalled, wearing fangs. It had been quite difficult to persuade her to stop wearing them. It was a tiny, dusty little place, full of fake spiders, black face soap and weird masks that brought back, in a single phrase, the childhood he and Nigel had shared over thirty years ago. He would go there. Now.

The shop was crowded.

A plump man in front of him was buying a rubber sausage. He said he was also looking for large ears. 'All the large ears have gone, I'm afraid,' said the man behind the counter.

Henry looked up at the shelves behind him. There seemed to be quite a lot of wigs and beards. There was a large bushy white one, labelled FATHER XMAS SPECIAL. Underneath it was a ginger effort, complete with moustache, that Henry suspected might make him look a little like Bernard Shaw.

He bought it. He also bought a curly wig, a huge pair of dark glasses and an amazingly realistic nose. He had not planned on the nose, but was unable to resist it. It was a big, fleshy affair. The shop-owner asked him if he wanted to try it on. Henry found that it fitted him perfectly.

Then, in a sudden fit of guilt, he bought Elinor a present. It was a small pot of what looked like mustard. When you opened the cap a small rubber snake leaped up at you on a coiled spring. The mustard effect had been achieved by painting the inside of the glass yellow.

After this he went off to look for a long mackintosh. He thought he would get a blue one (his own was brown) that stretched down to his ankles.

Perhaps he should get shoes as well. Wellington boots maybe. Once you got started on this disguise business it was hard to know where to stop. And it was certainly going to be safest to wear gloves. He went to an outsize menswear shop, bought a blue rubber mac and, for a reason he was unable to explain, a large white shirt. He decided his own shoes were dull enough to be anonymous. He went to a different shop to buy the hat, deciding, after some time, on a large black sombrero from a woman's boutique in the High Street.

'Who's it for?' the woman in the shop had said, and when Henry, without thinking, answered 'Me!' she raised both of her elegantly pencilled eyebrows.

He tried on the outfit in the gentlemen's lavatory at Wimbledon Station. At first he was a little nervous about the nose, but when he looked at himself in the mirror above the washbasin, he decided the nose made it. It grew, so naturally, out of the foliage of the beard!

He looked, he decided, vaguely Jewish. He tried a few shrugs and expressive hand movements but came to the conclusion that the costume worked best when its owner was completely immobile. There was something quietly alarming about it. He tried walking up and down in front of the mirror, bending the knees and keeping the upper half of the body still, à la Groucho Marx. Then he worked on surprising his own reflection so that he could see how the ensemble might strike someone seeing it for the first time. He walked away from the mirror and, when almost at the lavatory door, spun round, whipped off the dark glasses and stared at himself. The effect, he found, was truly terrifying. If he was being followed by a man who bore even a passing resemblance to the one in the mirror he would have rushed to the nearest phone box and dialled 999 as soon as his fingers had stopped shaking.

He was beginning to feel ready to face the world when the door opened and a small boy walked in. He took one look at Henry, gave a low scream and bolted. Henry looked at himself once more in the mirror. It was good. It was very, very good. It was too good to waste. He would go to the newsagent's, lurk a little, and, when she finished her shift, he would follow her home.

It was curious. Now, from behind the beard, the dark glasses, the wig and the hat, he felt he would really be able to look at the girl. When he, Henry Farr, was with her, even though she linked her arm into his, he hardly dared lift his eyes to her face. But now, like an ornithologist in a hide, waiting for some rare species of grebe to emerge from its nest, he felt he would be able to concentrate all his energies on the act of watching. That heart-shaped face, those golden curls and those big, brown eyes would unscramble themselves and, broken down into a code only he could understand, leak up the lines of his sight to become part of him.

'Darling!' he said, aloud, to his reflection. 'What I feel for you is something I have never felt before. It has wrenched my heart out of shape. It had made me see the world in a new way. It has opened me up to those big, animal passions that blow about the world. Oh, my God, my darling girl – '

Something made him stop.

A small man in a trilby hat had come into the lavatory and was looking at him, cautiously, from over by the closed cubicles. Henry turned and, with the gesture he had only just perfected, whipped off the dark glasses and stared deep into the man's eyes. The man gave a kind of croak and backed up against the wall. Without speaking, Henry strode out of the lavatory and on to the concourse of the station. *Soon, my darling!* he said to himself as he marched on towards the dying February day. *Soon, soon, soon!*

*

'What have you got in that bag?' said Elinor, suspiciously.

'Swimming stuff, my angel!' said Henry. He had, in fact, put a towel and a pair of trunks at the top of his sports bag. Underneath it lay the beard, the dark glasses, the wig, the hat, the rubber mac and the magnificent latex nose.

He had hidden them in the one safe drawer in Maple Drive – the second lower down on the right-hand side of his desk, in which he had also kept a black-and-white photograph of himself aged nine, at Cranborne Junior School, Wimbledon. He had also concealed Maisie's only good school report, from her third year at primary school. It didn't start well: 'Maisie has a power to disturb unusual in a child of eight and she can seem, at times, almost unmanageable . . .' It went on to say some brutally frank things about her maths, her nature studies and what she herself called 'her socialist skills', but there were a fulsome few lines on the subject of her English language compositions that Henry had always treasured.

He patted the bag as he let himself out of Maple Drive. It was seven o'clock on a Friday night. It was clear and chilly. There was no moon. She would be out in fifteen minutes. In the darkness, once he was fully dressed, he would be able to do something he had not yet been able to do: to follow her *all* the way home. And, once she was home, to wait out there in the darkness, unseen, while . . .

While what? He had no desire to see her undress. He was about as uninterested in her naked body as he was in his wife's. That, he thought to himself, was what made his feelings for her so precious. Sometimes he allowed himself to consider what it might be like to kiss her, but the moment when their lips touched always receded, like a dream at waking. Sometimes he imagined it *had* happened and the memory of it was unbearably sweet. But he never, even in fantasy, considered anything apart from the prospect or the memory of such a supreme moment. Of one thing he was certain. If it ever *did* happen, it was not going to be anything like the awful, chin-led collision between him and Sharon Hutchins in the back row of the Wimbledon Odeon in 1964. It would also have nothing in common with the unpleasantly dental encounter with Ellen Scarisbrooke in her bedsitter in the spring of 1968.

It would be, well, love.

'Love,' he muttered to himself, as he dodged on to the Common opposite the War Memorial and looked for a quite place to change. 'Love, love, love.'

He had never really loved Elinor. Their marriage had started as a blend of lust and inertia and ended as a mixture of dislike and weary tolerance. It had survived, like Kurt Vonnegut in Dresden, by bizarre accident. It might as well, he decided, as he wriggled his jaws into the beard, have been one of those arranged marriages. At least then he might have made a bit of money out of it.

Love meant a kind of ache, didn't it? The only ache he could recall experiencing with Elinor was a touch of arthritis in the shoulder. Love meant seeing the world in a new way, didn't it? The only way of seeing the world when you were with Elinor was seeing it her way. If he had been offered a series of futures at the age of twenty-five, they would not have included listening to her drone on about early music, the Wimbledon Craft Fayre, the –

The one thing he could never have imagined himself doing was donning a false nose, a beard and glasses in the darkness of Wimbledon Common one evening in early March because it represented his only chance of being near a girl who represented innocence, freshness, gaiety and all the other things that were missing from his marriage.

'Oh darling!' he said, aloud, to the huge dome of the sky above the silver birches. 'Oh my love! Oh my sweet, sweet, darling girl!'

His voice cracking with sobs, he fitted the nose carefully into the beard, stuck the hat on the wig and stumped off towards the newsagent's.

He had timed it perfectly. She was just leaving the shop as he turned into the street. He saw her wave to someone inside, and then, with a shake of those blonde curls, she walked, with that delicious, knock-kneed way she had, into the damp winter twilight. Henry gave chase.

She was wearing a black raincoat. As she walked, she pulled from her pocket a small beret and crammed it on top of her curls. There was something unbearably sweet about this gesture. The cap was so entirely decorative, the way she pulled it on to her hair so jaunty, that it seemed to Henry to light up the darkness that blew in from the Common, like mist, closing in on the yellow lights of the village. On this damp evening of the unfinished year, she was a natural challenge to the gloom. Henry wanted to shield her, the way he had seen working men cup their hands around a match flame, its red ochre warmth lighting up their faces.

He wanted to be her. He wanted to feel what she was feeling. Think what she was thinking. Wear what she was wearing.

He checked himself as he turned into Leopold Road. He had quite enough clobber on already without adding a bra, knickers and tights to the outfit.

At the thought of these words – *bra, knickers, tights* – a sudden stab of lust caught him. For the first time in the weeks since he had been following the girl, he found he was thinking about her sexually. The transition was awesomely easy. One minute there he was thinking about flames and stained-glass windows and the next –

No. No, no, no, no.

He knew, though he could not have said how, that she was a virgin. *She is*, he repeated to himself, *virgin*. He liked the absence of the indefinite article. She was as virgin, as, as . . . the forest! She was virgin and she was also *a virgin*! Adjective and noun burned in the young girl he was following through the dark suburban night, down towards the railway, until she seemed almost holy.

He must keep well out of sight. He did not want to frighten her. As she walked down a street that led away from Wimbledon towards the Merton Road, he caught sight of himself in the wing mirror of a parked car. He gave a little cry of dismay at what he saw. In the open, the nose and the wig seemed almost more shocking. She must *not* see him. In case she should turn – she was reaching for a key in her handbag now – he crouched down behind a car on the opposite side of the road from her and peered round as she clattered up the path of a small, semi-detached house.

She *did* live with her parents. He had known that that would be the case! A man older than Henry in a grey cardigan and slippers would answer the door. He would lead her in and ask her about her day while her mother sat opposite him, knitting. 'That'll be Sandra!' he was probably saying even now as he rose from his armchair, the evening paper in his hand.

Sandra! Oh, Sandra! Dear, dear Sandra (assuming that was her name). But it didn't *matter*, decided Henry, as he crouched down low behind the car bonnet. She could be called Phyllis or Dorothy or Sheila or Juliet or May or Stephanie! She was there, that was all that mattered.

She was at (Henry squinted at the gate) 59 Dene Avenue, Wimbledon. She was safe.

As he watched the light in the bedroom went on. She crossed and re-crossed several times. She was undressing. Henry averted his eyes. It was only when the light was off that, at last, he dared to stand by the car, feasting his eyes on 59 Dene Avenue.

In the front garden was a small plaster gnome in a red hat. He was carrying a fishing rod. Henry found he was chuckling at the little fellow. Next to him was a tiny patch of lawn. In the middle of the lawn was a black plastic bag that looked as if it was full of Michaelmas daisies. Henry had never warmed to Michaelmas daisies. They grew in a rank, arrogant way he did not like. Even when alive and well they seemed full of the gloom of autumn. These flowers were long dead. Their heads were as dry as paper. But they weren't just Michaelmas daisies.

They are the death of love, thought Henry. *They are the grave that waits for us all*. He really should write some of these things down. They were deserving of a wider audience.

Everything else on the lawn – a stone bird-bath, a broom resting against the front window-sill, a small, not very attractive shrub by the low wall that separated *her* home from the street – seemed amazingly clear and distinct. He found himself wondering whether she ever sat in this garden. Did she look at it from her upstairs window before getting ready for another day at the newsagent's? Had she crossed it and re-crossed it as a child, staggering against the gnome or the bird-bath and –

He was standing by the garden wall. And there were voices coming from behind the front door. Someone was coming out! With a hasty look behind him, Henry ducked down. But even when bent double he found he wasn't able to hide himself completely. He got down on all fours. Even then, the tip of his rear end felt exposed. He ended up looking like someone who has just aborted a press-up – resting on his two forearms while his toes kept the rest of his body clear of the pavement. The door was opening!

'There's no one there!' he heard a man's voice say.

'But there was!' This was the girl. 'There was this horrible man. With a huge nose. And a beard. And glasses.'

The man laughed. 'Don't be silly, love!' he said. 'There's no one! Look! There isn't anyone there!'

The two of them came a little way down the path. Henry held his breath.

'There's no one!'

'I've seen him before!' said the girl. 'Lurking. I didn't like to say. But tonight he was . . .' She gave a little shudder. '. . . He was after me.'

They moved a little way down the path. For a moment Henry thought they were going to step out on to the street. But then the man, who sounded unkeen on meeting the stranger with the big nose and the beard, clucked and pressed her back into the house. As soon as he heard the door slam, Henry got up and ran towards the railway.

She would probably call the police. Any minute now, they would be cruising the streets of Wimbledon looking for a man answering to her description. He must take off the beard and the nose. He stopped on a deserted stretch of pavement and groped at the back of the wig for the string that fixed the nose to his face. He couldn't find the knot! And when he found it, it was tied too tightly. He couldn't get his nails into it. He scrabbled desperately but the knot wouldn't give. Calmly now. Calmly.

He let his hands fall to his sides. He breathed out. Counted to ten. Slowly. Then, very gradually, he let his hands come up to the level of his head. The important thing was not to panic. To take your time. To simply get the fingers round the string and then to –

'Hullo there!'

Henry jumped six inches in the air.

'Hi de hi!'

The voice was coming from the other side of the road. Henry kept very still. Did he have time to run?

'I didn't recognize you at first!'

Henry still didn't respond. But now he thought he recognized the voice.

'I shouldn't think you do your shopping like that!' It was the man from the butcher's.

At last Henry had found the knot. He untied it and yanked the nose, savagely, from his face. The beard, too, came loose.

'Are you going to a fancy-dress party?'

Henry turned to face him. 'That's it!' he said. 'Or rather . . . just coming from one!'

The weasely man from the butcher's crossed the road towards him.

'Who are you?'

Henry stammered. 'I'm . . . er . . . Rasputin,' he said, eventually.

The little man gave him an appraising stare. 'You look, well, frightening!' he said.

Henry pulled off the hat, the wig and the dark glasses. The little man was looking at the nose with a grey expression that Henry found unnerving. It was the way a child might look at a new toy. Something made Henry start to put the thing away, out of sight, but before he could do so the little man was upon him, sniffing the nose, like a dog.

'Just the job!'

'Just the job for what?' said Henry.

The man leered. 'Give the girls a fright!'

Henry thought, but didn't say, that the butcher would not need a rubber nose to make any decent girl afraid to ever walk the streets of Wimbledon again. He looked at the little man's mac. It was entirely possible he was stark naked underneath it.

I'm one step away from this, thought Henry. *I'm the next best thing to a bloody flasher.* He felt suddenly old and lonely and sad.

'Turn up in the old wig and beard!' said the little man – who, if he *was* out for an evening of pointing his penis at unsuspecting women, was at least happy in his work – 'and a hooter like that and they'll wet themselves!'

He came close to Henry. A little too close. 'Poke 'em then!' he went on. 'Scare 'em and then poke the arse off them! That's my way!'

'Is it really?' said Henry.

The little man leered. 'Take them to see *The Blob*,' he said, 'and the old quim gets as wet as a dishrag!'

Henry was almost certain that he had never met anyone as repulsive as this man. He found he was walking away from him. The little man was following him. 'Give us a go, then!' he was saying. 'Let's try on the nose!'

If you hang around here in that outfit, thought Henry, *in a matter of moments you will run into the lads from Wimbledon CID on the lookout for a perve answering your description!*

He stopped and turned back to the little man. 'OK!' he said. 'It's all yours!'

The man smirked. 'And where's the party?' he said.

'Down there!' said Henry, pointing down the road from which he had come.

This seemed to please the butcher even more. He slipped the rubber nose on to his own and laid his index finger alongside it. 'I was going that way,' he said.

As he struggled into the beard, the hat and the wig and the glasses, Henry said: 'I can't remember the number. Just hang round the street and listen for the noise.'

Of police sirens!

The little man was delighted with his costume. He paced around the street, trying out what was supposed to be a Russian accent. He folded his arms and performed a ludicrous impression of a Cossack dance in front of Henry. Then, when Henry had also given him his mac, he paced up and down giving a mock Hitler salute.

'Drop into the shop tomorrow,' he said. 'I'll tell you how I got on!' Then he made pumping movements with his right arm. 'Will I shag or will I shag?' he said.

Or will I get six months for creating a nuisance?

Henry managed a smile as he turned to leave. 'Remember,' he said, 'just keep hanging around. You'll hear it eventually. If you don't, ring on a few doorbells and ask them where the action is.'

The man returned his smile with one of immense satisfaction. 'Don't worry,' he said, 'I know where the action is tonight!'

Henry didn't go into the newsagent's for nearly a week. He thought about the girl several times. But he was, as suddenly as he had been struck with her, sickened and puzzled at his behaviour. He was frightened, too. Perhaps the next time he saw her she would point one delicate arm at him and scream to the waiting shop, 'It's him! It's him!'

What had he been thinking of?

One brighter evening he decided he would look in on her. The spell, if that was what it was, had been broken. He hoped, now, that the obscene little man from the butcher's hadn't suffered as he had intended him to. The man, like the girl, like the unaccustomed words that had so tormented him in the second month of the year – *stained-glass window, luminous grace* – seemed ludicrous, almost unreal.

He would walk in, buy a paper. That would be all. And, with that totally normal transaction, the affair of the girl in the newsagent's would be over.

He let himself in very carefully. He closed the door so softly that the bell did not sound. The girl was talking with her friend, a plump creature with black hair, at the back of the shop. Neither of them saw Henry. There was no one else in the shop.

'It was last Friday,' the girl was saying, 'and I was *sure* I'd been followed home. But Mum and Dad went out anyway. Left me all alone.'

Henry kept very, very still.

'Then – I'm sitting there and the doorbell goes. I go to answer it and guess who's on the doorstep. Only the boyfriend. Only Kevin from the bloody butcher's!'

Her friend started to laugh.

'In a wig and a hat and glasses and a false nose!'

Her friend's laughter rose up the scale. It had, Henry thought, a hard, hysterical quality to it.

'I screamed blue murder when I saw him. I said, *Was you following me 'ome*? 'E said, *I got them off a geezer in the street*. I said, *Likely story!*'

''E's a terror, is Kevin!' said her friend.

The girl's voice dropped to a whisper. 'I nearly pissed myself,' she said, 'and we had sex. Right there on the sofa. I can't say no to Kevin. *Sometimes*, I said, *you go too far!* He said, *You love it though, doncher?*'

She stretched, catlike, behind the counter. 'It was almost as good,' she said, 'as when he took me to that film. *The Blob.*'

Neither of them looked up. Neither of them seemed to notice, even though the bell sounded, lightly, as Henry closed the door after him and climbed back up the hill towards his wife and daughter.

Keep Wimbledon White

IT WAS THE first day of spring. There were daffodils in Mrs Fountain's garden. The sun was shining. Henry's opposite neighbour (Is the Mitsubishi Scratched Yet?) had been seen in his garden in a large pair of khaki shorts. And there was a removal van outside 79 Maple Drive. Last week, Jan and Charlie and the twins (who everyone said were so sweet) had moved. Charlie had been made redundant. So had Jan. There were rumours that the twins weren't in great shape either. But everyone had come to their farewell drinks party, which they planned to hold on the patio. Charlie had built it, with his own hands, in the summer of 1989.

As it was the wettest March day since 1911, they had to entertain people in what their immediate neighbours called the drawing room. Charlie, rather bravely, did the barbecue in the garage and carried the smoking meat into what he called the lounge. Jan, who had designed the room herself, broke down and had a little weep on one of the packing cases.

Jan and Charlie had moved to Maple Drive from an estate in Southfields, just before Charlie got the job from which he had been recently fired. 'But,' as Is the Mitsubishi Scratched Yet? said to Man Who Painted His Brickwork Yellow, 'the children are always beautifully turned out.'

Everyone wanted to know about the new people. All Jan could say through her tears was, 'I hope they don't change the wallpaper!'

Charlie took Kevin Praed, the divorced publisher, to one side, squeezed his left arm very, very hard and said, after his third drink, 'Kevin – all I can say is – I'm sorry.'

So it wasn't really a surprise to anyone in the street when, from out of the removal van, came a small Indian, with a beaky nose and a rather dirty white suit, followed by a woman who was wearing what Mrs Gross, the retired architect's wife from number 82, described as 'a rather bold length of curtain material'. Behind her came no less than five small children. None of them, as far as Mrs Gross could tell, was white.

The Indian man stepped into the middle of the road, raised his hands above his head and, in a high, squeaky voice, spoke to the empty windows on both sides of the street. 'The wogs have arrived!' he said. 'Put your houses on the market now!'

Then, from out of the back of the removal van he took an elderly bicycle and an elderly man in white pyjamas. He balanced the old man on one arm and the bicycle on the other, then started up the garden path that Charlie had laid with his own hands in the autumn of 1991. As he got to the front door the old man started to sing something in a high, quavering voice. Mr Gross, who had, by now, joined his wife at the window, said later that he thought he recognized it as a traditional Punjabi folk tune.

'Shut up, Daddy!' said the Indian. 'It is either you or the bicycle!' With which he dropped both of them on the flowerbed, and sauntered back to the street.

Mrs Gross kept her eyes on the van. There might, she decided, be a few more wives to come. Instead, another, rather larger Indian emerged from the driver's cab and addressed the whole street in a voice about two octaves lower than his companion's.

'I must apologize for my relative,' he said. 'He is an incorrigible fellow. But I think he will prove a first-class neighbour.'

Henry recognized the man as J. Malik, the headmaster of the Wimbledon Independent Islamic Boys' Day School. He was wearing a dark suit and a grey silk tie. Henry had often seen him in the pub, where he was to be seen ostentatiously calling for tomato juice, alcohol-free lager and every conceivable kind of mineral water.

Henry was out jogging. Elinor had bought him a green track suit and a pair of trainers that inflated like a Li-lo. Maisie had bought him a sweat-band, a pedometer and an ordnance survey map of Wimbledon 'in case he got lost'. Then they had pushed him out of the door and told him to get on with it.

His 'jog' was an arthritic shuffle, slightly slower than a fast walking pace, and as he was passing Mr and Mrs Gross's house he was able to catch the expression on the face of the wife of the ex-architect. He recalled it often, in the light of subsequent events. The sixty-five-year-old Cambridge graduate looked as if someone had been sick over her shoes.

The old man in white pyjamas was crawling down the front garden of Jan and Charlie's house. He seemed keen, Henry thought, to get back in the van. But, when he was halfway to the gate, the small Indian with the beaky nose ran towards him, swept round behind the old gentleman and booted him, quite hard, in his raised buttocks.

'Fingers out of bottoms!' he said. 'Chop chop, Chinaman! To it, Father!'

He turned once more to Maple Drive. His voice seemed even higher and squeakier than before. 'We have a lot of very tasteless furniture to unload,' he yelled, 'and a few thousand stolen videos, principally of badly dubbed dramas from the Bombay area!'

J. Malik went up to him and put his arm on his arm. In deep, slightly stagey tones, he said, 'For God's sake, Hanif! First impressions are lasting impressions!'

'First impressions my bottom!' said the little man. 'First impressions my fine old Irish bum!'

Henry leaned against Mr and Mrs Gross's wall. He could see Mrs Gross's eyes flick, briefly, in his direction. Normally his behaviour would have had her out on the street in seconds but, for the moment, there were even more unpleasant things than Henry on the horizon. He saw her parrot's nose peck angrily against the glass.

Hanif was certainly not lying about the furniture.

First out was a sideboard about the size of a small motor cruiser. It was carved out of some cheap, white, lacquered material. There were little turrets, small shelves with mirrors and what looked like a cardboard cut-out of the Taj Mahal. On one side of this someone had added a fretwork impression of the Manhattan skyline, and on the other what looked like a three-dimensional reproduction in balsawood of the Leaning Tower of Pisa.

Hanif, his wife, and three of his children, carried the thing through the front gate and laid it carefully on the exposed back of the elderly man in white pyjamas. At first Henry thought the little old man was going to be ironed flat into Charlie's crazy paving, but, instead, with a whinny of pride, he performed half an immaculate three-point-turn, pulled his chin down into his neck, tucked his knees up to a crouch, and scuttled, crabwise, towards the front door with the sideboard on his back.

Hanif turned to the street. 'Seventy-four years old!' he yelled. 'And still sexually active!'

There was a crash as the left wing of the sideboard collided with a free-standing coach-lamp, installed by Charlie in the summer of 1987 – its cable laid so deep by the DIYer that he had been quoted a price of six hundred pounds for removing it to the new family home in Thanet.

'Watch out, beautiful Judies!' yelled Hanif, as he dived into the van and emerged with an armful of standard lamps and a large number of back numbers of the *Reader's Digest*. 'He likes it long and hot and strong!'

The little old man was crawling out from under the wreckage of the sideboard. 'Bastard!' Henry heard him mutter. 'Bloody buggering bastard!' Nobody paid any attention to him.

The children were carrying out other things that Henry could not remember having seen in an English domestic interior since the 1950s. There were nests of tables, pouffes, G-plan armchairs and (this set Mrs Gross's nose tapping even more furiously against her windowpane) a huge pair of speakers in walnut casings, with a television whose screen was concealed behind a pair of inlaid mahogany doors.

The woman had disappeared inside the house. From behind him Henry heard a low, throaty voice. It was Norbert DuCane from 98, a.k.a. Man Who Loves Shopping. 'She's probably inside painting a twenty-foot mural on the sitting-room wall,' he said, 'with palm trees and so on. They do that.'

Henry, who had always disliked Norbert, and who disliked Mr and Mrs Gross even more (Mrs Gross was now making shovelling gestures to DuCane), moved forward and took a small plastic stool off one of the children. 'Let me give you a hand,' he said, waving cheerfully to Mrs Gross as he did so. 'And welcome to Maple Drive!'

J. Malik, who had put himself in charge of a large glass ashtray, beamed at him approvingly.

'The Prophet,' he said, 'would wholeheartedly approve of your actions. Are you by any chance Muslim?'

Henry picked up another stool and followed him into the house. 'I'm afraid not,' he said, 'but I've always rather fancied it. I wouldn't mind another couple of wives.'

Mr Malik shrugged. 'Me neither,' he said, shrugging regretfully, 'but we cannot all have the sexual charisma of the Prophet Muhammed.'

Hanif came round the drawing-room door. He was clutching a large fish-tank. In it was a jumbo-sized goldfish. The old man in the white pyjamas followed him into the hall. He was carrying an electric fire in one hand and a large beach umbrella in the other.

'Put Henry in the kitchen!' he said.

For a moment Henry thought he might have violated some religious taboo. Then he realized the old man was referring to the goldfish. He felt curiously pleased about their choice of name.

'Hanif is my cousin,' said Mr Malik, 'and he needs a great deal of looking after. I am pleased to think he will have a new friend in the road!'

Hanif took the fish-tank through to the kitchen. He came back to find his wife and children marching through the hall carrying a selection of saucepans, cutlery and some large earthenware pots. He beamed at them. 'Culinary equipment!' he said. 'For creating unpleasant, lingering cooking smells with which one can antagonize the neighbours.'

Close to, he seemed even smaller than he had at a distance. As well as a large nose he had gigantic, intricate ears and a mouthful of bad teeth. As he looked around at Charlie and Jan's colour scheme, chosen by them in the winter of 1990 (peach marbled walls, ivory dragged woodwork and curtains from Peter Jones), his nostrils twitched like a prospecting rodent's.

'This is all in worryingly muted colours,' he said. 'We will have to attend to it.'

Hanif's father came back from the kitchen. He was now carrying one of the children, a small, fat girl who answered to the name of Fatima. Perhaps, thought Henry, they all carried each other round on a rota basis. Perhaps, now he seemed to be part of the group, the small fat boy who had just walked in with a bronze statuette, would pick up Henry and carry him off to another room.

'What line of business are you in?' said Henry.

'I am involved in the distribution of crack,' said Hanif, 'and also with the export of English virgins to the Third World.'

J. Malik cackled as the three of them went out once more to the van. 'Hanif is an electrician,' he said. 'So if you have any appliances that need mending or servicing, give them to him.'

The little man laughed. 'If you want your toaster to explode,' he said, 'I am your man. I can also effectively disable almost any brand of electric fire within a matter of minutes.'

He looked up and down the street, and, spreading his arms wide, once more addressed the citizens of Maple Drive: 'Sell now!' he called.

'Before the rest of us arrive! There is a large contingent bivouacked on the Common, waiting for the order to move in! The game is up!'

In spite of his opening performance, Hanif turned out to be rather popular. He was also, to Henry's surprise, a very good electrician. Electricity was not his only talent. He was good at plastering, brick-work, rubbish disposal, baby-sitting and cooking. In addition to this he was a competent pianist and, after only three days in Maple Drive, had painted and sold a watercolour of the exterior of number 79.

'It is so you can remember it before the wogs got at it,' he said to Mrs Gross, as he sat at his easel, directly in front of her house, 'and painted the whole façade bright yellow.'

Henry and Elinor adopted him. He was the first project on which they had been able to collaborate since the beginning of the year and, when he was around, their relationship showed signs of improvement. Like some alien monster, their marriage seemed to need periodic injec-tions of new flesh, or other lives. As if aware of his importance to them, Hanif made it his business not only to charm each of them but to pay flirtatious compliments to their coupledom.

'You two,' he would say, 'are better than a cabaret. It is only when I hear you pretend to dislike each other that I know the meaning of love.' Or, 'What I adore about the Farrs is that you are so perfectly *unperfect*. And so romantically unromantic. You are the great love affair of Maple Drive.'

Elinor, who was almost pathetically grateful for praise even if it included Henry, started to behave as if this might actually be true. She spent long hours with Hanif in the kitchen, discussing the state of the world.

'I am an Englishwoman!' she would say, waving her arms crazily. 'And you are a Muslim man from far away across the sea! And yet we have this . . . *rapport*!'

Hanif did not point out that he had been born in Bromley or that he charged a flat rate of fifteen pounds an hour for the rapport between them since he regarded sitting in the kitchen talking to Elinor as heavy domestic work.

He even lightened Maisie's life.

Her relationship with James Seebohm was at an even lower ebb than usual. Her friend Erica had told her that Seebohm had told Jeannette Goodwin, who had told her, that Maisie was too demanding. Jeannette

Goodwin had told Mary Leemis, who had told Birgitte Bjerkin, that she fancied James Seebohm. When Henry had said that he couldn't understand why anyone would fancy James Seebohm and that he thought James Seebohm looked like a rat, Maisie burst into tears and ran from the room.

'You don't know what it's like to be fifteen!' Elinor had snarled.

'I was fifteen once,' Henry had replied.

'You were never fifteen!' Elinor responded. 'You were born forty-five-years-old!'

'I was only trying,' said Henry, before leaving for the pub, 'to cheer her up!'

Hanif's arrival improved her temper beyond all recognition. She sat for hours in his front room listening to him play the first two *Goldberg Variations*. She went out with him on calls and even passed on some of his advice on marital relations to her parents.

'Hanif says,' she told them one night, 'that springtime is the time when you should renew trust and love!'

All of which helped to explain why Henry was so shocked to see, on the low wall outside 79, faced in concrete and painted white by Charlie in 1986, the message WOGS GO HOME!

There was a trail of red paint leading away from the wall and across the road, in the direction of Norbert DuCane's house.

Which made Henry suspect that the graffiti was not the work of DuCane. It was too obvious. And, besides, DuCane, a man who was reputed to wear a three-piece suit to brush his teeth, was known to be incapable of performing the simplest domestic task. He would have had to have hired a fashionable builder and obtained a free quotation even to write WOGS GO HOME on someone's wall.

Although several neighbours offered to scrub the slogan off, Hanif said he was going to leave it where it was. 'It's a strong statement!' he said. 'It focuses attention on an important issue. Anyway – it is evidence!'

Elinor had a coffee morning the following Saturday, and Maisie ran out a poster on her computer. It read:

STAND BY THE MAPLE DRIVE SEVEN!
HANIF MALIK IS ONE OF US!
WE STAND BY HIM!

He is an electrician and available for most kinds of wiring and machine servicing. Ring him on 081 9463725 or on his mobile number*

* Not available at time of going to press.

It had been Hanif's idea to combine an anti-racist leaflet and a business address card. In fact, although Elinor asked him to address the ladies of Maple Drive on the subject of MY STRUGGLE AGAINST THE WHITE SUPREMACISTS, he said he would rather get on and try to master the third *Goldberg Variation*.

'The fact of the matter, my dears, is,' he said to the Farr family, 'you don't breed white supremacists. Most of your chaps roll over and wave their legs in the air at the first sign of trouble.'

They had the coffee morning anyway. And, as a sign of the improved relations between Henry and Elinor, Henry was allowed to attend. He sat at the back trying not to make slurping noises with his coffee and watched the company. Mrs Jeeps, in a pair of pistachio leg-warmers, was sitting on the floor next to Mrs Allen, one arm draped over her friend's knee. In the far corner, Miss Dunwich and Mrs Lubin were giggling together. Were any of these people capable of daubing racist slogans on walls? thought Henry. Surely not. It was someone from outside the street.

But there was something strange about the gathering. He could not for the moment say what it was.

'I think,' said Maisie, 'we should march!'

'March where?' said Elinor.

'Up and down the street!' said Maisie.

Mrs Allen thought there might be violence. Miss Dunwich said she thought there wouldn't. Hanif said that he had contacted the police and that they were certain it wasn't anybody from Maple Drive. Elinor said that they had once had a paper-boy who, when he didn't receive a Christmas box, had broken two of their front windows.

But it was Henry, who, in one of the infrequent pauses in the conversation, said, 'Why isn't Mrs Gross here?'

Mrs Gross had not been known to miss a ladies' coffee morning once during the last ten years. 'Snooper' Gross, as she was known, had even been rumoured to secretly record them in case anyone said anything incriminating. She missed nothing. As she cycled between her house and the local Presbyterian church on the Gross family tandem she would rake the windows of every house in the street with her bright-blue, piggy little eyes.

Why isn't Mrs Gross here?

As soon as everyone realized she was absent they started to discuss her.

'She's probably behind it!' said Mrs Jeeps.

'She is an admirable lady,' said Hanif. 'She is a Christian of the best type!'

Some people doubted this. Mrs Allen said she had once caught Mrs Gross training a pair of binoculars on the window of a woman suspected of having extramarital relations. Miss Dunwich said she could be savage in a queue.

But it was Henry who said, 'There was something about the writing. On Hanif's wall. That looked familiar.'

After this, it wasn't long before someone suggested that they all go out and examine the slogan. Although no one said so, everybody knew that Mrs Gross's handwriting was liable to be the most easily recognized in the whole street, since hardly a day went by when she did not slip an invitation to a bazaar, a request for charity or a warning about some impending traffic plan through every letter-box in Maple Drive.

The coffee morning drifted out of number 54 and up towards Hanif's house. It was a clear, bright day, and the ladies, spread out across the road reminded Henry of exotic birds as they laughed, touched each other's arms and whispered confidences across the brilliant street.

He was the first to see that somebody had daubed a message on the pavement outside Hanif's house. This time they had used white paint, but the characters were formed in the same way. NIGGERS BEWARE was what it said. A trail of white paint led away from the last letter of the last word into the middle of the street. Henry and Maisie followed it on to the opposite pavement. It led, with what seemed like artificial directness, to Norbert DuCane's front garden.

Norbert's front lawn was protected by a six-foot-high privet hedge, but, on the upper leaves, Henry could make out a few flecks of white paint. When he and Maisie pushed open the front gate and tiptoed up the path, they saw, under his window-sill, a large can of emulsion and a brush, fully loaded, leaking whiteness on to the rank grass. As Henry and Maisie stood looking at it they heard a voice from the front gate.

'Oh dear!' said Mrs Gross. 'Has Norbert been a naughty boy?'

It did not really matter whether Mrs Gross was trying to frame Norbert, with whom she had had a bitter dispute about a lawn mower, or whether she and Norbert were in it together, or whether, as Elinor suggested, a third person was trying to frame the two of them – since they were the most unpopular people in Maple Drive.

Whoever was scrawling on Hanif Malik's house was getting away with it. The police sent round fingerprint experts, counsellors and a large West Indian sergeant called Wesley but, after several weeks, they admitted failure.

Not only was he getting away with it. Hanif refused to erase any of the messages scrawled on his walls or his patch of pavement. He even took a selection of hate mail and pinned it on a noticeboard in his front garden. Indeed, the more virulent the letters (all of which were in crudely scrawled capitals), the more determined he seemed to be to keep them before the public's attention. Several people said they thought his behaviour was in bad taste.

After two weeks his house looked like a parcel that had been re-addressed to the point of illegibility. Whoever was leading the campaign had scrawled on almost every available square of brickwork. On the garage roof they had written WE DON'T WANT PAKKY BARSTIDS HERE and on the front path Aerosolled the legend OUR KIDS WANT TO SPEKE ENGLISH, to which Hanif responded, 'The man has a point! There are clearly so many wogs here you can't even speak your own language any more!'

The person most offended by the gradual stencilling of Hanif's house was Mrs Gross. 'I have to look at it every morning!' she said to Miss Dunwich at the bus-stop one afternoon. 'He must be made to clean the things up!'

In fact the daubed messages only seemed to inspire Hanif to yet more decorative motifs. Out of the top front bedroom he hung a Union Jack and on several of the inscriptions he added footnotes, commenting on their spelling, probable date and literacy value. He even put out a selection of chalks, crayons and paints in his front drive, labelled DO-IT-YOURSELF RACIST SLOGANS. He was often seen asking Mrs Gross to comment on a particular graffito and, on several occasions, was heard to remark to Norbert DuCane that the racist abuse in Wimbledon was 'of a much higher order than in Tooting'.

The effect on Mrs Gross was profound. She started to be nice to people. She was even seen talking to Norbert. The two of them went to Wimbledon Police Station to complain about the state of Hanif's house. Not long after the police had told them both, 'Mr Malik's décor is up to him!', they were seen shopping together in the High Street. People in Maple Drive used to say that there was no greater form of intimacy as far as DuCane was concerned.

One evening, Henry was called to the window by Elinor, who had heard shouting from up the street.

Hanif and his father were yelling at Mrs Gross and DuCane, who were scrubbing his front wall. Henry and Elinor retreated to the kitchen but they heard afterwards that the entire Malik family had pelted DuCane and Gross with bric-à-brac, while they, with British imperturbability, scrubbed away furiously until Hanif's front wall read, WO   OME.

It was this, rather than the writing daubed on his house, that seemed to depress Hanif. Although he came round as usual the next day and dropped his usual pretence of having a high regard for 'Snooper' Gross, something about her behaviour had done what the anonymous campaigner could not do: it had depressed him. His step was slower. He would sometimes fall into a reflective silence and, after his third cup of tea, he said, 'That woman is immovable. There is something about her you can't shift. She could conquer damned continents. She thinks she's right, you see.' And he added, looking mournfully out at the street, 'Maybe she is.'

Early April brought rapid, grey clouds and winds that rattled the glass in Henry's windows. After the shouting match in the street, Hanif seemed to give up his attempts to draw attention to the campaign against him, and, a few days later, he allowed Mrs Gross, Norbert and a team of local boy scouts into his house. After a few hours number 79 was as perfect as it had been when Jan and Charlie first decorated it in the spring of 1985.

But Hanif was not the same man. He didn't spend as much time with Henry and Elinor. He no longer had the power to cheer up Maisie. Once, he connected up the wrong wires in the fridge. He was rumoured to have started a small fire in Edwina Sprott's radio.

When he said he was taking his family away, Henry knew he was beaten. 'Only for a few days,' he said to the Farrs. 'We have a *pied-à-terre* in Broadstairs.'

But Henry had the feeling, when he and Elinor waved goodbye to his battered camper van, that the little man had lost a battle. He couldn't have said what it was.

'Perhaps,' said Maisie, 'he really thought they *were* evidence. Perhaps he knows now that he'll never find out who was doing it!'

Gross and DuCane were smirking at each other the day Hanif left, as if at some shared secret. The little man looked across at them.

'You know what is amazing about the British?' he said.

Henry said he couldn't think of anything amazing about them at the moment. 'Their ability to cover their tracks!' said Hanif. With these words he climbed into the van and jolted off down Maple Drive. Mrs Gross and Norbert watched the van until it was out of sight. The retired architect's wife's face wore an expression Henry had not seen on it since the wedding of Prince Charles and Lady Diana Spencer – it was beyond satisfaction. She looked more than anything like the hawk in Ted Hughes's poem, determined to *keep things like this*.

At about four o'clock that morning, there was a loud explosion from the carport built by Charlie in the winter of 1988. By four-fifteen, when Gunther, the German violinist from 61, a.k.a. Nazi Who Escaped Justice at Nuremberg, called the fire brigade, the whole of the west side of the building was alight. The neighbours who gathered in the road (neither Norbert nor Mrs Gross was among them) said that, when the flames spread to the living room the place went up as if someone had sprayed a few gallons of kerosene all over Hanif's furniture.

Which, it later transpired, they had.

Not only that, the original explosion in the carport had been caused by a fire-bomb, activated by a time-fuse. If Charlie had not personally erected a ten-foot, blast-proof wall between himself and the neighbours in the autumn of 1990, Mr and Mrs Nigel Frayn, whose son was so intelligent that he had taken GCSE maths six years too early, would probably have been blasted into the front garden of number 75.

'It's *awful*!' Mrs Gross was heard to say when she finally appeared, in her dressing gown. 'Just *awful*!'

And she was seen to cast a glance towards Norbert DuCane's. Norbert managed to sleep his way through the arrival of four fire engines, under the command of Larry 'Big Boy' Ransom, who sprayed everyone in Maple Drive, including Henry, with high pressure foam.

Jim 'Hard Man' Waring, his second-in-command, insisted on going into the blazing building, although everyone told him there was nothing in there but a lot of blazing, tasteless furniture and a parboiled goldfish. He insisted he had heard human cries. Waring's friend Ted 'Massive' Duclerc, who, people at the station said, had an almost unhealthy attachment to Hard Man, followed him, pursued in his turn by Bobby 'Hack 'Em' Pratchett, who, some said, felt much the same way about Massive. The three of them smashed in the downstairs front window and, after blundering about inside for a few minutes, and, in Big Boy's words, 'nancying up the stairs with oxygen masks', emerged with the goldfish, which was warm but sentient.

It was too late to save the house. The roof had gone by five-fifteen and at a quarter to six the water tank in the loft fell through the insulated loft floor (1986), through the bathroom below (cork tiled, 1987), past the blazing staircase (sanded, stained and varnished in the same year as the bathroom) and landed slap bang in the middle of a kitchen designed and built by Charlie that some said was worth nearly twenty thousand pounds on the open market.

'If we hadn't been called in time,' said Big Boy, 'the whole street might have gone up!'

And it would have served the bastards right, thought Henry.

He did not, as a rule, allow himself to ask what he felt about his neighbours. But something about the little man had touched him. His perverse humour, his unfailing courtesy, or perhaps, as Elinor acidly pointed out, the fact that he was so amazingly useful. 'You can't even change a plug!' she said. 'You can't even ring someone up to ask them if they could change a plug. And now you've lost someone who did it all for us without asking!'

For Hanif did not return to Maple Drive after his holiday. In the end Henry went up to the pub and asked his cousin what had happened to the little man.

J. said, 'His heart is broken, my friend! He has had enough!' The headmaster told Henry that he thought Hanif had decided to go long before the fire. 'There's some woman there,' he said, 'a Mrs Gross? I don't know. Anyway – it sounds as if she got to him.'

Henry took the goldfish, which was the only thing that survived the blaze, across to the Islamic School, on the day the FOR SALE sign went up once more outside number 79. John de Brazier, the estate agent, was showing someone round the blackened shell of the place. As Henry passed him he was standing in the ashes of Jan and Charlie's bin-housing unit, waving his blazered arms at the south-facing walls and crying, 'Casement windows! Enormous potential!'

Over at the school, Mr Malik would not say where Hanif had gone. When Henry tried to discuss the case, the headmaster merely shrugged. When asked how a sixty-five-year-old retired architect's wife could have got hold of a fire-bomb, he became almost irritable. 'This is a more complicated question, Farr,' he said. 'This is a very complicated question indeed! I am not sure how to explain it myself.'

With a profound feeling of failure Henry wandered out on to the Common and started back towards Maple Drive. Did the headmaster know something he didn't?

He was a few hundred yards away from Queensmere when he saw a figure he recognized. At first he could not believe that the beaky nose, the thinning hair and the familiar drooping shoulders actually belonged to Hanif. But it was him. The little man was standing by his camper van. His father was inside with one pyjama'd leg up over the dashboard. But Hanif looked quite different. He was wearing a dark suit and carrying a smart, black briefcase. When Henry called to him he turned and gave a broad grin. 'Still here, Farr? You are too big for Wimbledon, you know that? You should get out! You need wide open spaces! You are a man of vision.'

Henry said he thought he was stuck in Wimbledon. He wished, he went on to say, that Hanif had not sold up. The little man looked at him shrewdly. 'You like having a wog around, eh?' he said.

'It's preferable to some of the people we have in the street!' said Henry.

Hanif nodded slowly. 'That Mrs Gross . . .' he said, '. . . she is quite something . . .'

Henry nodded.

'Racism is bad enough,' the little man went on in a slightly sententious tone. 'But those who pretend it doesn't exist are even worse!'

Henry nodded again.

'It's about the one flourishing industry in this God-forsaken country,' went on Hanif, with slightly more enthusiasm, 'and we might as well own up to it. You're all pretty racist. Even when you pretend you aren't.'

'So what do we do about it?' said Henry.

Hanif did not attempt to answer this question. He gave the kind of shrug that indicated this was something for Henry to think about rather than him.

The two men walked a little way away from the van. Inside, Hanif's father had fallen asleep and was snoring loudly.

'Was it her or DuCane?' asked Henry. 'Or both of them? Was that why they were so keen to scrub your walls? Was there something that tied them to the business?'

'No one likes being confronted with what they think,' said Hanif. 'It is why I have never kept a diary. But if you are asking who wrote all over my frontage, I should tell you, in strict confidence of course, that it was me!' He grinned. 'I was quite pleased with *Pakky Barstids*,' he went on, 'and it set the scene for the fire rather nicely. I had insured the contents alone for over a quarter of a million. They were valued by a relative of mine who works for the Bradford General Assurance Company Ltd.'

He winked and placed his finger to his nose. 'Keep Wimbledon White! I say,' he chuckled, 'and turn Virginia Water brown. I've got three acres and a swimming pool. Come down and bring that delightful family of yours!'

Real Men Throw Women in Ravines

'ISN'T IT GREAT to get away from it all?' said Henry.

Maisie, who was about fifteen yards below him on the path, grunted. Then she said, 'Away from what?'

Henry stopped, leaned on a rock and looked back down Sourmouth Ghyll or Milkmaid's Bottom or whatever it was called. Over to his right was something that might have been Clawpits Crag or Blindman or, perhaps, a completely anonymous chunk of pre-Cambrian rubbish that no one had bothered to dignify with a title. Below him lay the valley floor, green and brown in the April sunlight, winding its way towards whichever bit of the Lake District they had left this morning and to which – assuming his map-reading skills improved by three hundred per cent in the hours of daylight left to them – they would be returning this evening. They would be tired, they would be footsore, but they would have the satisfaction of knowing they had climbed –

Great Gable? Scafell Pike? Helvellyn? Ben Nevis?

Something anyway. He got out the ordnance survey map, wondering, as always, at the way the complicated whorls of the contour lines seemed to bear no relation to any of the hideously complicated three dimensions through which ramblers are doomed to wander.

'Away from Wimbledon,' he said. 'This is so different!'

'Is it?' said Maisie. Her face was bright red. Lumps of her hair, matted with sweat, trailed across her forehead, damp with the effort of the climb. She was wearing a Crevasse all-weather anorak, PVC overtrousers and a pair of Zammerland boots that had cost Henry a hundred pounds. Underneath her anorak, she had on two woollen jerseys, a woollen shirt and a thermal bodystocking. She looked, Henry thought, like the Michelin man.

'Where's Mummy?'

Henry started to beat out the ordnance survey map across the rock. 'Fallen off a cliff, I expect!' he said brightly.

They looked back down the path. It followed the course of a beck, round the side of a huge shoulder of rock, decorated by only a few twisted trees and the occasional sheep. There was one just above Henry and Maisie, chewing methodically at nothing. *You're only here for a week*, its expression seemed to say, *I have to live here the whole bleeding year.*

Although the path turned into the mountain about thirty yards behind them, Henry could see beyond that, to where it wound back out from the rock past another stretch of the beck, about a hundred yards below. It was along this stretch of stony ground that a huge, shapeless figure, crowned with a yellow woolly hat, now came slowly into view.

Every three or four yards, Elinor would lean forward, put both hands on one leg and put her head down between her knees. It was hard to be sure at this distance but Henry thought she might be crying. When she saw Henry and Maisie she started to do a kind of sema-phore. She looked, Henry thought, as if she was guiding a helicopter in to land. Perhaps there was one in the offing.

'Shall we go down to her?' said Maisie.

Henry shook his head. 'We can't afford to lose height!' he said.

Elinor stumbled. She seemed to have decided to do this section on her hands and knees.

Henry clicked his tongue. 'She's making very heavy weather of it!'

As they watched she fell forward on to her face and lay, spread-eagled on the rock, like a starfish stranded by the tide.

'She's just getting her second wind!' said Henry. He looked up from the map and squinted up the path in what he hoped was a convincing manner. Ahead of them scraps of mist were blowing over sharp edges of grey rock. His eye was caught by some red marks on the map that looked as if they might be close to where they were now standing.

'Where are we?' said Maisie, for the sixth time in half an hour.

'I think,' said Henry, 'we are heading into a Ministry of Defence free-fire zone! Prang the ramblers sort of thing. Get the old heat-seeking missiles zeroing in on the odd scout troop lost in the mist.'

Down below, Elinor had started to crawl forward on her stomach. This was presumably, Henry decided, meant to be funny. He folded the map into a neat square. As far as he could tell the footpath curved up to follow the beck then crossed the open moorland to the west. Or maybe it was the south. Or north, perhaps.

He got out the compass and its needle swung, wildly, in several directions at once. All he had to do was to find where north was. Then he had to point the map north. Then he had to face north as well. Then he would know where he was. Well, not exactly where he was. He would know he was somewhere in the Lake District, facing north. That would be a start.

But how would he know that the right bit of the map was facing north? He might line up a bit of the map that was in fact south-south-west of where he was with the direction of magnetic north. That would be a lot of help, wouldn't it? Maybe he should leave the map out of this. Maybe he should line up the compass and head north until he came to a main road, assuming he didn't fall off a cliff first.

Maisie was looking at him suspiciously. Henry tried to look as if he knew where they were.

'What you've got to do,' Maisie said, 'is find a detail in the landscape and match up the map to it!'

Henry tried to look as if this was what he had been doing. He looked down at the map, and, aware that Maisie was watching him closely, raised his eyes from it and panned his eyes across the landscape. There seemed to be a marked absence of detail in it. All he could make out was grass, the occasional rock and a few sheep. He peered once again at the small square of brown contour lines. In the top left-hand corner was a tastefully shaded replica of what looked like a row of teeth. Next to it, in Gothic script, was the word QUARRY. Henry peered into the mist, scraps of which were now swirling round them.

'There should be a quarry ahead!' he said in bold, forceful tones.

Before Maisie could comment on this remark there was the sound of a colossal engine from further up the hillside. The noise suddenly altered pitch and, as Henry realized it was fizzing directly over their heads, he looked up to see a camouflaged fighter tearing out of the mountain towards the valley. It buzzed, like a huge insect, over the valley floor, and, almost as soon as he had made out its shadow skimming across the green spring grass, it had gone.

'One of ours,' said Maisie, narrowing her eyes. 'Out of RAF Dunsmore, I expect.'

The sight of the plane seemed to cheer her up. Henry knew how she felt. Any fragment of the civilized world, even if it was headed away from them at a speed of a thousand miles an hour, was welcome. What he could really do with was an ice-cream van.

Something was coming to them from below. It was huge, about

seven or eight feet in length and it seemed to be almost the same distance across. It was making a hideous, moaning noise, a bleak restless whine that seemed formed out of the wind, the rain and the heather of this God-forsaken place. It was not, as a casual observer might have thought, some Cumbrian variant of the Yeti; it was Elinor.

'Why don't you wait, you bastard?' she said. Her arms, encased in a quilted Pinnacle anorak, stuck out at right angles to her body, as rigid as a doll's.

Henry looked at his watch. 'We have to press on!' he said, as Elinor fell forward on to the scree. Then, refreshed by the pause, he started up the mountain at a brisk pace.

'Don't leave me here!' moaned Elinor. 'I am going to collapse!'

Had the woman no sense of humour? Hadn't she heard of grace under pressure? He had thought, ever since the Hanif Malik business, they had been getting on quite well. He had even hoped, once or twice, that they might manage a bit of sex. But somehow sex was never forthcoming. He was always too busy or she was too busy or they were both too tired or perhaps, like Leo Nikolayevich Tolstoy in his later years, both pissed off to the back teeth with the mere idea of taking out your chopper and sticking it in someone's hole.

'I need to be seduced!' Elinor had said in a service station on the M6 on their way up here. 'I need to be ravished. I need a *real* man, Henry. Who needs me in a real way.'

Henry squared his shoulders and tried to look real. He did not find this easy.

'Not far now!' he said.

Maisie had shouldered her rucksack and was following him. It had been clever of him to make sure the sandwiches were in his pack.

He called back over his shoulder. 'Nothing like this in Wimbledon!' he shouted, in what he hoped was an encouraging tone. 'They're all slumped in front of the telly back there!'

He didn't like to think about Wimbledon. It seemed impossibly remote. It reminded him, too, of the fact that he had asked Angelica to come in and clean the house while they were away. He had offered her five pounds for six hours work which, at the time, had seemed a bargain. But he could not rid himself of the idea that she might, even now, be loading all their possessions on to a cart and heading off for Heathrow with a one-way ticket to Guatemala City tucked in her brassiere.

'No,' said Henry again. 'We may never see Wimbledon again!'

As he was saying this, he found he was looking at Emily Drossor of 116b Maple Drive, Wimbledon. She was wearing a green cagoule, knee-length breeches, a pair of amazingly elaborate leather boots and, looped about her shoulders, about a hundred yards of lightweight climbing rope.

'Henry!' she said. 'What are you doing here?'

She had an accusing expression on her face. But before he had a chance to ask her what the hell *she* was doing here and why she was posing about with about five hundred pounds worth of the sort of climbing equipment that should only really be worn by trained mountaineers, Mary Pleckett, the gym mistress at the Mary Louisa Haddock School for Girls, Wimbledon, sauntered into view. They seemed to be wearing the kind of garments seen on dummies in the shopwindow of Fellwalker, the establishment in Keswick from which Henry had bought his whistle, torch, survival pod and cellophane ordnance survey map holder. She was also, as far as Henry could tell, carrying an ice axe.

'My Christ!' muttered Maisie behind him. 'It's Jamrags Pleckett! And Loopy Matheson!'

It was important, Henry realized, that Jamrags should not catch sight of Elinor. Jamrags was Maisie's French teacher. Once Elinor realized she was on the mountain, they would never get off. She suffered from a delusion, Henry had noticed, infecting several mothers of his acquaintance – that a teacher's judgement of a pupil could be affected by its parent's opinion.

Other people from Wimbledon were coming at them through the cloud. All of them seemed to be women. And many of them seemed to be vaguely familiar, although Henry could not have said why.

As they swarmed up to Henry, Maisie started to make small, imitation retching noises. 'Sicko!' she whispered. 'It's Filthy English and Dildo Farmer! The whole staff room is here!'

That was where he had seen them all. At parents' evenings. Every single one of them was a member of staff of the Mary Louisa Haddock School for Girls, Wimbledon. And filtering through, in ones and twos, were members of the Upper Fifth.

Maisie continued to mime vomiting. 'It's Reeny,' she muttered, 'and Ardmilla! And the Ghosht twins! And the Balrog! It's the Easter field trip!'

Today was Good Friday. But, this year, Henry remembered, it was also April Fool's Day. Was this, perhaps, part of some elaborately constructed plot against him? Before he had time to consider the implications of this thought, or to dive over the thirty-foot sheer drop to the beck below, Elinor appeared.

'Miss Pleckett!' she said. The tiny area of her face exposed to the elements showed the effects of a smile.

'Elinor!' said Jamrags. 'How marvellous!'

More girls and women were approaching them. Maisie's arch-enemy, Stephanie Wyse-Fanshawe, a thin girl called Dawn who never spoke, Emma and Jackie, and a small, dark girl known as Mordor. There was Mrs Ruckett who had once given Maisie A-minus, and Brenda Lickspear who had said she had no aptitude for pottery. There was Jessie Bulldike White who had made her run round the games field in the middle of January, and Vera Dupuys who had cast her as Macbeth in her disastrous promenade production of that play. There was Creepy Rawlings who had lied about more than her age, and her friend Jenny Short who had said that Maisie had no aptitude for anything apart from causing trouble.

Before they could all start discussing Maisie's GCSEs, Henry stepped forward on to the path and planted his boots squarely on the damp ground. 'Are you lost?' he said.

Jamrags looked at him, pursing her lips. Bulldike White gave a loud guffaw. 'Are we hell!' she said. 'We're going to do Nosegay. By the Titchfield route!'

'If we don't get stuck in the Crack!' said Jamrags. Everyone bellowed with laughter at this sally.

Henry tried to look as if he recognized some of these names. 'Don't, whatever you do,' he said, 'get stuck in the Crack!'

'Where are you off to?' said Jamrags.

Before Henry had time to invent a suitably Norse-sounding name, Elinor said, 'We're lost. Hopelessly lost. Henry has no sense of direction whatsoever.'

All the women started to laugh. It was hard enough pretending to be a real man at the best of times. Faced with this lot it was a clearly impossible task.

'Come along with our posse!' said Bulldike. 'We'll take good care of you!'

Henry looked up the path. Whether it was that the mist had cleared, or simply that his masculine powers had been awakened by being sneered at by a group of demented lesbians, he suddenly felt he was very sure of where he was. That bumpy thing, up to the right, was the crag he had picked out of *One Hundred Tough Walks in the Lakes* last night, and beyond it, that dark shape on the side of the hill was, yes, it had to be, a quarry.

He moved in front of the women and positioned his trunk and rucksack parallel to the ground. He then turned through a hundred and eighty degrees and, while working his rucksack up on to his shoulders, pawed the ground, thrust his hindquarters in front of the assembled company and gave them about thirty seconds of lead bottom display. If they were going to play the fellmanship game, they had better know with whom they were dealing.

'We're going up Farson,' he said, 'and through to Gable by the back way. Then we'll hold to the tops and drop down into Buttermere!'

Jamrags Pleckett looked impressed. 'It's thirty mile to Buttermere,' she said, in a not very convincing rustic accent.

Henry straightened up. He gave a small smile. Then he waggled his right boot slowly to and fro. 'That's what, my good friends, my feet are for!' he said.

The women were clearly thrown by this. Even Bulldike was silent. Henry turned to his family, and put a protecting, patriarchal hand on Maisie's shoulder.

'Come on, girlies!' he said. 'Shanks's pony!'

With a groan, Elinor and Maisie followed him as he started up the path.

Henry was not exactly lost.

He could not, if he was honest, remember a moment of the day when he had really known where he was. There had been a brief glimmer of recognition as he drove up the Newlands Valley from Keswick, and he was fairly certain that the large patch of water he had passed earlier in the day was Derwentwater. But to be *lost* implied that at some point one had had some control over one's bearings.

What he had done, in essence, was to move through various phases of being lost. He was, he told himself, *experiencing different types of disorientation*. He had been not very sure, very uncertain, hopelessly confused and frighteningly isolated; he had wandered off the path, gone round in circles, retraced his steps, consciously and unconsciously, and was now undergoing a severe existential crisis with each step that he took.

But he was more determined than ever that no one in his family should be aware of this fact. It was something he had to deal with on his own.

To start with he had had the illusion that he was going somewhere. The horizon, as was often the case on mountains, had gone on for longer than he expected. He would labour up a patch of scree and stones to the white band of sky above it, only to find yet more scree and yet more stones above the skyline, still, apparently, at the same teasing distance from him. He had found a beck that he had thought must be something called Coates Gill and then, as he clambered up it, realized, with terrible certainty, that it had to be something called Skaira Force. For half an hour or so he had been convinced that the mountain ahead was familiar. He had even run ahead of Maisie and Elinor and sneaked a look at his *Illustrated Guide to the Lakes* to see if it matched any of the pictures; he had come to the conclusion that it could be any one of nine different peaks, some of them thirty miles apart.

They had seen no people. Not even a crisp packet for the last three hours. Even a lesbian would have been welcome.

Henry shouldered his rucksack and turned back to Elinor. 'I think,' he said, 'if we carry on up this path we should see the lake over the brow of the next hill.'

'What lake?' said Elinor.

Maisie puffed up to them. 'What hill?' she said.

Henry looked ahead of him.

Something had happened to the landscape. It had never had many points of interest. It had not, as far as he could recall, offered any trees since the morning. It tended to get a simple idea, such as, say, heather, or big grey rocks the size of a small car, and work it to death. But, at some point, there had been a quite striking display of a mountain range in the distance, and once the path they had taken had led them round the edge of some spectacular black cliffs with a drop of hundreds of feet to their left. But now, everything ahead of them was grey. After about fifteen yards, the scraps of cloud merged into long tendrils of grey mist that whirled and danced into each other like steam rising from some hellish kitchen. This wasn't like anything Henry had seen before. It wasn't simply opaque. It was a new element, asserting itself across the landscape, shouldering its way over grasses, pools and sodden earth until solid things seemed doubtful and all the available air as thick as some hideous soup.

'Mist!' said Henry in the clipped tones of a man who knew what he was talking about. 'That is mist!'

'I can see it's mist,' said Elinor, who seemed to find his calmness irritating, 'but what are we going to do about it?'

Henry narrowed his eyes and worked the lower half of his body into his Mathiessen cord breeches. 'We'll have to go back,' he said. 'There's a basic rule on mountains. If mist comes down, retrace your steps.'

They turned.

The mist seemed, somehow, to have sneaked up behind them as well. It hadn't been there before. But since the last time Henry had bothered to look behind him, it had moved in on every available square foot of moorland. It lay behind them like some ghostly army summoned by magic incantation – mysterious, apparently yielding, but obviously in control of everything to their rear. If this was their rear. It might well be their side. *I am*, thought Henry, *at last, literally in the position of not knowing my arse from my elbow. I am already hopelessly lost and now I am about to move into the ultimate stages of geographical self-doubt. I am about to be confused about my confusion. Oh help me, God, I am double bleeding lost!*

It was important not to let any of this show on his face.

'What do you do,' said Maisie, 'on mountains when you are totally surrounded by mist?'

Henry gulped. 'There are several things you can do . . . ' he said.

Elinor sat, heavily, on the grass to the left of the path. 'Let's hear them!'

'We could get into our survival bags,' he said slowly, 'and wait for help to arrive . . .' He tried to keep his voice on an even keel as he said this. Nobody seemed very impressed. 'We could follow the path back . . .'

The trick here was to sound as if you were considering all of these alternatives but, because you were a level-headed mountain man, you already knew what you were going to do. You were just letting them in on the process. It was important not to allow them to suspect that your favoured option at the moment was to roll around in the damp grass screaming for your mummy.

Elinor was looking at him.

'We could,' said Henry, in measured tones, 'let off flares!'

'But what,' said Elinor, 'are we going to do?'

'First,' said Henry, trying to suggest he had done this before, 'we check the survival equipment.'

Then we roll around on the damp grass and scream for our mummy.

The survival equipment, when they got it out of Henry's pack, was found to consist of a condom (for storing water), a large knife, some Kendal Mint Cake, a torch, three large polythene bags and a whistle.

'What do you do?' said Maisie. 'Eat the cake, pull the condom over your head, blow the whistle, climb into the bag and cut your throat by torchlight?'

'Not necessarily in that order . . . ' said Henry.

Maisie laughed. Elinor did not. Henry then read, aloud, the label on the polythene bags. 'This 7-foot by 3-foot quality polythene bag will protect from rain, wind and snow. Care should be taken when entering the bag. Enter it feet first.'

Elinor said she refused to enter a polythene bag, backwards, forwards or upside down. She said she felt like throwing Henry into one, head first, for having persuaded them to come up here in the first place. Maisie said she should be allowed to eat all the mint cake because she was the youngest. Eventually Henry packed the things back into his rucksack and peered into the mist. He could make out the next few yards but beyond that, nothing.

'I think,' he said, 'I recognize the rock formation!'

It was important to keep their spirits up. Elinor goggled at him. 'You don't really have a clue, do you?' she said.

'Trust me, my darling!' said Henry. Why was he saying this? He was only making it worse for himself. But, even at this late stage, he was quite unable to admit that he was completely and hopelessly lost.

'Do you really know?' said Maisie.

'Trust me, my dear!' said Henry. 'Guys have a feeling for these things . . .' The more he carried on saying things like this, absurd as they obviously were, the more they seemed true. At nearly two thousand feet above sea level in a thick mist, masculine decisiveness, even of a patently ridiculous kind, was somehow welcome. Maybe that was why he had got them up here.

Elinor got to her feet. She sounded doubtful, but anxious to believe in him as a navigator. She said, 'Do you *really* know where we are?'

Henry looked back along the path. 'It's not just the rock,' he said, 'it's the grasses. That patch of heather over there. See?'

What he really needed was a mobile phone. And the number of the Mountain Rescue Service. *'Where are you?' 'Somewhere in the Lake District. And my wife is wearing a yellow bobble hat!'* But, to his surprise he found he was rather irritated at her refusal to trust him. Why shouldn't people trust you simply because you were known to be unreliable? If he could get them out of this, maybe she would start respecting the person he wanted to be – brave, cool, kind, clever – rather than the person he actually was.

This isn't just about a mountain, he thought to himself, *this is about our relationship. I'm not just fighting for survival here, I'm fighting for my rights.*

'Look,' he said, 'I'll go first. OK?'

Elinor pouted. 'You're always coming on like you *know . . . '* she began, but Henry cut in.

'You have to trust me!' he said, and put his arms round both his wife and daughter. 'We're miles away from anywhere and – ' His voice was in danger of breaking into sobs. He collected himself. 'This is a *Stone Age* situation. And we have to act like Stone Age people. You know?'

Maisie seemed to brighten up at this thought.

'Me Tarzan, you know? You Janes. Me the Boss up here. Me the male. You the women. This is the way it has to be!'

Elinor's mouth sagged visibly. Why was he saying this? If he *didn't* get them out of it – and there seemed no reason why he should – he would never be allowed to forget it. Mind you, if he didn't get them out of it, they would all probably be dead of exposure long before his behaviour could be reported to any of Elinor's feminist friends.

'And who knows,' Henry went on, feeling he had nothing to lose, 'maybe it's the way it'll always be. From here on!'

After quite a long silence she got to her feet. With only a touch of irony she said, 'You're the boss, boss!'

Henry strode off ahead of them into the mist. As the damp cloud stung his face, he listened for any sound, ahead or behind, that might suggest there was anyone at all in this God-forsaken place apart from them. But nothing, as they walked into the gathering darkness, came between them and the sound of mud on rubber soles, the harsh rasp of cagoule against rucksack, and the wind, as lonely and undecided as the landscape, howling across the tough grass and the weathered stones.

'I think it's time,' said Elinor, 'to get out the survival bags.'

'Have faith!' said Henry.

Maisie stopped. 'I think I can hear voices!'

Henry and Elinor exchanged glances. He had not thought that Maisie would crack so easily. 'What kind of voices, darling?' he said, gently.

Maisie knitted her brows and looked between her parents. *Don't behave*, her expression seemed to say, *as if I am a fruitcake.*

Henry had heard of the phantom strangers who would often show up when an expedition was headed for the wrong kind of explorer's notoriety. Was it on Scott's ill-fated journey to the Pole that the members of the party reported being joined by a mysterious figure in the wastes of snow? *Ill-fated*, was, now he thought about it, the kind of adjective the *Cumbrian Gazette* would soon be applying to their little jaunt.

'I thought I heard the school song!' said Maisie.

This was obviously serious. Elinor glanced quickly at Henry and then went to her daughter. 'You'll be OK, darling!' she said in an unconvincing voice. 'Have some Kendal Mint Cake! We'll camp here.'

'I did!' said Maisie.

It was now dark as well as misty. If it was still misty. It was too dark to see if it was misty or not. It was doing something but it was too dark to see what it was. All Henry knew was that something – rain, hail, sleet, snow or possibly hordes of iced-up midges – was coming at him from out of the blackness. The weather had gone beyond atrocious. It was an organized attack on any life form foolish enough to venture into this particular corner of the British Isles.

'We're almost there!' said Henry. 'Not long now!'

'I think we should get into the bags,' said Elinor.

'We could get into them,' he said, 'if you girls think you could manage to hop forward while inside one!'

This joke did not go down well. He was in danger of losing them. They must have been walking for four or five hours. But the physical effort of wading through bogs, over sharp rocks and down terrifyingly steep stretches of ground was as nothing compared to the acting required of the team leader.

'I just can't go any further,' said Elinor. She added in a whisper, 'And Maisie is having hallucinations!'

Maisie was looking suspiciously at her mother.

'It's just round the corner!' said Henry. This seemed to him, as he said it, one of the most patently absurd remarks he had ever made. But it seemed to have a calming effect on the women in the party. He moved on down the path.

'I did hear something,' said Maisie. 'Sort of ghostly singing!'

This was very worrying. It wouldn't be long before she was seeing the Great Boyg or the Wendigo or some other native spirit that showed up just before you were due to sign off from the human race. Henry moved a little further away.

It was then that he heard it. Very faint, very far away. But, quite definitely, the noise of singing.

> We are steadfast, steadfast, steadfast
> Mary Louisa Haddock
> We are steadfast, steadfast, true and fine!
> We are steadfast Mary Louisa
> Mary, Mary o' Mine!

He looked back. Neither Elinor nor Maisie seemed to have heard.

It wasn't a natural noise. It was as if it was being carried up to them through tunnels of rock, from somewhere miles below. At first Henry thought he might be entering into the kind of delirium that descends shortly before people start sorting out one's funeral guest list.

But then, as he listened, he heard it again. It was weirdly amplified. It was as if it had passed to them through the heart of the harsh rocks that lay so close to the surface. He looked back at Maisie and Elinor, trying to check the sudden, irrational optimism that had seized him.

'I'll just check out the path!' he said.

Elinor turned to him. 'What *path*?' she said. 'You don't know what path. You are completely and totally lost. You are just blundering around helplessly miles from anywhere and trying to bluff us! And now Maisie is . . . is . . . *seeing things*!'

When Henry spoke it was with a new confidence. 'Leave it to me,' he said, 'just leave it to me!'

Leaving the two of them he walked off into the darkness. He walked as he had learned to do in the Cadet Force at school, feeling his way before placing each foot on the ground ahead. As he moved forward he prayed, silently, *If I ever get out of this, I will be a better person. I will not lie or be cowardly or in any way be like the person I was before I climbed this horrible bleeding hill!*

And, as he prayed, he heard the noise again. It seemed closer now, still ghostly and strange as if coming from a cave deep in the mountain, but it was, without a doubt, the song penned by Julia Martinez in 1896 to commemorate the founder of Maisie's school.

> We are lonely, lonely, lonely
> Mary Louisa Haddock
> We are lonely, lonely, sad and lost
> We are lonely Mary Louisa
> You are the one that we trust!

The path went down much more steeply here but Henry still had no idea where it was leading. Perhaps it ended in a sheer drop and the girls from MLH Wimbledon where sheltering in a cave beneath the overhang. He went down very cautiously now, picking his way from stone to stone until he came to a frighteningly smooth patch of rock that seemed to grow out of the side of the hill.

Apart from the occasional ridge caused by two stones lying on top of one another, there was nothing on to which he could grip. The rock seemed to rise almost vertically away from him. He started to edge to his right. One step, two steps, three steps, four steps –

Oh no! His right boot encountered vacant space. Not only his right boot. His right hand, too, had come to the end of the rock, which seemed to conclude in an almost uncannily neat edge. At last, however, he managed to get his hands round the damp surface of the stone and, scrabbling and kicking with fingers and toes, he started up the incline. He would go a little way and see if the noise got any louder.

It did.

As he crawled further up the rock he could even make out individual voices. Jamrags Pleckett's famous, glass-shattering soprano soared above the other voices in the last chorus.

> We are triumphant, triumphant, triumphant
> Mary Louisa Haddock!
> We are triumphant, brave and free
> We are triumphant Mary Louisa
> O Mary, Mary are we!

If this was a hallucination, it was a very convincing one. It seemed to be coming from somewhere over to his left. If it was floating up from some gap in the rock, he had better make sure he didn't fall into it. And still the smooth surface sloped upwards, the rocks knitted impenetrably together. Another pull. Another pull and –

He found he had got his hands on a ridge. A terrifyingly narrow one. It seemed to go directly above him, from left to right, and on the other side of it the rock sloped downward at almost the same incline as the side he was ascending.

He found, to his surprise, that he wasn't frightened. He pulled himself up to the ridge, although for all he knew it sloped away thousands of feet on the other side. But he had beaten it. Whatever it was called – Razor's Edge, the Knife, Slice Your Balls – he had conquered it. He swung one leg across it and found he was sitting astride the mountain like a child on a wooden horse.

Except it wasn't a mountain.

Now, suddenly, he could see what the stone was. It was a slate roof, set into the hillside from which he had come. He had climbed up the far edge and was now looking down into a courtyard made of paving stones. He could make out beautiful, beautiful things he had thought never to see again. There was a Bedford van and a couple of bicycles. There was a notice-board and a sodium lamp and a fence. And on the notice-board was the sign of the Youth Hostels Association.

The noise of the singing was coming up through one of the chimneys to his left, which gave it that eery, amplified sound. Down here he could see that the mist had lifted. Beyond the youth hostel was a broad track that led up to the hill from which he had come. To reach it all he would have to do would be to walk parallel with the line of the ridge of the roof on which he was perched.

Henry eased along the crest of the roof. The singing had stopped. He grasped the chimney with both hands and put his ear to it. He heard, quite clearly, the voice of Bulldike White. 'Tragic little bloke!' she was saying. 'Suburban macho man battles with the elements!'

Jamrags Pleckett, equally easy to distinguish, replied: 'I don't know how poor Elinor tolerates him,' she said. 'He's one of those men who have to *construct* their masculinity out of nothing. Every time he wants a bunk-up.'

There were noises of clucking sympathy at this. Then Bulldike said, in her fruity, bass voice, 'He's lost, poor lamb, isn't he? In spite of all this *real-men-throw-women-in-ravines* act!' A gale of laughter greeted this sally.

Henry got out his compass and held it for some moments. The

needle swung round. When it settled, Henry saw it had aligned itself with the roof. So the broad track must be headed due west, the direction he would have to take to get back to Maisie and Elinor.

The singing had started again. They were on to the other school song, written by Mary Louisa Haddock herself. All Henry could remember about it was that it contained the word 'girlhood' and that the penultimate verse was capable of being interpreted as violently obscene. He swung his legs over the roof and slithered back to the hillside. When he was on the track, he lined up the compass and started up the hill towards his wife and daughter.

As he trudged up the hill, he heard a faint voice coming out of the darkness.

'Henry!'

It was Elinor. 'Darling!'

Darling yet!

Henry could not remember having been at such an advantage at any point in the twenty-five years of their marriage. It was important not to throw it away. With the stern confidence of a man who knows there are bicycles, Bedford vans and central heating just round the corner, he called, 'Coming, darling!'

He kept his voice firmly in the bass register. When he saw them ahead of him he remembered to step out strongly and when he got up to them he looked, long and hard, at his compass.

'Daddy,' said Maisie, 'are you all right?'

Henry smiled. 'Daddy's fine!' he said. 'Daddy can look after you! Daddy knows these mountains!'

This obviously untrue statement seemed to go down fairly well with his team. Deprive people of food and water, force them to hike across stony ground for five hours in sub-zero temperatures, thought Henry, and they will believe anything. He was starting to enjoy this trip.

'I was worried,' said Elinor.

Henry smiled. Again. 'You still don't believe me, do you?' he said. 'You still think I'm bluffing!'

'How can you know where we are?' said Maisie. 'It's pitch dark and it's – '

Henry gave a manly laugh. Then he got out the ordnance survey map and, by the light of the torch, selected at random a patch of contoured ground. He stabbed his forefinger into the paper. 'We,' he said, 'are about . . . *here!*'

'How do you know?' said Elinor. 'And where's here?'

Henry folded the map and muttered something about cairns. Neither of them looked as if they believed him. But that was all to the good. He put the compass on the map and pointed due north into the pitch blackness. 'Follow me!' he said.

After some protests, they did.

The ground was rough. Once or twice they fell into huge pools of water, and after a few minutes Maisie started to complain. Henry started to sing.

> Keep right on till the end of the road
> Keep right on to the end!

Sometimes he would get out the map, shine the torch at it and click his teeth. Once or twice he pretended to triangulate. He rather enjoyed it. Map-reading was pure pleasure once you knew where you were.

They hit the broad track after about fifteen minutes, although Maisie and Elinor were too tired and frightened to notice what was underneath their feet. Instead of turning right, Henry turned left, back up the mountain and gave them a little more mountain-speak. 'I'm doubling back by the cairns,' he said. 'Along Windspeare's Bottom and then I'm heading for Carling Nick and Brown Nose Ghyll!'

Elinor merely groaned. Maisie said he could stop pretending now. They would all get into the same polythene bag and slit each other's throats. It would be a relief, she said, to be dead. So long as it got her off this mountain, death was her everlasting friend.

Henry rounded on the two women. 'You don't trust me, do you?' he said, as he struck off the broad path to the right, circled once or twice and then headed back to it again. 'You have to trust me, my dears!' he said. Elinor and Maisie were still quite unaware that they had ever been on a path or that they had left it and returned to it.

'Just *here* . . .' said Henry, making great play with map and torch, is a sort of . . . *broad track!*'

When Maisie and Elinor looked down they found that this was indeed so. They were, he was glad to notice, impressed. Now he turned left, back down the hill. He summoned both women to him. If he was to get back to the hostel he would have to travel . . .

'Due east!' he said, proudly.

'But where are we?' whined Maisie.

Henry held the map up to his face, making sure that neither woman could see any part of it. He stepped out vigorously down the path. As he walked he looked from map to path constantly. 'Well,' he said after a few minutes, 'I would say . . .' Two minutes? Three? 'In five minutes we will see . . .' And as he rounded a bend in the path he saw the glimmer of the sodium lamp. 'A youth hostel!'

When they saw that he was right, both wife and daughter embraced him. Henry, folding the map up very small in case anyone should start trying to do a geographical post-mortem, said, 'It's simple! Me Tarzan! You Janes!'

Beyond the yard was a road. He had no idea where it might lead. The important thing was to get on to it and walk until they came to some dwelling that was not sheltering some thirty-odd females from the Wimbledon area.

'This,' he said, 'will take us back to Keswick!'

It was forty-five minutes later. Henry was walking with the quiet confidence of a man who is on a road that he knows leads somewhere even if it isn't to the place to which he is supposed to be going.

Maisie suddenly said, 'I wondered what that noise I heard was!'

Henry looked back at the dark shapes of the mountains behind him. 'The hills can play strange tricks on you,' he said, 'and you can't always trust your senses. Never go up there without someone who knows their way around.'

'But I did hear something!' said Maisie.

Henry patted her on the arm. Then he went forward to join Elinor, who was stumping along ahead of them. She seemed, for Elinor, comparatively calm. Henry breathed in deeply and in an easy, rugged sort of way he took her by the hand. 'How was I up there?' he said, lightly.

She looked across at him shyly. 'You were really good!' she said. 'I take it all back. I thought you were lost and you weren't.'

Bonking tonight! thought Henry. He allowed his arm to creep across her shoulders and in the same easy, natural way he squeezed her to him.

'I'm not a *real* man, of course,' he said, in a voice intended to convey that he was but that he was also not the type to boast about it. Elinor continued to smile at him. Henry squeezed her again. There was the heavy thud of boots behind him and Henry's daughter appeared next to her parents. She looked, sideways, at her father.

'I bet,' said Maisie, 'I did hear singing. They were probably in the youth hostel. You went ahead and found them and pretended to lead us there by map-reading.'

There was a horrified silence.

'That,' said Elinor, 'is a horrible thing to say. Can you imagine Henry doing something as despicable as that?'

The three of them walked on without speaking, and, around them, from the dark mountains the April wind moaned across the valley floor, as if in primitive reproach of man's efforts to achieve the smallest thing.

The Authentic Noises of Her Heart

'Twas in the merry month of May
Heigh ho!
Heigh ho!
When folk do sing a roundelay
With a heigh
Nod niddy
Nod niddy
And a heigh heigh heigh ho
With a heigh nod niddy no!

Esmond Brice, BA (Mus.) Oxon. and honorary fellow of the Wimbledon Analytic Society, held up his hand. A pained expression began to deform the lower offside of his mouth. 'I think,' he said, 'some of us are singing niddy nod when we should be singing *nod niddy*!'

He looked round at Doublet and Hose, the Wimbledon Early Music Group. Behind the singers, Norman Spritz, on the viol da gamba, and Herbert de Freitas (tenor recorder and bass viol) smirked to themselves.

'We can sing niddy nod if you like,' went on Esmond in his calm, reasonable voice. 'I'm not such an early music buff that I'd go to the stake for nod niddy. But – ' He began to belabour the music stand with his index finger. 'It's either nod niddy *or* niddy nod. Not a halfway house.'

He was so strong, thought Elinor, as she nodded agreement, so decisive! And he cared. He really cared about how they played the bass viol in 1587 and whether Scarlatti should ever be played on a forte piano. He cared passionately about them in a way Henry would never understand.

At the thought of Henry she felt suddenly depressed. The thought of what he had tried to do her in that hotel room in Keswick still made her shudder. Just because, by some fluke, he had managed to stumble off that stupid, stupid mountain, it didn't mean that he had the right to –

Now she thought about it, he had not been himself since the beginning of the year. His attitude to Angelica had been definitely peculiar, ever since he had taken those weeks off work in January. He had been even more odd during February. He had spent most of the month hanging around the newsagent's on the way to the station and, on one occasion, come home with pet food and a pornographic video. And since they had come back from the Lake District he had seemed listless and apathetic, as if he had lost all confidence in his own judgement.

Brice walked to the window and looked down at the Common. 'From this window,' he said, 'from this *very* window in 1587, William Byrd, who was staying in this *very* house, on his way to a secret meeting with his Catholic friend de Beynyon, performed, with his musicians, his specially composed piece *A Maying*, while the solo voice of Mistress June Howking rose through the clear air, and, so a contemporary tells us, *delighted all the folke of Wymbledune!*'

Elinor closed her eyes. She could imagine it so clearly! The sun glistening on the halberds (there were bound to have been a few halberds about), the raucous voices of the ale wives and the scriveners! The ostlers unyoking the potboys! And Mistress Howking singing out to the Great Fayre of Wymbledune!

Things hadn't changed. They still had the Great Fayre. It now included demonstrations by the local Fire Brigade, the Wimbledon Sea Scouts and the local branch of the Territorial Army, but it was essentially the same. There was continuity. And one of the women in Doublet and Hose was going to *be* Mistress Howking.

> With a la la ho
> A ha la lo
> 'Carpe Matronem' sing we!
> With a dang dong day
> A dong dong dee!
> Let us have good ale
> THOU KNAVE
> Let us have good ale!

She looked round at the other women. They were, for the most part, pathetic specimens. Julia O'Dowd with her great, fat bottom, her hippy dresses and her hair down to where her waist would have been if she had had one. Louella van Heeming who was no more a soprano than Elinor was a fruit bat. Ellen Harrison (The Viper) had the nearest thing to a voice, next to Elinor, in the group but after the things she had done with the man from the Westley Garage – presumably in order to get a reduction on parts and labour – no one took her seriously. Esmond was talking again. She must concentrate. She must drink in his every word.

'Imagine it!' Brice was saying. 'The smell of horse manure! The *swoosh* of a hawk as it stoops to the falconer! The viols and recorders strike up and one beautiful creature, one of *you* . . .' He looked along the line of women. '. . .*One* of you, chosen to stand at that window. No longer Mrs So and So or Miss Such and Such but a living part of our heritage. "Mistress Howking" whose "eie", Byrd tells us, was "fine", whose features, "rare and lovely", and whose "voyce" was "exceeding sweet"!'

The fifty-two-year-old psychotherapist picked up his music and signalled to the ladies of Doublet and Hose that the rehearsal was at an end. 'I will be looking,' he said, 'for *authenticity*. And I don't mean that when you ladies come to audition you say "I trow" or "Forsooth". Authenticity in music is like authenticity in human relationships. It is about being true. As true to the past as we are to the present. That's all!'

I will be authentic, Elinor murmured to herself, as she jostled down the narrow staircase towards the bright May morning. *I will be authentic*. She turned at the door and looked back at the other women. Julia O'Dowd was, as usual, hanging round Esmond trying to get his attention. You could tell that she was irritating him. Let them wait for the auditions. Then we would find out which of the twelve was a real soprano. Ellen Harrison was leering at him and displaying her bottom for his benefit.

As she set off, on her own, towards the Volvo, she sang for sheer joy, and, as she sang, it seemed to her that the young leaves on the trees, the grass, the birds and the shy spring flowers were as authentically English as her voice, as she warbled –

> 'Twas in the merry month of May
> Heigh ho!
> Heigh ho!
> When folk do sing a roundelay
> With a heigh
> Nod niddy

And a niddy nod niddy noddy
Or something
Let us have good ale!

'Where are you going?' said Henry.

He was sprawled on the sofa, watching the television. From time to time he farted loudly, raising his buttocks from the floral cushions as if he wished people to pay attention to the noise he was making.

It was hard to believe, really, that he and Esmond were from the same planet. She had never seen Henry moved by any kind of music, except when he had thrown a book at Maisie for playing RUN DMC too loud. All that seemed to interest him was lying around the house and having ponderous conversations with Angelica in Spanish. Perhaps he had persuaded the stupid, fat cow to offer him her mouth and her rear-end. They were up to something. It certainly couldn't take her four hours to do the amount of cleaning she was doing.

'I am going to audition!' said Elinor.

Henry grunted.

'Where's Maisie?' she added, trying to keep the irritation out of her voice.

'She and Erica went to James Seebohm's,' said Henry. 'They said they were going to revise.'

'Revising' meant sitting in Seebohm's bedroom listening to loud American music, usually with obscene lyrics. Elinor worried, sometimes, that her daughter was going to end up like Henry.

She took a sideways look at her husband as he inserted the index finger of his right hand into his left nostril, scooped out a quantity of green flaky material and, when he thought he was unobserved, popped it into his mouth.

He hadn't listened when she had told him she was competing with eleven tough, ruthless women for the important role of Mistress Howking. He never listened to her. When he made a gesture to how she felt, there was always a sneer in it. Like that business with Valentine cards. Why couldn't he say what he really, *authentically* felt?

Henry turned up the volume on the television.

'Wish me luck!' she said.

'Best of luck!' said Henry.

Just as she got to the door he called after her, 'Watch Brice doesn't try the old casting couch routine!'

She started back from the front door to the television room. She was about to tell Henry that he disgusted her. That she couldn't bear any more of his grossness, his narrowness, his utter lack of spirituality. That, in case he wanted to know, Esmond would not even deign to *look* at her – even though she often found herself wishing he might. He has his work as a counsellor, his musical interests, his wonderful – if disturbed – son, Orlando, and his wife Inge, a Gestalt therapist who specialized in performing sixteenth-century music for the zlitny, a kind of primitive harp that had its origins in Poland.

She stopped in the hall and peered at her husband through the crack. She wanted to tell him that she longed, yes *longed* for Esmond Brice to put his strong arms round her and for their lips to meet in endless yearning. But she did not do so. He would only say something coarse. Henry did not understand endless yearning. She went out to the car.

Esmond had commanded them not to discuss the auditions amongst themselves. 'I will simply call people on an ad hoc basis,' he had said. 'Some I may not call at all. But I don't want this to be a source of friction in the group. All I will say is that those I do call . . .' He looked along the line of women. His big, grey eyes were serious. '. . . should be aware that it is a privilege. And not to be taken lightly. I won't tell you when the call will come. I will give you very little notice. I don't want artificial "preparedness". I want the authentic noises of your heart!'

It was a beautiful day. Perhaps, thought Elinor, as she drove across the Common, she was the only one chosen. Perhaps he hadn't bothered with the other fat-bottomed, tone-deaf creatures who made up the Wimbledon Early Music Group.

She had had the call last night. Susannah Greenstreet had told everyone that *she* had had the call last Tuesday but nobody had believed her: Susannah Greenstreet had a voice like chalk being dragged across a blackboard. He had simply said, in that curt, musicianly way he had, 'My house. Three o'clock. This is, of course, confidential. I am close to making a decision.'

Then the phone had been replaced. Esmond was not a man to use too many words when he needed to make an important point.

At his house! Where, as Henry had often pointed out, there were enough authentic instruments to start a small orchestra. Elinor had only been there twice before – once when Inge had given a zlitny recital in aid of the Timex workers and once when Esmond had had Orlando barmitzvah'd. None of the family was Jewish but Orlando had very much wanted to experience the ceremony, and although one or two people said not all the details were correct, Elinor had found it a profound and moving way of spending Saturday afternoon.

Everyone in the Brice family had a car, but, as she arrived, Elinor was surprised to see that there were no other vehicles in the drive apart from Esmond's camper van. Perhaps, she allowed herself to think again, perhaps I am the only candidate!

Esmond's house was a white villa, its frontage wound about with clematis and wisteria and its gravel drive fringed with evergreen bushes. As she got out of the car, Elinor could see, through the ground floor window, the grand piano, the wooden rocking horse and, behind it on the bookshelves, a sober looking row of volumes that she knew to be the *Collected Works* of Jung. There was a thrush in the plane tree to the left, practising its song, over and over, as the light winked back from the window. She rang the bell. There was no answer. She rang again.

'Come on in!' said Esmond. 'The door is open!'

Elinor pushed her way into the hall.

On the floor opposite her she could see a viol da gamba that, as far as she could remember, had been given to Orlando shortly after he went to the University of Reigate. By the hat-stand were seven or eight pairs of green wellingtons, and, over by the spinet, which was next to the lavatory, was a gigantic picture – in oils – of someone who Elinor was fairly certain was either Jonathan Swift or Mozart.

There was no sign of Esmond. Elinor went into the music room, and, as she did so, heard a noise behind her.

It was Esmond. He was steaming gently, and, apart from a towel round his waist, was completely naked. 'I'm sorry,' he said, in his deep, gentle voice. 'I simply cannot get out of the bath when I'm listening to Thomas Tallis.'

Elinor tried to look as if she understood this remark.

'Tum tum tum a- a- a-men! A-a-a-men!' Brice hummed as he came towards her across the parquet floor. 'I am so glad you could come, Elinor. I'll just slip out of this towel and then we can get down to business!'

He had a magnificent chest. Unlike Henry's, it was sprinkled with fine, black hairs and, also unlike Henry's, it was not sabotaged by sagging packets of flesh. Esmond, who did not appear at all embarrassed about appearing in front of her like this, started to roll his left nipple through the third and fourth fingers of his right hand.

'I want us,' he said, 'to work in depth!' He smiled. Elinor smiled back.

He was so open and frank. That was what people like Henry didn't understand. He could appear before her like this because Inge and Orlando and Wieland (Orlando's half brother – or was it sister?) *were* his life. He was, as he had once told her in the bar of the Fox and Grapes after a rehearsal, secure in his sexuality.

'Wait by the piano, Elinor!' he said in the same deep, careful voice he used to coax Doublet and Hose through a tricky madrigal. 'I'll be back!'

Elinor looked round the music room. There was always this sense of quiet, intellectual effort in Esmond's house. A feeling that, if you stayed here long enough, you would simply soak up things like 7/8 time or the rudiments of ancient Greek. Over by the fireplace, the cat Diogenes sat in exquisite repose, while Sartre, the family lurcher, nosed his snout over his front paw and shot Elinor a long, sorrowful glance.

Suddenly Esmond appeared at the door.

He was wearing a blue towelled dressing gown. He was still barefoot. He seemed quite unaware of the effect he was having on her. He was almost totally absorbed in the soprano part of *A Maying* as he came towards her. But Elinor was almost visibly shaken by the maleness of him. He was so firm! So compact! So full of contained energy!

Perhaps she should ask him to go and get some clothes on! She felt, in spite of herself, the beginnings of a longing that, if she were not careful, might well affect her vocal performance. Esmond, still totally oblivious of her, said, 'I am going to skip the niddy nods and start with "Speak Thou True Mine Heart"!'

Elinor gulped.

'I want us,' he said, allowing his hand to stray inside his dressing gown, 'to really go into this thing in depth this afternoon. I want us to get eyeball to eyeball. You understand?'

Elinor nodded. 'You want us to really study the music,' she said.

Esmond's eyes narrowed. 'You could say that,' he said.

He was so oblivious of the kind of cheap *double entendre* Henry might have indulged in on this occasion. His absorption in the music was total. Even when he sat at the piano stool and his dressing gown rode up over his exquisitely formed knee, he did not throw it back in place or give any acknowledgement that this was a sexually charged situation.

It isn't to him, Elinor thought to herself, *it's me. I mustn't let him see.*

Esmond shifted forward and the dressing gown rode up even further. His upper thigh (God alone knew what he was wearing under the dressing gown) was as firm and hairy as his upper body.

'Speak Thou True Mine Heart!' he said in a no-nonsense voice. And Elinor sang.

> Speak thou true mine heart
> As in thine eie I gaze
> O speak thou true mine heart
> Let true love mee amayze
> For if this Love bee seene
> In this mine eie
> Hey nonny no!
> Hey nonny no!
> Then will spring come by
> And by and by
> Will sing me Nonny no
> Heigh ha!
> Nid nod non nonny no!

When she got to the bit about gazing into his eie, Esmond looked up from the piano and gazed into her eyes searchingly. His hands were moving across the piano in a way that suggested that William Byrd had written this one with Esmond Brice specifically in mind. She held his gaze, as she assumed she was meant to, until she got to the second lot of hey nonnies. She found she was blushing. Not only that. Her voice was faltering. Just before she got to 'heigh ha nid nod non nonny' she dissolved into a coughing fit.

Esmond lifted his hands from the keys. 'Is something wrong, Elinor?' he said gently.

Elinor looked down at her hands foolishly. 'I was wondering . . . who else . . .'

Esmond smiled. 'There is no one else Elinor. We are the only people in the house. Inge is playing the zlitny in Norfolk.'

'I mean – '

And he laughed. 'The *competition*!'

He shifted easily on the piano stool. Elinor looked away. 'There are only a couple of my singers who are a *patch* on you, Elinor!' he said. 'What you bring to Doublet is unique. And if this audition goes the way I . . . er . . . want it to, then I will have no need to call them!'

He pushed his right hand into his dressing gown and, once again, began to do things to his nipple. In spite of herself Elinor had to bite her lower lip to stop herself offering him some assistance in this task. There were, she noticed, beads of sweat on his forehead as he peered at the manuscript.

'Authenticity,' said Esmond, 'is authentic emotion. When you *gaze into mine eie* you must gaze. Go with the emotion and see where it leads you!'

His left hand slipped beneath his gown and began to scratch vigorously at an area, where, if Elinor was correct, his private parts were to be found. 'We have all afternoon,' he said. 'Inge does not return till tomorrow and Orlando is seeing someone about the business with the magistrates' court. To it! Abandon yourself, Elinor, to the authentic feeling and see where it leads you!'

Elinor had a nasty feeling that if she did abandon herself to the authentic feeling it might lead to her leaping over the piano at him, pulling off his blue towelled dressing gown and drawing the male centre of him into her yielding, throbbing, womanly essence.

Esmond was talking about music. His life was music. He was starting to play again.

> Speak thou true mine heart
> As in thine eie I gaze
> O speak thou true mine heart
> Let true love mee amayze
> For if this Love bee seene
> In this mine eie
> Hey nonny no!
> Hey nonny –

She became aware that Esmond had left the piano and was standing next to her.

'As in thine eie I gaze!' he was saying in that deep, brown voice of his. 'Where does that lead you? Authenticity, Elinor, remember this, is authentic emotion. When you gaze in mine eie – gaze!'

He was seeking her eyes out. He was, thought Elinor, living the music. He was so absorbed in the lesson that he did not seem to realize that the dressing gown had slipped over his left shoulder so that his nipple was once more visible. The skirts of the dressing gown swished around his thighs as he walked. He turned swiftly, as he came back to her and the towelled fabric spun round him. When it settled again Elinor found herself bewitched by the amazing youthfulness of the man's behind.

'Go with the emotion and see where it leads you! Where does it lead you?'

Elinor went with the emotion and saw where it led her. She gulped twice and said, 'Er . . . to the key of C major . . .'

Something about the sudden cloud that passed over his face as she said this led her to suspect that this was not the correct reply. But then, he was so far above her as a musician! How could she match up to him? If this was some kind of test she had clearly failed it. She was utterly unworthy.

Esmond was drawing his dressing gown about him and studying the floor. When he did look up there was a look of infinite sadness in what Elinor had started to think of as his 'eie' – as if a favourite pupil had failed to deliver what was expected of her.

'I think,' he said, 'we had better leave it there . . .'

'Esmond,' said Elinor, 'have I . . . should I have . . .'

Esmond's lips curved upwards in a mysterious smile; but his eyes were misty with regret. He pulled the dressing gown more tightly about his shoulders and said, 'The authentic moment has gone. But we must look for it again. We must keep looking for it, over and over and over. The music making is the *search* for that authentic moment. Farewell!' And he kissed her, lightly, on the cheek.

Elinor, who thought this was the most beautiful thing anyone had ever said to her, somehow found her way out to the bright May day with the conviction that she had lost something that, if her life was to have any meaning at all, she must one day recover. If only she knew what it was!

Elinor was halfway home when she realized that that was where she did not wish to go. She had a sudden, clear vision of Henry. He was sitting on the sofa, staring at the television. The television did not appear to be on. He grinned satirically at her as she passed him and said, 'Bonky-boos with Brice?'

He seemed horribly real to her as she said this. When she tried to

88

shake off the image, it was replaced with one even more vivid. He was sprawled, now, with his legs out in front of him and he was picking his nose. 'Shagging Esmond?' was what he said. And then he winked at her broadly. 'I hear early music isn't the only thing Brice can't get enough of.'

She could not bear to be in the same house as the man. He blocked her at every turn! When she wanted to grow in a certain direction, there he was – standing in her light like that ancient Greek with the shears. Or was he Norse?

And yet it was Henry's grossness that had suggested to her an idea so surprising and wonderful that she stamped hard on the Volvo's brakes as she was driving across Cannizaro Road, nearly causing a BMW to shunt her in the rear. Maybe, *maybe* Esmond felt the same way about her as she felt about him. Maybe the correct thing to do when he asked her where the authentic emotion was leading her was to say 'to *you* Esmond!' Maybe he was trying to tell her that he needed a little help with his nipples. Maybe she had just been stupid enough to pass up the chance of a lifetime.

She would say that she had forgotten something, or she would say that she wanted to borrow some Jung. They would look for the book together. Maybe at some point his fingers would brush against hers and she would look up from the book and their eyes would find each other and she and Esmond would be . . .

She did not know what they would be. But whatever it was they got up to it would not be anything like what Henry tried to do to her in the Lakeland View Hotel, Keswick. She would be drawn to him as is a tide to the moon, an iron-filing to the magnet or a rabbit in the headlights of a car. *I am a rabbit in your headlights*! she sang to herself.

And Henry need never know. There was little chance he would even notice the change in her. It might be that giving herself to Esmond, physically, might even improve her marriage. Only last week she had read an article by a qualified doctor entitled 'Men Who Have Gone Stale and How to Liven Them Up'. One of the things you were supposed to do, as far as Elinor could make out, was to have an affair.

She was still singing as she drove into Esmond Brice's drive. The first thing she saw was Julia O'Dowd's 2CV. It was amazing the woman fitted into it really.

Poor Esmond!

No sooner had he finished with her than it would be Mary Parker, the Beast of Blenheim Drive, and after her Ellen Harrison would be panting her way up the front path. They probably wouldn't even wait to be phoned. They would just turn up. Or else invent pathetic little excuses. She had a vision of Louella van Heeming smarming her way into the front hall muttering, 'I thought you *rang*, Esmond!'

She was now absolutely convinced that the expression in Esmond's eyes during her audition had expressed passion for something else as well as the correct way to phrase William Byrd. It was meant for her. And she had rejected it. She had not listened to the authentic noise of her heart and followed it to where it should have led her. And now the poor man was having to listen to a tone-deaf, fat, neurotic mother of five squawk on while the woman he really cared about sat at his gates, unable to return to her own tragic, lifeless marriage.

I am all suffering woman, though Elinor. *I am Simone de Beauvoir. I am Emma Bovary. And Henry is . . . Monsieur Bovary!*

She had no very clear picture of Monsieur Bovary except that she vaguely recollected he was not a man to set the dinner table alight. He was probably an improvement on Henry, however. Henry was incapable of the kind of love for which any sensitive woman craved. And now she had thrown away the one chance of romantic happiness offered to her in the last twenty-five years.

I am Natasha Thing in that book by Dostoevsky, thought Elinor, *I am Isolde in the opera of the same name. I am –*

Unable, for the moment, to think of any more women she was like, she got out of the car and went to the front door. She would ring the bell, briefly, make a dignified enquiry and then leave. Maybe she would find a way of letting him know that she understood what he was feeling. She would smile lightly and look straight into his 'eie' and she would say: 'Esmond – '

Just like that. And he would understand. He would leave fat Julia O'Dowd frumping away by the piano and in a matter of seconds they would be . . . they would be . . .

She was getting horribly clear about what they would be. About how they would be and when they would be and for how long they would be and if they would be again and after they had been how they would be able to plan how they could be *again* in the very near future even if Inge *wasn't* playing the zlitny in Norfolk. My God, what was wrong with a hotel after twenty-five years of being *entirely faithful* to a fat, flatulent insensitive slug who made Monsieur Bovary look like Paul Newman.

Something made her decide not to ring the bell. Perhaps it was the fact that she could hear the piano. And Esmond was playing the same passage that they had been rehearsing. She recognized the masterful, clear lines of the bass and the flourishing treble with which, only minutes ago, she had been harmonizing.

> Speak thou true mine heart
> As in thine eie I gaze
> O speak thou true mine heart

Elinor started to walk along the front of the house until she was at the edge of the window of the music room. She kept out of sight as the song went on. If you could call what O'Dowd was doing singing. It sounded more like someone in the throes of peritonitis.

> Let true love mee amayze
> For if this Love bee seene
> In this mine eie
> Hey nonny no!
> Hey nonny no!

She heard the sound of Esmond's naked feet on the parquet floor. One step, two step, three . . . was he standing beside her? Maybe he was trying to get out of the room. For someone with an ear as sensitive as his, being in the same room as Julia O'Dowd's version of William Byrd must be torment. Perhaps he was gong to slap her round the face and order her out of the house.

'As in thine eie I gaze . . .' he was saying in that deep, troubled voice of his. 'Where does it lead you? Authenticity is authentic emotion. When you gaze in mine eie, *gaze!*'

He probably, Elinor realized with a shock, said this to all the girls. The remarks she had thought were made specially for her benefit were simply part of his teaching technique. He was simply a careful, thorough professional. And she had very nearly made an enormous fool of herself!

She stole a glance round the edge of the window.

To her surprise she saw that he was still wearing the dressing gown. Perhaps, she thought, he had not had the time to change. She also noticed that it had slipped over his left shoulder in almost exactly the same manner as in her audition. There was nothing, she decided, unusual in that. Some people's socks were always falling down. Esmond's dressing gown just had a habit of slipping over his shoulder blade so that you could see the beginnings of the teeny tiny hairs that covered his firm, manly chest.

What did disturb her, slightly, was the fact that he seemed to be doing the nipple trick again. She felt a little cheated. It was such a carelessly intimate gesture. And then, when he spoke again (she was unable to resist a thrill of excitement when that dark brown voice got into gear), she was shocked to hear he used *exactly* the same words as he had used to her.

'Go with the emotion and see where it leads you. Where does it lead you?'

In auditions, of course, you had to be scrupulously fair. Even to fat, ugly women who could not hold a crotchet together. For the audition to be really authentic, you had, presumably, to go through exactly the same routine with each candidate. Social events were so easy to manipulate, and there were, Elinor well knew, any number of fiercely manipulative women about the place.

'It leads me,' Julia O'Dowd was saying, '*here*!'

There was a silence. Then Esmond said, 'Oh my God!'

There was another, slightly longer silence. 'And,' went on Julia, 'it leads me *here*!'

'Oh Jesus!' said Esmond. 'Oh Jesus Christ! Oh sweet, holy Jesus!'

There was then what seemed to Elinor an almost unbearably lengthy silence, broken by the rustle of material, the thud of joints against the parquet floor and the unmistakable sound of heavy breathing.

'And then,' went on Julia, 'it leads me . . . *here*!'

After that her voice became muffled. She said something but she sounded as if someone had just shoved a large bread roll in her mouth.

'Oh Christ!' said Esmond. 'Oh Jesus Christ! Oh my God! Oh my fucking Christ!'

Julia O'Dowd said something else. It could have been, 'I've got a ticket for Hastings!' or it could have been, 'Why don't you give me a pasting?' but it was most probably along the lines of, 'Oh my God, this is tasty!' because she now sounded as if someone had added a few slices of ham to the bread roll and that Julia, at the same time, had decided to drink some hot, sweet tea out of a saucer. Whatever she was doing – Elinor had a fairly good idea of *what* she was doing – it had led Esmond to make some very authentic noises indeed.

'Oh Jesus Christ!' he cried. 'Oh Jesus Jesus Christ! Oh God! Oh yes!'

But it was only when Elinor had forced herself to move, once more, a little further to the left, so that she had unrestricted access to what was going on in the music room, that he exclaimed: 'Suck my penis! Yes! Oh suck my penis! You are sucking my penis! Do it like that! Oh my God, yes, suck it like that!'

He brought, thought Elinor, the same relentless thoroughness to sexual relations that he brought to Monteverdi. Never had he shown so clearly what a conscientious conductor he was as when he urged Julia O'Dowd through the not-always-easy business of fellatio. There was something almost pedantic about his concern for what was being done by her lips, tongue and fingers ('Oh, you must squeeze my arse now! Oh yes, yes, yes!'). There was certainly no doubt that Esmond, now fully naked and in plain view of anyone rash enough to wander up his drive unannounced as he plunged his equipment into Julia's face, wrestled with her hair and rolled his superb hindquarters, left, right and left again, was in the grip of a really *authentic* experience.

There were moments towards the end of May when Elinor felt like telling Henry what had gone on between Julia O'Dowd and Esmond Brice. It wasn't particularly that she wanted to cheer him up, although she knew it was the kind of story he loved to hear. It was simply that she could not bear to keep it to herself and she was unable to think of anyone else to whom it was safe to tell it.

It was probably this fact that made her feel more warmly disposed towards him. But Henry seemed still out of reach. 'He has gone into himself. He has gone to a place where I cannot reach him!' she confided to the widow of Gordon Macrae, or Jungian Analyst Beyond the Reach of Winebox, as Henry insisted on calling him.

The last weekend in May, when she went in to hear the results of the audition, Henry had gone to Brighton, by bicycle, with Sam Baker QC (almost). 'It's in aid of something or other,' he had said to her, with a near snarl, as he set off at a quarter past five in the morning, wearing khaki shorts and a large white helmet that made him look a little like a mushroom. Maisie had been asked to lunch by James Seebohm's parents.

We are growing apart, thought Elinor to herself, as she went up the stairs to the rehearsal room overlooking the Common. *We do not communicate. How can we learn to reach each other*? All the women were already there. Their heads turned towards her. Was it her imagination or had they been talking about her?

She went to sit down and found herself next to Julia O'Dowd, who was studying her score with elaborate care. Next to her Ellen Harrison was saying something pretentious about counterpoint. There were moments, Elinor decided, when Henry's coarseness might come as a relief. The trouble was – the relief always came too late.

Would he be all right on the bicycle? Would he get beyond Clapham?

'How long,' said Elinor, turning to Julia and trying to keep the anxiety out of her voice, 'did your audition last?'

Julia O'Dowd smirked. 'Some time,' she said. 'We really went into it in depth!'

'Did you indeed?' said Elinor.

Julia smirked again. 'We were at it from four till six.'

Louella van Heeming was sitting near them. She was wearing a green trouser-suit and a white blouse with a ruffle. All she needed, thought Elinor, was a pair of platform shoes and she could have applied for a job as an extra in a seventies theme park. None of which would have mattered if she didn't look so like a witch.

'Well!' said Louella. 'You surprise me!'

Julia tossed her head. 'And why is that?'

'Because,' said Louella, 'I was there from seven till ten-thirty! Inge was playing the zlitny in Norfolk, you see.'

Several of the members of Doublet and Hose raised their eyebrows.

It was eight o'clock. Outside the May evening was still bright. Esmond had promised to announce the results of the auditions that evening, and the twelve 'singing women' as Esmond called them were sitting in Susannah Greenstreet's front room waiting for the maestro to arrive.

'Oh,' said Susannah, 'I didn't realize he had even *seen* anyone else last Sunday. I was there in the morning – from nine till eleven. We had a very intensive session.'

What a mess they all were, thought Elinor. Pathetic, moustachioed, middle-aged women, no longer sure of what to wear or of what to say; not an idea in their heads except to try to let you know how well little Damien was doing at Cambridge or –

Surely the woman wasn't implying that –

But before she had time to think what the woman might be imply-ing, Mary Parker thrust her odious little nose into the conversation. If *that* haircut was her idea of *gamine*, roll on Selfridge's shop window!

'I was there from eleven through one!' she said, allowing her pointed little tongue to poke out from her cupid's bow mouth. 'Esmond and I really got down to it!'

'We covered a lot of ground too,' cut in Gemma 'Dumpbin' Farmer, 'because I took over at one-thirty. He didn't even stop for lunch. Once he gets the bit between his teeth he is unstoppable!'

She wriggled around in her seat as she said this in a way that Elinor found distastefully suggestive. But before she could go on any more about how masterful and impressive Esmond had been, Julia Bergman and Ellen Harrison revealed that they had been there, together (they seemed to think there was something particularly clever and funny about this), between seven and a quarter to nine in the morning.

'He must have had a very busy Sunday,' said Jennifer Prescott, the librarian nobody liked, 'because I didn't arrive till eleven and we were at it till one-thirty. In every room in the house!'

Julia O'Dowd started to say something about how some people liked to imagine they had done something when they hadn't done something but several of the other women started to compare notes, in slightly worried tones. Most of them wanted to know when Esmond had phoned, what he had said over the phone, what he had said when they arrived and, this seemed most important to them, what he had been wearing during the audition.

The answer to that question seemed to be – *a blue towelled dressing gown*. And though no one was yet ready to discuss his nipple-rolling proclivities or for how long he had remained in the garment during the audition, it was fairly obvious that, for all of them, the trials had been more than a merely musical experience. He had seen every single female member of Doublet and Hose, even Linda 'Wallaby's Bottom' Makepeace, between six forty-five on Sunday morning and four ack emma on the Monday.

What a man! Elinor found herself thinking. What a musician!

None of this made him any the less attractive. If possible, he seemed more so. And, as the women, sometimes giggling, sometimes icy, sometimes openly lustful, sometimes merely curious, offered scraps of information, delicately turned into and then away from the obvious innuendo, she found, to her surprise, that it made her fellow chorus members more, not less, bearable. The thought that they were all *his* women made her shudder with something between fear and desire. He was like a sultan, a pasha. They were his slaves. All he had to do was to lift his baton and any of them would sink to her knees and take it between her –

She found she was going over the scene she had witnessed between him and Julia and was putting herself into it. She wasn't any longer at the window – she was in the room, her knees on the parquet floor and she was –

Why hadn't he asked her? She moved from erotic reverie to total despair. Why, of all twelve women, should she not be asked? It wasn't just that she hadn't forced herself on him. There was something about her, wasn't there, that was, well, frankly, repulsive. That was why she was stuck with Henry Farr in 54 Maple Drive. That was why she had had a daughter as ugly and fat as her. And one day Maisie was going to grow up and marry a man as fat and ugly as Henry. And so it would go on. Horrible, fat, bitter, twisted people would keep being born in Wimbledon on and on and on until the next millennium unless some merciful nuclear explosion came and blew the lot of them sky-high.

You're the only one he didn't get his leg over! came Henry's voice. *He bonked the lot of them in twenty-four hours and somehow you slipped through the net. Is this something to do with the perfume you use or what?*

'I think,' Julia O'Dowd was saying, 'it was when he said – '

Louella van Heeming cut in: 'Authentic music is authentic emotion – '

And Mary Parker said: 'Go with the emotion and – '

Ellen Harrison: 'See where it leads you.'

'Where does it lead you?'

Almost all the women voiced this question at the same moment and, as they did so, Esmond Brice came through the door, a baton in his left hand, a bunch of manuscripts under his right arm. He looked at his women with a dark and serious expression and, holding up his hand for silence (which he got), he said, 'Yes. Where does it lead you?'

The women surged towards him. He pulled them towards him. They are like plants, thought Elinor, long confined to cupboards. Esmond had opened the door, let in the light and now they were rising towards it. Living with Henry, she reflected, was very like being in a cupboard with the door closed.

'It leads you,' said Esmond, 'to *authenticity*. Authenticity of feeling and of emotion. Of testimony and of moral worth. We are here to decide which of you can *be* Mistress Howking and *be the authentic voice of William Byrd.*'

It was only now, quite suddenly, that Elinor realized she disliked Esmond Brice intensely. There was something absolutely disgusting and phoney about him. It only took her one second to decide this. One minute he was a sultan – the next he was a pathetic poser whose only claim to fame was that between Pentecost and Victoria Day he had managed to shag no less than eleven unbelievable frumps. He had probably made up this whole Mistress Howking business. William Byrd had most likely had the good sense to keep well away from Wimbledon, which was, probably, as dull, unrewarding and pathetically small-minded a place in 1587 as it was in 1994.

'I know you all,' Esmond was saying, his eyes fixed on Ellen Harrison. 'I know you deeply, intimately, as women. I feel for all of you a deep, deep concern and love and trust.'

Julia O'Dowd gave a low moan. All the women, apart from Elinor, started to shake like long grass in a small wind. Brice held up his arms before the choir. 'So who will it be?' he said. 'Who will be Mistress Howking?'

His eyes went along the line of women. Susannah Greenstreet gasped audibly.

'There is one among you,' he said, 'who has a quality none of the others has. A quality *key* to this role. A quality that is at the very heart of Byrd's harmonies.'

His eyes came to a stop. With a start Elinor realized he was looking straight at her.

'Mystery,' he said. 'There is something about her that I can't quite . . . grasp. And it is this quality that has made me award the role of Mistress Howking to Elinor Farr.'

Elinor felt eleven glances of pure hatred upon her. But she could not remember being as authentically happy as this since the day her sister Henrietta – who had always been her father's favourite – failed all her A-levels. She shook out her hair, stepped out from the line of local uglies and said, in a low, serious voice, 'I will try and do the role justice, Esmond! I will try and do my best for you. As we all do, don't we?'

Behind her, Julia O'Dowd sounded as if she was being sick. Elinor didn't look back. She kept her eyes on Esmond's. It was, she now realized, one of his tricks. To stare at someone without blinking. It made you look sincere. What a ghastly little worm he was! Why hadn't she seen that earlier?

Now she knew what he was, everything about him – his jacket, his ridiculous cord trousers, his brogues, his slightly greying hair, even his admittedly compelling eyes – seemed totally artificial. There were things wrong with Henry – so many things that she hardly knew where to begin – but, if you could rub off some of the crudeness, give him a little of Esmond's deceptive style, he would prove the better of the two men. Over the summer she would take him to concerts, read him the short stories of Ian MacEwan, she would make him a fully rounded human being. And she would be happy with him.

With these thoughts in her heart she smiled at Brice. 'You inspire us, of course. Of course! You see, Esmond,' she said, 'you're so . . . so very . . .' He smiled back at her, clearly unaware of what was in her heart. '. . . *authentic!*'

GCS What?

'SO LONG, MOTHERFUCKERS!' said Maisie Farr. She said this, first time, under her breath. She rather liked the sound of it. When she got to the front door she said it again, this time quite loud. 'So long, mother-fuckers!'

There was a grunt from Henry. He hadn't gone into work before eleven since 15 May. Were they making him redundant? But how could you make someone so obviously useless redundant? Neither of her parents did anything as far as she could see. They spent most evenings going to concerts or to the theatre but they never listened to or watched anything interesting. It was Chekhov and Shakespeare and Beethoven and all that shit. Then Elinor called, 'Goodbye, darling!'

She had obviously not heard. Or chosen not to hear. When she had opened the door Maisie screamed up through the hall, 'So long, motherfuckers!' Then, without waiting for a reply, she slammed the front door.

They were both going to sleep all morning. Sleep or hump. If they humped. Mind you, if they humped, they probably humped in their sleep. They were disgusting.

'I hope I die before I get old!' she said, out loud, as she walked up Maple Drive. In a few days she would be sixteen years old. She was horribly close to getting the vote. Once that happened to you, as far as she could tell from looking at the Upper Sixth, you were finished.

It was already disgustingly hot. Why did they have exams in June? Because they wanted you to suffer. They thought of new ways of making you suffer all the time. It wasn't enough that you had course work and timed course work and ongoing assessment and the whole Stalinoid apparatus of the National Curriculum. They also had to lock you up in a room with three hundred other people at the height of summer and ask you questions about surface area, the velocity of projectiles, electrical circuits and other things about which you knew absolutely fuck all.

You are the terror
You are the burning
You are the white heat
Muthafucka!

Singing stuff from The Twisted's album made life a little more bearable. Even though she was wearing the amazingly stupid *grey skirt* and *grey jumper* forced on all personnel of the Mary Louisa Haddock School for Girls, Wimbledon, she had managed to score heavily in the hat, footwear, sock and tie departments. Her shoes, a pair of de-studded football boots that had once belonged to 'Loony' Ned Parker, a friend of James Seebohm's, really said something. Her socks – one of which had once belonged to a member of the Cranborne School hockey team, the other of which was one of a pair of Myocin support tights which she had painted bright green – were also, she felt, indicative of the things that drove her: despair, anger and a deep hatred of the false or the half-hearted.

But the hat (hats were not required at the MLH School for Girls, Wimbledon) was the real stroke of genius. It was a small, blue-rimmed job that she had found in a junk shop. Once upon a time it had crowned the head of some poor little tart in one of those schools of yesteryear where it was the done thing to feel strongly about the gym mistress. It had, when Maisie had bought it, an elastic strap and a badge that said FORTITUDO ET CASTITIA. She had jumped up and down on it in the football boots, sprayed it with silver dust and written WHO LOVES YA? on the side.

At least she was going to fail in style.

She knew so little about physics that she had decided to make today a day of protest. She was not quite sure yet what form the protest would take, but it would almost certainly involve not answering any of the questions. There was absolutely no point in trying to do so anyway.

You take my taxes
Spend them on guns
You are the pain
You are the magma
Muthafucka!

She had the impression that James Seebohm was avoiding her.
Last week when she had sighted him in Sainsbury's, he had broken

into a run. Although she gave chase, she lost him somewhere around the tinned vegetable area. She wasn't sure that he had seen her but she was taking the possibility seriously. Sometimes she wondered whether the whole world might not be against her. Not just Elinor and Henry. But Elinor and Henry and James and the Midland Examining Board. They were all in it together, she decided, as a double-decker bus roared up the hill towards her. As usual there was another one behind it. She ran along the side of the first bus. No James. Not downstairs anyway. He always went downstairs. Upstairs made him feel sick. She ran on to the second bus. No sign of him there either. Had she missed him on the first one? Maisie wheeled round and, as she did so, saw something that looked like James Seebohm rear up from one of the seats. He looked – although she could not quite credit this – as if he had been hiding from someone.

'James!' she called, and started back towards the bus. As she did so, the figure that looked like James seemed to make a half-hearted dash for the exit, then start up the stairs to the upper deck.

It couldn't be James. He never travelled on the upper deck. But by now the bus was pulling out. Maisie jumped up on the platform and peered inside the bus to see if the little rat was hiding behind another passenger.

He was nowhere to be seen.

Clucking noisily to herself, Maisie turned and climbed the stairs to the upper deck. As soon as she had bobbed and swayed her way up there, she saw James. He was crouched down low in a seat up near the front. Something about his shoulders reminded her of a small animal trying to blend into its background.

She started down the aisle. 'James?'

He crouched even lower in his seat.

'Are you avoiding me?'

He didn't answer.

James Seebohm had had, and indeed was still having, a disturbed childhood. The only son of Laura and Violet Seebohm, who ran a secondhand bookshop in South Wimbledon, he described his life as 'hell', 'really painful' and 'slow death, really'. It was hard to work out quite why this was the case. When Maisie and Amina Ghosh had gone round there on the night of Benjie Rabstein's party, Mr and Mrs Seebohm had seemed delighted to meet them. They did not, as Henry tended to do, lurk in their sitting room muttering about their compact discs. 'It's so nice for James to have friends!' Mr Seebohm had said. 'He hasn't really had friends, have you, Jimbo?'

James had not replied to this.

He was quite a small boy and although, when you looked at him for the first time, he did not appear striking, there was a gentleness about his pale blue eyes that, after a month or so, began to haunt a girl. He had a pale, thoughtful look about him that you did not find in many of the boys of Cranborne School, and, unlike them, his conversation was not confined to the words 'Woah!' and 'Nutter!' He didn't just do Lloyd Grossman impressions. He did not speak much but when he did he gave the feeling that what he said mattered to him.

Maisie liked his hair too. It was almost always tousled and un-combed. It made him look, she thought, like something out of the small mammal house. Every time she saw him she wanted to pick him up and cuddle him, or wave bits of cheese above his nose and make him dance on his hind legs. Maisie had once tried to do this in Nuala O'Dowd's kitchen and James, who had drunk three pints of lager, responded by twitching his nose and sticking out his teeth like a beaver.

But something had gone wrong with their relationship.

Elinor was always saying that men were not to be trusted. Maisie had always assumed that when she said 'men' she meant Henry. And the fact that her mother always looked at her father when she said this confirmed this suspicion.

But maybe James Seebohm and Henry, although superficially as unlike each other as any two people could be, were bound together by some dark thread.

'You are avoiding me!' said Maisie.

'I'm not!' said James.

He got up from his seat. Maisie grabbed his arm.

'You see?' she said. 'You're off!'

'This is my stop,' said James. 'I have to get out. I have to go to school. I have to take GCSE physics!'

Maisie steered him back into his seat. 'We never talk these days,' she said.

She realized as she said this that it was something her mother was always saying. Would she, one day, end up exactly like Elinor? The thought was so horrific that she loosened her hold on James's arm and Seebohm, like a mouse going for its hole, headed down the stairs.

'You are ruining my life!' Maisie called after him.

That, she realized, as Seebohm scampered off into the road, narrowly avoiding the bus behind, was another of her mother's favourite phrases. Was she doomed to waddle around like a robot, repeating her mother's well-rehearsed views on art, cookery, politics and human relations?

Might she, in spite of herself, end up by marrying someone like Henry?

This thought was so appalling that she had to put her head between her knees. If Rita Dunsford from 5E hadn't tapped her on the shoulder, she might well have missed her stop.

James had not yet kissed her, although once or twice he had looked as if he was summoning up the courage to try something along those lines. Whenever he looked like this Maisie tried not to seem like a girl who would greet an approach of this nature with a blow to the face. The trouble was, she looked like just that kind of girl. She looked just like her bloody mother.

She would have given anything to look yielding. But how could you look yielding when your arms hung down at your sides like a gorilla's and your eyes, even when plastered with Immaculate eye shadow, made you look like some primitive British warrior out of his skull on mead and herbal cocaine substitute?

Why didn't school tell you how to deal with all this stuff, instead of their half-assed bollocks about sines, cosines and the cubic volume of swimming pools? Why didn't they do GCSEs on James Seebohm?

1 Why, and to what extent, is James Seebohm 'gorgeous'?
2 'James Seebohm – a Man Apart.' Discuss this in relation to Linda Wakefield's party.
3 Write down everything you know about James Seebohm. Maps and diagrams may be used.

Why was she walking to the MLH School for Girls behind Nuala O'Dowd, when the sun was pouring down like honey on the street behind her? Why was she going in to answer questions to which she did not know the answer, when the trees were thick with opulent leaves and the blackbird, masked by the foliage of a plane tree, raised its yellow bill to summer sweetness?

Raised its yellow bill to summer sweetness! Not bad! First line of a poem. Maisie wrote a lot of poetry. Much of it, lately, had been in the style of Gerard Manley Hopkins, who was a set text. It had started as a joke and now she was unable to stop. Every subject she covered, even the things she felt deeply about – such as James Seebohm – seemed to get the Hopkins treatment.

> All's past sweet Seebohm, gone
> Gone – drained down sweet Seebohm sweet ah gone!
> How shall I now you in nooks rediscover?
> How lightly lollop into your lap, lover?
> How are we changed Seebohm? How heft?
> Sweet Seebohm? Or are we not? Is all strong sweet
> Sweet Seebohm slowly say now is the sour sweet?

She was not entirely sure this was how it went. She was frightened of writing it down in case someone found it. Even in her head it felt like a compromising document.

The exam took place in the Great Hall. Girls were ranged in neat rows the whole length of the place, their desks a weirdly discrete distance from each other. There was a rumour that Angela 'Rubberneck' Beveridge had been placed in a kind of Bermuda Triangle of her own directly underneath the stage. Anthea Porter, who never mixed, was already sitting at her desk when Maisie came in. She was surrounded by pens, rulers, set squares, rubbers and amazingly sharp pencils. There was probably, thought Maisie, a mobile phone in there somewhere, so that the fat frump could call up her ever-loving mother and ask her advice about heat efficiency or the Brownian motion of molecules.

Maisie did not look out for any of her friends. She wasn't sure she had any, anyway. Stephanie Wyse-Fanshawe was smirking to herself in the corner. Perhaps she had somehow got to James Seebohm. It was perfectly possible. The girl would do anything to make Maisie's life a living hell.

It was so hot!

The windows in the Great Hall were not designed to let you see the world outside unless you happened to be a giraffe or pitched up with a forty-foot ladder. This was presumably because the things that happened in the Great Hall were so paralysingly boring that the merest glimpse of the real world beyond would create a stampede.

Why did so much depend on the stupid piece of paper now being carried towards her by Jamrags Pleckett, a woman who seemed to take a special, perverted pleasure in the act of invigilation? She looked at Maisie as she placed the exam paper reverently on the desk in front of her and her upper lip twitched. Maisie did not look at the paper but kept her eyes on Jamrags's upper lip. If the woman's moustache got any bigger, she would have to start making it a feature.

Maybe she was going for the full Monty – a George VI beard and 'tache combo. Maybe, like a lot of the other creatures who crawled out of the staffroom of the Mary Louisa Haddock School for Girls, Wimbledon, Jamrags was really a man. Which could explain why she wore what looked like a bivouac tent during netball practice.

To let them know she really didn't give a stuff, Maisie, without looking at the paper, turned it face down on her desk, folded her arms and glared round at the other candidates. Anthea Porter, who had not got her paper yet, was waiting, mouth open, and pencil poised, like an Olympic sprinter on the starting blocks. When Jamrags laid it, with the reverence due to a star pupil, on her desk, Anthea gobbled it up with her eyes and, almost immediately, started to write. 'Yes! . . . Yes! . . . Yes!' she cried to herself as she scribbled furiously. 'Mmmm! . . . Oh yes! . . . Yes! Yes! . . . Mmmm!' As she found yet more things that she had prepared specially the night before and as she recognized old friends – surface area, torques, vectors, angles of incidence, ohms – she crooned to herself as if in the throes of orgasm: 'Mmmm . . . yes, yes, yes . . . Oh *yes*!' While this was going on, Stephanie Wyse-Fanshawe smirked round at the rest of the hall, shaking her long blonde hair out behind her as if to say, 'I may not know much about physics, but I am easily the best-looking girl in this room!'

Maisie folded her arms even more tightly. She still did not turn over the paper. What was the point? Jamrags Pleckett was glaring at her. Maisie glared back. Then she looked up at the picture above Jamrags's head. It was an oil painting of Dame Mary Louisa Haddock, the hideous old bat who had founded this place. It was, thought Maisie grimly, an oil painting, but she was no oil painting. 'Why did you bother?' she said to Dame Mary.

The woman did not reply. She was wearing a sort of blue cushion on her head. In her right hand was what looked like a shrivelled banana. Perhaps it was a vibrator. The old cow was, so Miss White was always saying, at the forefront of the struggle for women's equality. In front of her, on a small wooden table, was a tennis racket. Or perhaps, thought Maisie, it was a bondage aid. Everything else in the picture was drowned in a sea of oil paint. If ever the art historians got to work on this one, they would find it told them depressingly little about society and culture in Wimbledon in 1889 – the date on the bottom of the picture. If you hadn't known the stupid old trout was in Wimbledon, there was no way of telling, unless the tennis racket was intended as a clue. She might have been on the fucking moon. If she was on planet earth, there was no clue as to which bit of it she was on. There was no indication of whether she was in or out of doors, upstairs, downstairs or underwater, or whether there was any significance in the odd, dark shape looming up out of the blues and browns behind her as she stared complacently down at the young people whose lives she had ruined.

Maisie pulled a blank sheet of writing paper towards her and wrote, rapidly, 'What is science? What is physics? Do we care?'

This, she decided, was what they needed:

The world does not, repeat, not, exist to be measured. Physics can tell us things about how the world works but, unfortunately, it does not answer any of the interesting questions we choose to ask ourselves about it. Who cares how long it takes to fill a bath? Are there not more interesting questions to be asked about the world?

Such as what? thought Maisie. And then, without pausing, found herself writing:

Such as what? Such as *why*? The great poet Wordsworth wrote that we 'murder to dissect' and nowhere is this more evident than in the operation of science, especially. Physics may tell us how quickly a cannonball travels down the Leaning Tower of Pisa (shouldn't Galileo have been *looking* at the thing instead of hurling cannonballs off it?) but it cannot tell us –

A very clear image of James Seebohm came to her at that moment. He was in another room struggling with the same impenetrable rubbish against which she was even now protesting. She saw his pale blue, gentle eyes, heard his delightful, oddly gruff voice and found herself writing:

– why the sight of a loved one may disturb our world more effectively than the discoveries of Einstein or Newton. The touch of a hand, the sound of a voice – these are, surely, more complex, and yet simpler, than the effect of nerve endings telling one human brain that a fragment of its DNA has touched another creature, whose genetic material may correspond in some way to the toucher's. As Keats wrote, 'Heard melodies are sweet but unheard melodies are sweeter!' and physics is the science of heard melodies not of sense impressions rendered through the best means of conveying them – poetry.

She looked at the scribbling masses around her. What did they understand of the world? They were struggling with concepts that were not designed to make sense of anything important – like the light on James Seebohm's hair –

The light on James Seebohm's hair is too complex a subject to be dealt with by talk of photons and angles of incidence. How can 'a drowsy dullness numb our senses as if of Lethe's water we had drunk' when some idiot is telling us about how to remember the exact velocity at which a rose petal is expected to hit the ground? Imagine a physicists' version of Shelley's 'Ode to the West Wind'. He or she certainly wouldn't tolerate any idea of the poor zephyr being the breath of autumn's being. It would be heigh-ho for the Beaufort scale and why the ambient temperature was affected by the wind chill factor!

She stared round at the other examinees. Didn't they understand what they were missing? At least some boring teacher out there was going to be shocked into some kind of life by this answer. Even if it got her nought per cent, it was worth it. At least the unknown marker would hear and understand about what she felt about Seebohm. There was a wonderful irony in this. As she poured out her heart in sentences that were absolutely private she *knew* they would be misunderstood, ignored by the person destined to read them.

Physics does not know James Seebohm. Why should it? He is beyond its grasp. He means nothing to it. But he means something to *me*. 'Poets', as Shelley wrote 'are the unacknowledged legislators of the world', and though you may try and calibrate them, measure them, murder them in order to dissect them, they will arise to sing the praises of James Seebohm!

Maisie stopped. Jamrags, who had been stalking the room for the last half an hour, was standing at her shoulder. Not only that. She was, without bothering to conceal the fact, reading what Maisie had written.

There was a special pleasure in this. Invigilators, like prison warders, were as much victims of the system as the people they guarded. Jamrags was trying to look as if she wasn't bothered by Maisie's performance. To irritate her even more, Maisie pushed her paper into her line of vision as she wrote:

Seebohm is impossible to describe. He cannot be trapped in an equation or plotted on a graph. He is himself, as I am myself, and any attempt to pin him down is doomed to failure as total as that which will greet the person who tries to cast the second law of thermodynamics into blank verse!

Jamrags was grinning stupidly. She leaned over and said, 'I don't think I know Seebohm. Is he good?'

Maisie's jaw dropped.

'Is he worth getting hold of?' said Jamrags in a matey whisper.

You weren't safe anywhere. First Stephanie Wyse-Fanshawe, and now this ugly old hag, were trying to pinch James Seebohm from under her nose. In the middle of an examination! Jamrags was practically digging her in the ribs as she said, 'I must look him up, anyway. You've obviously got hold of an interesting property, Maisie!' And she swept on through the lines of girls, bowed over their papers. Maisie glared at her retreating back and wrote on, as the time ticked away:

How can we 'get hold' of James Seebohm? We cannot. His essence is too complex to grasp. How can we say we love what he is? What is love? DNA reaches out for more DNA. Nerves transmit to the fingers or the eyes or the hands certain information but this is not all. When we say we love James Seebohm we are not saying we have 'got hold of a property', since, as Wordsworth said, 'getting and spending we lay waste our powers'.

As she wrote, the hall, her neighbours, the noise of the huge clock ticking over to her right seemed to disappear and she was in a place that was here and now and yet was a lot of other places as well. Even Seebohm was no longer the subject. Although she was nominally writing about him, she was really writing about everything – herself, Henry, Elinor, the paper in front of her, the girls to the right and left of her – they all dissolved into the act of recording, of marking white sheets of paper with black ink.

Science cannot explain, finally, what I feel about James Seebohm any more than it can explain why dust dances in the sunlight before my uncomprehending eyes or what is the 'still, sad music of humanity'. Seebohm is a mystery. He is, it seems to me, life itself and I do not wish to know how long it takes him to fill a bath or at what speed he will hit the ground if I cast him out of the window of a moving train!

Jamrags had crept back to her. She was grinning idiotically. In a larky, little girl sort of way, she whispered, behind her hand, 'Is he German?'

Maisie looked up at her. What on earth was the woman on about? Had she got nothing better to do than to fantasize about getting her hands on fifteen-year-old boys?

'I can't find him anywhere!'

'Good!' hissed Maisie. 'He's English. And don't bother trying to find him, because you won't!'

Jamrags merely smirked again. Maisie, oblivious of her now, wrote faster and faster. Where was she 'looking up' James Seebohm? In some kinky directory for frustrated spinsters? She had gone back to her desk and was flicking through a gigantic tome in a furtive kind of way. It wouldn't surprise me, thought Maisie, if the Girls Independent Schools issued a kind of *Toyboys Who's Who*. She urged the pen over the page:

Sweet Seebohm! What he has to say to me is something that science can never be – and that is personal. He dwells 'amongst th'untrodden ways' far from the reach of lever, pulley, or particle accelerator. Dull would he be of soul who could pass him by – and yet I am not sad that many men of science do just that. For James Seebohm is a secret to be shared between me and him. He belongs beyond the prying eye of teachers, in a place that scientists, that physicists, can never, never reach – the human heart!

As she wrote this last sentence the bell sounded. They had five minutes to go. It was too late to do anything else. Let some poor bastard from the Midland Examining Board of the Oxford and Cambridge branch of the General Certificate of Secondary Education read that!

What had Jamrags been going on about? With a half smile of contempt she turned over the paper, and, at the same moment, she saw that the volume Miss Pleckett had been reading was the *Oxford Guide to Twentieth-Century Poetry*. The paper was headed ENGLISH COMPOSITION.

She could have sworn it was physics! She stared at the paper.

ANSWER ONE QUESTION

1   'We murder to dissect' – discuss the opposition between art and science in the light of Wordsworth's line, paying especial attention to the Romantic tradition in English poetry.

Maisie did not look at the other questions. There were four minutes left. She went through the essay carefully substituting William Wordsworth for James Seebohm. Apart from the line about the mysterious effect of sunlight on his hair, it seemed to make pretty good sense. And the thing about English – the reason why she was good at it – was that, if the broad lines of the argument were all right, it was sometimes quite OK to talk absolute rubbish, provided it sounded as if you meant it.

The Right Set

'THIRTY ALL!' said Norman, in an accent that was clearly not his own. Norman owned an off-licence. Unkind people in Wimbledon maintained he put two pounds extra on a bottle of Beaujolais simply because he talked like a member of the royal family.

Why, thought Henry, am I always playing on the next court to Norman? He is the person I hate most in Wimbledon – or rather, one of the people I hate most in Wimbledon.

Norman always knew the score. No one else did. Nor, for that matter, understood why he should always have such a detailed knowledge of it. It rarely did him credit. Norman weighed about fifteen stones. This did not stop him from wearing tennis whites, or from thrusting his buttocks out as if about to solicit sexual favours from the assorted dentists, lawyers, computer salesmen and graphic designers who filled the courts of the Wimbledon Tennis Club at this hour of a Sunday morning.

Why, thought Henry grimly, did they call it the Wimbledon Tennis Club? It was confusing. Especially during these two hellish weeks in July when athletic young millionaires from New York, Lisbon and Sydney descended on the suburb Henry liked to think of as his. He should probably have leased the house out to one of the bastards and moved the family into a hotel.

Mind you, that would only have encouraged Elinor. Ever since the beginning of summer she had been dragging him to concerts, plays and art galleries. She had forced him to walk through the Picasso exhibition at the Tate and thrown up her hands in delight at everything of the horrible little Spanish phoney that was on offer. She had forced him to sit through a play at the Royal Court that was called *Loathing the Dawn*; she had even tried to read him a whole book by someone called Jeanette Winterson.

What she hadn't done was waltz into the bedroom in a black negligée and said things like, 'Give it to me long and hot and strong,

Henry!' Henry had taken to desperate measures in order to escape. Any company and any environment seemed preferable to sitting next to Elinor at the Wigmore Hall or the National Theatre. And so here he was, with Maisie at the Wimbledon Tennis Club.

The Wimbledon Tennis Club. One of these days, Bjorn Borg was going to turn up and ask to play a few sets.

It wasn't Bjorn Borg these days, was it? Henry couldn't even remember the names of the tennis players any more. He was getting old, he thought, as he paced inconclusively up and down the base line. And the club wasn't even *in* Wimbledon. Anyone who knew anything about sw19 – and Henry was a world expert on the subject – knew that every single figure out on the courts this Sunday was at least fifty yards inside Southfields. Which was probably why the subscription rates to the club were so low.

At least Elinor was not a member! Not yet, anyway. In her present mood she was quite capable of signing herself into the club so that she could rush on to the court with a volume of medieval French verse just when her husband was at match point.

Henry started to bounce the ball in front of him, trying to look like a man who had a serve on which he could concentrate. He was only playing his daughter, but it was still important to win. Maisie did not look like a player on whom anyone would put money. She wasn't even putting up a show of attention to the game. As far as Henry could make out, she was not bending at the waist, the way you were supposed to when waiting for one of Henry's killer serves.

Not that you would have been able to tell if she *had* been bending at the waist. Erect or crouching, Maisie, these days, presented five feet eight of concentrated flab to the world. Her nickname at school, this term, was Jabba the Hut. It was partly to try to reduce her weight that Henry forced her out on to the courts. Someone had to supervise her exercise with the utmost care. They had tried to send her, on her own, to the Lime View Health Club. It was only after she had been going for three months that Henry and Elinor found out she was spending all her time in the Vegetarian Slimmers' Bar.

'Come on, Daddy!' she said. 'Let's get it over with!'

They had suggested she go to a plastic surgeon for Spot Fat Reduction. But Maisie, once she had seen the menu of possibilities, had demanded receding chin correction, eyebag and eyelid replacement, lipolysis, breast enlargement and a particular kind of nose job that would have cost about as much as Henry's car.

In spite of all this she still maintained she was making progress with Seebohm. 'He likes 'em big!' she had said last week to Henry, and Henry, who could not understand why his daughter should show any interest at all in that rat-faced little twerp, had grunted in disbelief.

Henry threw the ball high in the air and whacked it across the net. It bounced inside the inner court and bounced again past Maisie's ear. She looked after it resentfully. 'That's not fair,' she said. 'You're supposed to hit it *to* me!'

What made it worse was the fact that Norman was playing 'Steel Thighs' Jessup, the Putney architect who had once boasted that he could take on the entire club with both hands tied behind his back.

He looked, this morning, as if he was trying this technique out on Norman. Jessup was not in the traditional pre-service position. Both right and left arm (and, presumably, racket, unless Jessup was now so amazingly good at tennis he didn't *need* a racket) were draped, yearningly, over his buttocks. With a shock, Henry realized that the star of the Wimbledon Tennis Club was doing some kind of breathing exercise. The combination of Jessup's performance and Norman's crouch made it look as if the two men were engaged in some complex mating ritual of the kind found in the pages of *A la Recherche du Temps Perdu*.

As he hit the next ball past Maisie's head, he saw both Norman and Steel Thighs, as if in deliberate synchronicity, turn their heads sharp left and leave them facing in that direction. Was this, wondered Henry, some new pre-match ritual enjoined on all serious members of the club?

Following the line of their gaze, he realized it was not.

Coming round the side of the clubhouse, in immaculate tennis whites, dangerous-looking tennis shoes and a couple of designer sweatbands, was a black man.

There had been, a few years back, a German member called Heinz, although he let his membership lapse after Jessup did his Hitler moustache act in the bar late one night. There were rumours of a Chinaman called Ping Ho although, even if he had paid his subscription, the man had never actually dared show his face anywhere near the premises. As long as Henry had been playing there, the Wimbledon Tennis Club had been one hundred per cent white. Or, to put it more accurately, thought Henry as he looked around the courts, one hundred per cent pink.

How had the man got through the front door, let alone past the selection committee? Peter Bates, Peter Pearse, Peter Piper and Peter Parker had given Henry a fairly nasty couple of hours at his interview. Peter Piper had asked him, several times, whether Farr was a Jewish name.

'Surely shome mistake!' Norman was saying to Steel Thighs as the black man made his way towards the one vacant court – on the other side of where he and Jessup were playing.

How had the man done it? Had he worn a disguise of some kind? Had he sent someone else along to the interview? Or had he (this was entirely possible) simply wandered in off the streets? He did not, to the obvious relief of almost everyone there, appear to have a partner. But this did not seem to trouble him. He went to the base line of the empty court and, from an elegant shoulder bag, took out a plastic tube full of tennis balls, two rackets and a small bottle of mineral water.

It was, thought Henry with some satisfaction, the beginning of the end. South Africa had fallen. Wimbledon's turn was bound to come. No one, as far as he could make out, was even pretending to play. All attention was focused on the tall, elegant stranger.

It wouldn't have been quite so bad, said Peter Piper's wife, Elspeth 'New Money' Piper, if he hadn't been quite *so* black. Everything about him apart from his tennis clothes was quite incredibly black. He had high cheekbones, dark eyes and the kind of physique usually seen on advertisements for sports equipment. He was, Edith Walkman observed to her friend Lucy Broke, 'a very polished black man'. To which Lucy Broke, who thought of herself as a wit, replied, 'Polished as in Voltaire? Or as in furniture?'

Under the watchful eyes of about thirty or forty Wimbledonians, the black man threw the ball high into the air, did a worryingly efficient dance-like step and, with considerable force, smashed the first of his balls hard into the net. The mood on the courts relaxed.

'It's long-jumping they're good at!' said Norman, loudly, in Henry's direction. The stranger, meanwhile, unperturbed, reached for his second ball. Maisie, her racket drooping from nerveless fingers, was staring at him with the kind of attention she usually reserved for the American Hot served in the Pizza Express, Wimbledon.

With the second ball, he cleared the net but served out of court. With the third he achieved the kind of obvious ace that even Steel Thighs would have been unable to return. With the next ball, it was back into the net.

And so it went on. He seemed to have everything required to make a tennis player. He was tall. He was obviously fit. He could hit the ball very hard. When he served with any precision he was quite clearly of professional standard. But he seemed incapable of maintaining any degree of accuracy. As Norman said later to Henry in the club bar, 'They can't concentrate, you see. In a way it's sad. They have tremendous style and flair and some of them are marvellous athletes and musicians and so on. But they can't concentrate!'

It was Norman, curiously enough, who was the first to offer him a game. Probably, thought Henry, because the strain of trying to work out who the stranger might be was unbearable. 'Peter Piper might have made a mistake!' he called to Steel Thighs. 'Maybe the chap phoned up and asked if he could try out the courts or something! Some of them sound quite English over the phone.'

The stranger did, indeed, sound very English. He had the kind of natural, aristocratic accent that Norman had never quite managed to imitate correctly. For some inexplicable reason, Henry thought it sounded vaguely familiar. Why should that be?

'I'd love a game old chap!' he said. 'Shall we play doubles?'

Norman and Steel Thighs seemed to like this idea. 'You could play with Henry!' said Steel Thighs, adding, under his breath, that this would be the equivalent of forcing the darkie to run around the court in football boots. Maisie seemed very keen to watch her father being humiliated and, against his will, Henry went over to join the stranger.

'Henry Farr,' said Henry.

The black man seemed to hesitate slightly. For a moment, Henry could have sworn he had seen him somewhere before as well. But this was not possible. There were no black people in the solicitors for whom he worked, and no black parents at the expensive school to which, against his will, they had sent Maisie. The only black people he ever saw were on the street or on television.

'Call me . . . Julian,' he said, eventually.

Norman gave a puckered little smile. 'Nice little serve you have there!' he said.

'When it goes in!' said Julian.

It was at this point that Steel Thighs suggested fifty pounds on the match. The speed with which the stranger accepted made Henry wonder whether he could be one of those hustlers who frequent American films. Once the bet was sealed, perhaps he would start to serve with the accuracy of a brain surgeon slicing his way through the medulla oblongata.

'Have you been a member long?' said Steel Thighs as he and Norman regrouped on the other side of the net.

'Do you have to be a member?' said Julian.

Norman and Steel Thighs exchanged glances.

'Let's have the game anyway,' said Norman, 'and we can point you at the selection committee after you and Henry have thrashed us!'

This seemed, everyone said, the perfect, diplomatic solution to the stranger's arrival. There was, after all, as Emily Pratt said to Mabel Lawley, a waiting list, adding that the black man would not need to be told that the waiting list consisted of a seventy-year-old man who was not allowed to play on medical grounds and three ten-year-old boys.

Steel Thighs served first to Julian. Once he had recovered from his surprise at the fact that Henry's partner managed to return it, Jessup forced it over towards Henry. While Henry was still trying to work out where the ball might land, Julian bounded over to his left, flicked it back over the net and watched, impassively, as fifteen stone of off-licence proprietor thundered off in hopeless pursuit.

'Love fifteen!' said Henry, who had never been able to make a remark of this nature to Steel Thighs before. He sneered slightly as he prepared to receive the architect's serve, already under the delusion, as so often occurs in doubles matches, that he had played some significant part in gaining the last point.

There was the familiar blur of Jessup's arm, the kind of grunting sound Henry normally associated with visits to the lavatory, and somewhere ahead of him the percussive sound of something hitting tarmac. Henry looked around for a moving tennis ball but did not see one.

'Fifteen all!' said Jessup grimly.

'Bad luck!' said Henry's partner. 'He has a mean serve!'

Steel Thighs allowed himself a small smile.

'Have you ever played professionally?' said the black man to Jessup – which, some people said, was a question Jessup had been waiting forty years to be asked.

The first two points more or less set the pattern of the game. The only points that he and Julian lost were when Henry was serving or receiving service – apart from two double faults served by Norman. Julian's service was so terrifyingly hard and accurate that, for a time, Henry wondered whether he might actually *be* the first tennis hustler ever to be sighted in Wimbledon. Even Steel Thighs was powerless against it.

But the black man's manner was so unfailingly courteous! If he was a tennis hustler, he had managed the final test of the good con man – he made his victims enjoy being robbed. He was always quiet, gentle and discreet, especially at the moment of victory. He resisted the temptation to leap over the net and shout, 'Give me five, bro!' every time he slammed another ball past the racket of Ronald Jessup, a man who was known to put his architect's business before his wife and his tennis a long way ahead of either of them. He was even nice to Henry, resisting the urge to call him 'hopeless wanker', 'four-eyed git' and 'lumbering barrel of lard', all terms used at one time or another by members of the Wimbledon Tennis Club unfortunate enough to partner Henry in a game.

As the match proceeded, every other game on the court slowly ground to a halt. Henry heard Ella 'I-was-at-RADA' Makepiece whisper to a friend that this was the most exciting match the Wimbledon Tennis Club had ever seen. A crowd of spectators – some from the clubhouse, others from the other games in progress – gathered to watch Steel Thighs serve to Julian. With a shock, Henry realized that the score was 6–3 in favour of the architect and the off-licence manager. Jessup was serving for the match.

'Go for it, pardner!' said Henry in a tough, no-nonsense manner. Everyone looked at him rather curiously. Steel Thighs tossed the ball high in the air and, creasing his piggy little eyes with concentration, prepared to vindicate the honour of the club.

Henry was amazed that he and the black man were only 6–3 down. He was not the only one. Peter Piper observed to Peter Parker later that this was the only time anyone forced to play with Henry had ever managed to win a single game. It was often said at the club that even two competent players playing with Henry might stand a chance of losing against one determined opponent. Indeed 'playing Henry' had become a kind of folk expression to indicate any kind of disaster up to and including death. When Maureen Jarvis had died of a heart attack on holiday in Spain last year, Dave Spence, a particularly heartless younger player, had described as her as 'playing Henry'.

Henry crouched, with what he hoped was professional keenness, as Steel Thighs wound his racket back, hopped neatly to his left and smashed the ball over the net. It wasn't just that he hit it hard. He hit it, thought Henry, with the kind of passion that suggested that Julian had just asked to marry his daughter. It was as much of a statement on behalf of white suburbia as anything in the speeches of John Major or Margaret Thatcher. It was not only hard. It was well placed and mercilessly well timed. For a moment, it seemed as if Julian might not be able to return it. But he moved left across the court and caught it with a meaty, satisfying backhand that sent it back, low and sweet and marked for the attention not of Steel Thighs but of his less talented partner. Somehow or other Norman, whose face was now the colour of his overpriced claret, got behind the ball. Or at least, alongside it. Sliding along the surface of the court he managed to put the rim of his racket between the projectile and the ground. It bounded off, at a crazy angle, rose high in the air and started a downward path towards a spot about three yards to the left of Henry.

'I'll get it!' called the black man in clear, reasonable tones. And started, without any particular appearance of hurry, to amble over towards Henry's half of the court. The ball was still about twenty feet in the air.

'I think,' said Henry, in a small, tight voice, 'that I can cope with this one!'

'Are you absolutely sure about that?' said Julian, sounding like a consulting surgeon breaking the news to a terminally ill patient.

'I think I have the thing under control,' said Henry. 'I am not a *total* incompetent you know!'

The ball seemed to be taking an amazingly long time to get back to earth. Henry had the impression that he and Julian would have been able, had they so wished, to have a leisurely business lunch in order to discuss what to do about returning Norman's offering.

'If you're sure – ' said Julian.

'I'm positive!' snapped Henry. 'I may not be Bjorn Borg but I am a pretty good player when I choose to and – '

With a shock he realized the black man was signalling to him. What was the man on about? Why was he pointing in the air like that – and with his mouth open too? He looked most unattractive.

Henry suddenly realized that Julian was pointing at the ball which was now about six feet above his partner's head. He seemed to be offering to take it off Henry's hands. But it was already too late. Henry whirled the racket round his head, swatted the air feebly and watched the ball drop about three yards away from him and, unaided, bounce solemnly away across the court.

'Game, I think, gentlemen!' said Steel Thighs, allowing himself a thin smile.

People at the club said they had never seen a man with such perfect manners as Julian. He did not – as many members would have done – run screaming at Henry and try to sever his head with the side of his Malkham Fetherlite full-size racket. He did not even pout sullenly or run through what was known as Norman-shoulder-acting. He strode manfully up to the net and, with the air of a man who had been expecting just such a result, produced a fifty-pound note which he handed to Steel Thighs with a slight bow. Then he turned to Henry, who was giving the watching crowd his 'I-pay-my-subscription-don't-I?' look.

'Bad luck, partner!' he said in beautifully modulated tones. 'I was rather hogging the ball. You played a very honest game!'

Afterwards, some people said it was Henry who had asked the black man to the clubhouse for a drink. Later, when the whole business was out in the open, some people said that Henry had introduced him to the club for the express purpose of making trouble.

But in fact it was Steel Thighs who asked Julian for a drink and Steel Thighs who, over a half of lager, asked him whether he would be interested in joining. The fact was that the Putney architect had never had such a satisfying victory since he beat Hairy Duvalier, the former French professional, at an exhibition match designed to raise money for Juliana Barnes's hip replacement in 1989. And Steel Thighs was, as he pointed out to close friends, nearly forty. He was looking around for a successor.

'I'll be honest,' he told Jumpy Prang, the former RAF pilot. 'I hold no particular brief for the average black man!' (This was the understatement of the year.) 'But for me tennis comes first. The man's a damn good sportsman. I don't care if he's bright green.' His expression, as he said this, gave his listeners to understand that he would rather have preferred it if Julian *were* bright green.

When Steel Thighs made his offer, Henry expected Peter Piper, Peter Pearse, Peter Bates and Peter Parker, who were all in the bar, to take him outside and have a quiet word. Or possibly to kick his head in. But they, too, seemed to wish to adopt the stranger. After Steel Thighs had bought them all a drink with Julian's fifty pounds, they agreed to waive the usual membership committee meeting. And after Steel Thighs had bought them all a second drink, Peter Piper said it was nice to see a few new faces around the place and he, personally, would stand up for any man's right to be a tennis player first and everything else second. No one asked him what he meant by this.

There was only one moment when, afterwards, people said they should have suspected something. When Peter Pearse asked Julian for his address – although Peter Piper tried to ask him what he did for a living, he would not be drawn on the subject – the black man said he lived in Heathview Gardens. Henry, who knew a thing or two about the street map of Wimbledon, said 'Don't you mean Heathview *Crescent*, old man?'

Julian smiled and said of course he did. There was, as Henry pointed out to anyone prepared to listen, a Heathview Gardens in Morden and two of them in Raynes Park. It was an easy mistake to have made.

But, when Peter Pearse asked him how he would be paying, Julian said 'by banker's order'. And, when the first monthly payment arrived, it was from a branch of Coutts in central London. The name on the account was J. Thomson. There was nothing unusual in that. Except, as Peter Parker pointed out, this was the first time any of them had been given any clue as to Julian's surname.

'I've seen him before somewhere!' said Henry. 'I could swear I've seen him before. Or heard his voice or something . . . ' But no one listened to Henry. No one ever listened to Henry. And, even if they had listened to him, by that time it was too late.

'Care for the next dance?' said Julian.

'I'd love to!' said Amanda Jessup.

There had never been, thought Henry morosely, a club member as popular as Julian. He stood his round. He was a good listener. In fact, he hardly ever opened his mouth to speak. He was always offering people lifts in his BMW. He was clearly going to be the star of the Summer Ball that traditionally took place at the beginning of Wimbledon fortnight.

Elinor had refused to come. She seemed to have given up on both her husband and her daughter. She was spending more and more time with Mrs Lingalonga Boccherini, the widow of Gordon Macrae, or

Jungian Analyst Beyond the Reach of Winebox. Occasionally she would sneer at Henry and say things like, 'How will we find each other again, my dear?'

Once, he had heard her talking to Maisie in the kitchen, when she thought he was asleep in front of the television. 'If only,' she had said, 'Henry would do something. Something that showed me what he was made of!'

Henry had no idea what he was made of. Except that there was clearly something wrong with him. Why else was he squiring his sixteen-year-old daughter to the Summer Ball?

'We'll have to be off soon!' said Steel Thighs. His wife gave a brief, pained smile and moved out on to the floor with Julian. Julian put one hand to her waist and, holding her right hand lightly with his left, started to sway, easily, to the music.

'Love fifteen!' said Henry to his daughter as they made their way back from the bar.

They found themselves a table in the corner. Maisie, as usual, was drinking pints of lager. Seebohm, with whom she had gone to the cinema the previous evening, was, she had told Henry, 'being horrible', although she had not said what form this was taking.

He couldn't be being as horrible as Elinor. Now he thought about it, it had all started at the disastrous Doublet and Hose concert at which the stupid O'Dowd woman had done an impression of a sixteenth-century hooker. Elinor had been vile ever since that day. He was almost positive she was shagging Brice. Not that he minded much any more. As far as he was concerned, she could shag the entire All England Lawn Tennis Club if she liked. All he required of her was that she be reasonably polite to him inside, as well outside, 54 Maple Drive.

Angelica had told him the other day that he was a wronged man and that he needed a good woman. At least that is what he thought she said. As they communicated mainly in sign language, he could not be entirely sure.

Maisie sat heavily in her chair. She took a deep swig from her glass and gave a ladylike belch. 'Jessup,' she said, in tones of some satisfaction, '*hates* Julian!'

'Just five minutes now!' called Steel Thighs to his wife.

She looked at him over Julian's upper right arm. The upper right arm that had taken nearly two hundred service games off the Putney architect. 'Don't be petty, darling!' she called. 'We're having fun! I've got the hots for Hunky Jules!'

Julian gave a slight, almost weary nod of the head.

'Love thirty!' said Maisie. 'Julian leads by two games to love in the first set!'

One game, thought Henry as he groped for his double Scotch, probably referred to an incident earlier in the evening when Julian had put Steel Thighs right on a point of fact about the rules governing the tie-break. What was the other? As if in answer to his unspoken thought, Maisie said, 'Julian always starts one game ahead because he's so amazing and you're all such fat, white, horrible racists!' She was always saying things like this in the club bars. Usually in a very loud voice.

Over in the corner, Steel Thighs could be heard asking someone, in a loud voice, 'Who is he anyway? Why doesn't he say who he is or where he's from?'

Everyone knew to whom he was referring. Julian was known in club circles as the Mystery Man. It wasn't simply that he never discussed his life outside the club. It was as if such a thing did not exist. He always arrived, and left, in tennis whites. He never used the showers, greatly to the relief of Verwoerd Hughes, the club accountant, who told his friends in the Frog and Ferret that he had no wish to be 'overwhelmed by the man's equipment'.

There was also the question of his briefcase.

He always arrived carrying a plastic bag in which were his tennis balls (he had twenty of them), a towel, a small thermos and a copy of his current reading matter. For the last three weeks, according to Maisie, he had been reading Antonia Byatt's *Possession*. But, as well as the plastic bag, he always had with him a small, black, leather briefcase. It was locked. Maisie had tried to open it three or four times. Once she had taken a hammer to it while Julian was in the middle of a ten-game marathon with Steel Thighs at the end of which the defeated architect had had to be taken home in a taxi. But no one had ever seen what was inside it.

There were other, inexplicable things about his behaviour.

The way he leaned forward, very closely, when he was having one of his intimate conversations with club members (no one in the club would tell anyone else what they had talked about). The way he would suddenly rise in the middle of one such encounter and thrust himself across the table as if overcome with lust for the person to who he was talking. The way he had talked one night when slightly drunk (the only occasion) wistfully and sadly of 'his treatment'.

'It's my treatment . . . ' he had said to Toby 'Watch the Au Pair' Gutteridge. 'Do you see . . . it's my treatment . . . ?'

Toby was of the opinion that he had not long to live. There were others who said he was a professional player trying to 'case out' the All England Lawn Tennis Club. Honky Miller, the club bore, said to Steel Thighs during the club theatre night at the Richmond theatre, 'He probably needs to get used to the climactic conditions over here!'

Amanda Jessup and Julian were dancing very close together. Steel Thighs – over the bar – had ordered a double brandy. He was deep in conversation with Norman, who was about to start his third bottle of Beaujolais. 'I never minded them,' he was saying, 'when they were bus conductors. But have you noticed that these days the bus conductors are *white*! The coons are riding round in Rolls Royces, high on cocaine!'

Norman did not (perhaps wisely) attempt to test his judgement against his immediate experience. He nodded, in a way intended to convey fellow feeling, combined with a certain lack of interest, and said, 'Monica Seles is a sloppy, sloppy player!'

Steel Thighs, looking over towards the dance floor where Amanda was now leaning her head against Julian's, started to grind his teeth audibly. 'Who is he?' he muttered. 'Who the hell *is* he? Whoever he is, he isn't who he says he is, is he?'

As Julian had never really said who he was, this was a hard state-ment to contradict. No one, anyway, seemed prepared to take Steel Thighs up on the point. Someone, as they often did at this stage of the evening, put on the 'Chicken Song' very, very loud. Amanda started to rotate her thighs slowly and then thrust her pelvis forward, hard, at her partner. Julian, instead of looking round humorously at the rest of the club (which was how you were supposed to behave when Amanda Jessup did this to you), rotated his thighs back at her. Not only that. He put his right hand behind his head and gave a worryingly convincing pelvic thrust all of his own.

'How de doo di doo da!' said Peter 'Husband and Father' Winterson. 'Isn't he wondrous?' said Maisie. Henry sank more of his Scotch.

Everyone said afterwards that it was Julian's fault. That Steel Thighs was drunk. That there must have been ways in which Jessup could have been calmed down. But in the view of expert Jessup-watchers (including Henry) there was nothing short of chloroform or a massive injection of valium in the left buttock that would have stopped Steel Thighs – once the club secretary had made the mistake of putting on 'Lady in Red'. 'Lady in Red', as Jessup was always ready to explain to anyone willing to listen, was his and Amanda's favourite tune. 'When I hear it,' he was fond of saying, 'my belly turns to water. I can only think of Amanda. I think of what a great wife she's been to me. I think of her body, and I remember she is the best-preserved forty-eight-year-old woman I know. And I melt!'

During this number, Henry could not help noticing, Julian put both arms round Amanda's waist, moved his cheek close to hers and in the far gloom of the clubhouse, started to nibble her ear. Amanda, instead of responding with a forearm smash to the face (as Ella Pearse declared *she* would have done), started to rub her right leg along the line of Julian's left thigh.

Jessup's face darkened. His right hand went down to his own right thigh, considered by many to be his best feature, and he started, with ominous calm, to move over in the direction of his wife and her dancing partner. His lips were moving slowly but no one could hear what he was saying. He moved through the dancers as the song reached its wailing, desperate climax. All around him, husbands and wives were groping each other, inexpertly, in the gloom. And, over by the wall, Amanda had slipped her right hand inside Julian's elegant black jacket and was beginning to massage his left breast. Julian – a faraway look in his eyes – was allowing his own left hand to cup Mrs Jessup's ample buttocks. Just as Steel Thighs came up to them, the black man began to knead Amanda's rear end and to align his handsome face a few inches above hers. Henry watched the architect nervously. This was the man who had broken Dennis Thompson's arm after Thompson had borrowed his racket press without asking permission. Henry was not the only one watching the encounter. All over the darkened room, club members separated from their clinches, put down their drinks and breathed in slowly as they waited to see what would happen.

Steel Thighs waited until his wife had started to pucker her lips up at the tall, handsome stranger before tapping him on the shoulder and saying, in a brisk voice, 'Hands off my old lady, sonny. She's only allowed chocolate at weekends!'

Julian turned round with what seemed, to those close to him, almost leisurely interest. Henry did not see his left hand go out but Honky

Miller, who studied boxing, said it reminded him of Frank Bruno's 'flick'. It didn't seem to have the whole of the man's body weight behind it, but it must have landed on Steel Thigh's nose with considerable force, because the architect fell backwards into the darkness, his strong right hand flailing wildly up at his opponent.

'Bastard!' he croaked to himself. 'Black bastard!'

As blood started to course from Jessup's nose, Arthur DuCane, the club drunk, said, in a loud voice, 'Steady on, Sambo!'

Julian wheeled round. All round him, in the darkness, men were separating from their women. Chunky Boyle, the film editor, pushed his common-law wife aside, and, his face dark with anger, assumed the kind of boxing crouch usually seen in sporting prints of the eighteenth century. 'Come on, then!' he muttered. 'Come on, then!'

Julian moved towards his opponent. Chunky made a loose right jab at his face, but, even while he was in the middle of doing this, Julian was giving him a high punch to the head followed by two short blows to the stomach.

Chunky, whose work on a Hollywood epic about Louis Pasteur had been nominated, by his neighbours, for an industry award, made a noise like a punctured Li-lo and fell to the floor. Two committee members, Peter Piper and Peter Pearse, then ran at Julian waving their arms. Somehow or other they, too, ended up on the floor. One of them, as far as Henry could make out, seemed to have sustained some form of spinal injury.

After that things went rather quiet, apart from Maisie, who was muttering, 'Zap the bastards!' into her lager.

Julian looked round at the assembled members of the Wimbledon Tennis Club and said, in beautifully inflected tones, 'I really am frightfully sorry. I was simply dancing with the man's wife.'

At which Amanda Jessup burst into tears and, howling that Julian should go back to the jungle where he had come from in the first place, went over to the father of her two children and started to wipe the blood from his face.

'I love you, monkey dear!' said Steel Thighs in a loud voice. It was the first time he had used his pet name outside their bedroom in twenty-two years of marriage.

Julian looked round at the assembled Wimbledonians and, with a brief, saddened laugh, started towards the door.

It was only after he had gone, and after Peter Piper had been given back massage by Otto Kahn, the club osteopath, that someone noticed Julian's briefcase, on one of the chairs at the bar.

'Probably got a bomb in it!' said Chunky Boyle, who, like everyone else, had been given a free drink by the club secretary and was explaining how black boxers often threw low punches and that someone, like him, trained to fight fair could not possibly hold his own against such tactics.

It was Steel Thighs who suggested they open it. 'At least we'll find out who the little bastard was!' he said.

Everyone felt the use of the past tense was appropriate. It was clear that, were he to show his face again, he would not be welcome. Peter Pearse said that the committee would personally guarantee that if he came within fifty yards of the premises, they would break every bone in his body. At which Maisie muttered, 'If he doesn't break all yours first!'

But who was going to open it? Nobody seemed willing to take the risk. Henry looked away from the mysterious black bag, out into the Wimbledon night. Somewhere away in the distance he heard Julian's BMW roar into life and drive off up towards the village. He was clearly not coming back for it. Club member looked at club member. But no one moved. It was as if, thought Henry, the briefcase, like its owner, had been sent to torment them. As if, for the first time in recorded history, the members of the Tennis Club had been confronted by something unique in Wimbledon – a moral dilemma.

Opening another man's property did not come easily to the membership of the tennis club. There was something about a man's briefcase, people felt, that was sacred. Away from its owner, Julian's precious piece of luggage acquired an air of respectable mystery. It looked as if it might contain something important and official.

'Maybe,' said one of the DuCane twins, 'he worked for the government or something.'

'You can never tell,' said Maisie darkly. 'They can have quite powerful connections these days!'

By the time a few more drinks had gone down, everyone had convinced themselves that Julian was an undercover agent for the CIA. Several people were prepared to swear that they had seen the briefcase chained to the man's wrist. Peter Pearse put his ear to it and announced that he could hear ticking; Amanda Jessup ran out on to the courts and would only come back inside after Pearse himself had told her he was joking and admitted the joke was in poor taste.

In the end Henry was deputed to open the case. 'Henry has a furtive look about him!' said off-licence Norman in his loud, braying voice. 'He looks like a man who would know how to pick a lock or two!'

'I know,' said Steel Thighs, who had now recovered his composure and whose face no longer showed any traces of blood. 'We could get Maisie to sit on it!'

Everyone laughed. Henry picked up the case and, beckoning to his daughter, went out on to the verandah. 'Anyone who wants to be implicated in the violation of Julian's privacy, please follow me!'

Nobody did.

Out on the verandah the summer air was sweet. The lights on the main road could be seen beyond the plane trees, and, beyond them, the dark spaces of Wimbledon Park. Somewhere further up the hill was the golf course, the Common and the green sweep of Surrey. Henry breathed in deeply, holding the briefcase at arm's length. 'Shall we open it?' he said.

'Of course!' said Maisie.

Taking a brooch from her blouse, she started to work its pin, carefully into the mechanism of the case's brass lock. She seemed to know what she was doing. At least, thought Henry grimly, she had learned to do something useful at the Mary Louisa Haddock School for Girls, Wimbledon. She made a quick thrust forward, pulled hard at the straps above the lock and slipped her hand inside.

'It's papers!' she said, pulling out forty or fifty typed sheets.

Henry felt a sudden qualm. 'I don't think we should –' he began. But he moved over to his daughter's shoulder as, under the yellow light on the clubhouse porch, Maisie read Julian's secret.

It was headed:

RACISM IN THE SUBURBS
by
JULIAN DE VERE THOMSON
A TREATMENT FOR A FIFTY-MINUTE RADIO
DOCUMETARY IN THE 'UNDERCOVER LONDON' SPOT

Henry only read the the first few words:

Racial attitudes in white bourgeois society are, inevitably, covert, and it is only by penetrating a classic fortress of reactionary racist attitudes – such as the Tennis Club – that we can –

Maisie's mouth had opened like a fish's. She seemed to have read further than Henry. 'He had a tape recorder!' she was whispering. 'He's got a transcript of Chunky Boyle talking to Norman. When he was drunk! They're discussing the average IQ of black immigrants!'

Henry gulped. 'That was where I'd heard his voice,' he murmured. 'On the radio!'

There was more than Julian's 'treatment' (at last Henry understood the meaning of the word) in the briefcase. There was a small recorder and ten or fifteen of the tapes themselves, all of which amounted to unanswerable proof of the unsavoury racial attitudes of the Wimbledon Tennis Club. He had Julia MacEwan talking to Mary Seymour in frank and candid detail about 'the fearsome size of the negro races'. He had Peter Piper and Peter Pearse using the words 'chocco', 'Sambo', 'coon' and 'nigger minstrel'. He had a spectacular display of ignorance, medical, geographical and cultural, from Steel Thighs in a taped conversation with Olga, the ugly accountant, which began with the words, 'Is Julian a common name among our Caribbean brethren?' and then got a lot worse.

On the plastic box containing the tapes was written:

ONLY COPY OF HIGHLY CONFIDENTIAL
RECORDINGS. IF FOUND PLEASE RETURN TO
JULIAN DE VERE THOMSON 'UNDERCOVER
LONDON' FREE SOUTH LONDON RADIO, SW19

Maisie looked back into the clubhouse. 'This,' she said slowly, 'could do the club a great deal of damage!'

'You're right,' said Henry. 'You can't argue with your own voice on tape, can you?'

'They might close the whole place down,' whispered Maisie. 'You have to be very careful about being racist these days!'

Henry had certainly always been very discreet about it. He tiptoed nearer to the clubhouse and, from the safety of the darkness, he peered in at the members.

Inside Steel Thighs was telling Norman how he had beaten Henry while having a conversation on his mobile phone. Peter Piper was proposing to add the word 'British' to the club name on the board outside and Chunky, who had had half a bottle of free vodka, was being sick into a fire bucket.

Henry patted his daughter's hand. 'I think,' he said slowly, 'that we should send it on to Mr Thomson, don't you?'

Maisie leered horribly. 'At least,' she said, 'we'll have a good excuse for not coming here! James says they wouldn't let his dad join. Because he's Jewish!'

Henry leered back.

'I'd like us to do more as a family,' said Maisie. 'You, me and Mum. I'd like us to do things together. Why did we join this club?'

Henry did not know how to answer this question. All he did know was that it was time to leave it. All he did know was that, no matter how many routes he tried to take that led him away from Elinor, something always led him back to her. And that that return, as now, was something he wanted, even when he could not see how he might achieve it.

Maisie closed the briefcase carefully and, hand in hand, father and daughter walked down the gravel path, under the club chestnut tree and out into the streets. As they walked back towards Maple Drive in the summer evening, Henry held his prize carefully. He had never liked Julian. He was never really able to like anyone who was good at tennis. But the man was certainly more bearable than most of the other members of the (British) Wimbledon Tennis Club, Southfields. Henry smiled to himself, sweetly and serenely, as father and daughter walked up the front path of number 54 and into the double-fronted house where all their feelings and opinions could be comfortably hidden from the outside world.

Henry, Satanism and the August Terror
of Doctor Doom

'WHY,' SAID ELINOR for the third time in half an hour, 'are we going to Saulieu les Trois Pigeons?'

Henry did not respond to this. Although he could think of several replies – 'it is one of the few places in coastal France to which large numbers of other people are not hurrying, even in August'; 'it is very bracing'; 'it is somewhere I have always longed to visit' – all of them were so transparently false that he did not feel equal to trying them out on his wife.

The one thing he could not tell her, as so often, was the truth. If he were to mention Dr Doom, Satanism or the distant town of Carey, Idaho, USA, she would probably call a gendarme and have him taken away.

James Seebohm did not speak. Would he ever speak?

Maisie had insisted on bringing him. She said he brought her luck. She had told Elinor that her GCSE results would be 'sensational'. James Seebohm, she said, had taught her 'a new way of looking at the natural world'. Henry glared at the boy in the driving mirror. He wasn't sure that the natural world, whatever that might be, included James Seebohm, unless you could squeeze him in under Pests.

'Have you got a floozy here or what?' said Elinor.

Matters had not improved between them. Whatever she was up to with Esmond Brice had certainly not improved her temper. Although Elinor's temper had never been improved by sex, from what he could remember, anyway.

'I mean *why* Saulieu les Trois Bloody Pigeons?'

'Because – '

No. He couldn't tell her about Dr Doom. He cast a quick, sideways glance at his wife. After she had given up her cultural improvement programme, she had become more and more bad-tempered. Or so it seemed to Henry. She kept saying she wanted him to 'do something'. She didn't specify what this something was but, from her behaviour so far this holiday, he guessed it wasn't just booking a passage for her, Maisie, Seebohm and the Volvo from Dover to Calais and then driving nearly three hundred miles across rural France. What she wanted, thought Henry grimly, was for him to be someone else. And that, as yet, he could not arrange.

Seebohm still did not speak. He looked as if he were about to burst into tears. Let him, thought Henry; serve the little bastard right. A grandstand view of Henry's marriage had put about twenty years on the boy since the Channel crossing.

He was probably macho enough with Maisie when they were alone. He probably swaggered around trying to remove Maisie's knickers and then boasted about it to his friends. Henry recalled with a shudder that, when he was young, he and a boy called Walters had worked out a private score-card. It was ten for above the knee, twenty for inside the knickers and –

'It's a lovely place!' said Seebohm, in a small, squeaky voice. 'I'm really looking forward to the hotel!'

Randy little bastard, thought Henry. Straight to the hotel for a bit of rumpy pumpy, eh? Well, sunshine, wait till you get there, sunshine!

He had put Seebohm in an annexe. He was at the end of a large garden, the proprietor had told him. Henry had told him that he wished to be as far away from Seebohm as possible. At least, he *thought* that was what he had told him. Henry's French was generally reckoned to be fluent and confident to the point of flashy, but not always *French*.

'Je suis bored!' said Maisie as Henry turned the Volvo into the main street of the town. Elinor peered up at the street signs.

'Are we in Avenue de la Liberation?' said Henry.

'Are we in Saulieu les Trois Pigeons?' said Elinor. 'Are we in the Charentes Maritime? Are we in *France*?'

Henry thought he saw that white space above the street that spoke of the sea. If they were in the Avenue de la Liberation (although, for all he knew, they could be in the Boulevard des Moines Assassinés or the rue Johnny Halliday), then the hotel was in a street off to the right.

If he could get to the right.

The traffic lights in this place all seemed to be suspended at a point where no Englishman would think of looking for them. Presumably as part of a plan to humiliate the traveller. Even when you found them you were not much better off. The locals seemed to ignore or obey them according to some complicated rule of their own. Sometimes they would leap up behind you, shouting and waving their arms and urging you to drive on past the red. At other times they would sit, as prim as maiden aunts, in front of green lights.

The only safe rule seemed to be to get into a space by yourself. But even when you had done this, Henry found, you still did not feel secure. There had not been a moment, from Calais to the Côte Atlantique, when he had not been expecting the loud crash of metal on metal and the howl of the sirens as foreign policemen arrived.

The accident – and he knew it was coming, with the same, hideous certainty that your average Theban knew that things were not going to work out too well with Oedipus – wouldn't be so much an accident as a public demonstration of the fact that he was an Englishman abroad. The damaged Peugeot or the old man in blue dungarees and beret crushed beneath the wheels of Henry's car would be there solely and simply to tell the locals, *There is a foreigner in your town! Hurry to humiliate him publicly!*

'Right! Go right!' Elinor was squawking. Henry started to try to edge right. Every so often Elinor's hands went up to her face. She was moaning quietly to herself. As he moved across the stream of traffic she wound herself into a small ball.

'I am going right!' yelled Henry.

The Volvo lurched right, in front of a lorry, and, to the sound of screaming brakes, the Farr family found themselves in a narrow alley with high brick walls on either side. Henry caught sight of the street sign.

Rue Georges Clemençeau.

He felt, suddenly, frightened. Why was he doing this? He should have ignored all the damn letters. He certainly shouldn't have taken himself all the way to the Charentes Maritime to –

The hotel would be all right anyway. He was having a holiday. He should concentrate on having a holiday.

HÔTEL DES BEAUX ARTS
SAULIEU LES TROIS PIGEONS
CHARENTES MARITIME 4109876

Visitors to Paul and Henry Leclerc's charming *auberge* in this out-of-the-way corner of the French Atlantic coast have been struck, not only by the warm welcome Paul and Henri offer to weary travellers, but also by the cooking (Gault-Millau *toque*.) Sandy Neumann writes of a 'striking' *caille aux épinards* although there have been complaints about 'peculiar' tomatoes. No matter. In spite of the strange green mould spotted last year in the outdoor swimming pool, this is a unique place. In winter, Paul, who is from the Lubéron, organizes Provençal games in the huge barn at the rear of the house, and many guests have felt that even after a few days at the Beaux Arts they feel as if they have been there for literally years. No children under twelve are allowed on or near the premises and the hotel is closed in November. NB 'On no account,' writes Julia Fauconberg, 'book into the annexe.' She goes on to tell us that it was 'cold, distinctly spooky' and 'miles away from the rest of the hotel'.

It sounded just the sort of place for Seebohm, thought Henry, as he drove on down the rue George Clemençeau. Perhaps it even contained a ghost of some kind.

Elinor switched from icy depression to the weird, hectic enthusiasm that seemed to affect her only in foreign parts. 'Oh my God!' she said. 'Look at that petit coin! C'est glorieux, n'est-ce pas? Oh, que la France est belle!'

Henry gave her a sideways glance. She relapsed, once again, into gloom. 'I hope the hotel will be nice,' she said.

Henry knew the sub-text of this remark was – *I hope for your sake it is nice, you little creep!*

'It's got a Gault-Millau *toque*!' he said.

'Is that a kind of bidet?' said Maisie. Seebohm snickered.

The rue Georges Clemençeau led them away from the town, across a flat, featureless stretch of land, broken by pine trees, drifting silver sand and folksy wooden cafés. All the French – and there was no sign of any English people – were working away at their leisure in the public, conscientious manner they all seemed to acquire in the month of August. In the shade of some pine trees, a little way away from the road, a large family were setting out a picnic. A fat man and his young daughter wobbled past on obviously rented bicycles. In the distance, behind a low range of dunes decorated with harsh grass, was the sound and smell of the sea.

Just before the dunes was a row of caravans and a sign announcing that you were coming in to Saulieu les Trois Pigeons (Plage). But before you got to the caravans Henry saw a small wooden arrow pointing off towards what looked like a car-breaker's yard. It said HÔTEL DES BEAUX ARTS. There was a narrow, sand-strewn track next to it. Henry stopped the car.

'Oh!' said Elinor.

The track skirted the car-breaker's yard and climbed a low hill about three hundred yards away from the sand dunes.

'That's not it, is it?' said Maisie.

Without answering, Henry jerked the wheel of the car and drove off up the track. It was too late to do anything else. He had sent Paul and Henri a cheque for three hundred pounds in order to stop any other jammy bastard jumping the queue and getting a free ringside seat of a low-grade *zone industrielle*.

They drove, in silence, up the hill. On the other side the road ran into the dunes, passed among pine trees and then came to a halt in front of two faded green doors.

'It's quite nice really, isn't it?' said Henry. Elinor gave him a slow, appraising glance. Henry got out of the car and pushed at one of the doors. Behind it was a very small Frenchman in blue overalls. He looked at Henry with neutral hostility, made a noise that sounded like 'Paugh!' and sloped off towards a clump of trees to their right.

'Are we going in?' said Elinor from the car.

Without answering, Henry got back into the driver's seat and started up the drive towards the hotel.

His father would probably have engaged the man in conversation. Mr Farr Senior, known for being a miserable bastard all over Wimbledon, became a sort of low-rent version of Maurice Chevalier every time he crossed the Channel, soliciting, in an almost sexual manner, waiters, policemen and shopkeepers in order to show off his dramatically life-like French accent.

Henry knew – had known since he was twelve – that he hated all Frenchmen. He hated the affected way they smoked cigarettes, their desperate punctuality at mealtimes and their ability to make even the most mundane remark sound like a philosophical proposition. He hated the small thin ones with downy upper lips and leather handbags and he hated the big fat ones with wobbly bicycles and berets. He hated the women worse than the men. He hated the old, leathery ones who, even at eight in the morning, looked as if they were on their way to a formal dinner party. He hated the young, athletic ones who, while trying to look like a subtle blend of English and American, managed to suggest that they had a style superior to both those cultures.

The Hôtel des Beaux Arts was a large, well-weathered villa, built, Henry guessed, some time in the early nineteenth century. Its stonework, bleached by the sun, was softened by vines and climbing flowers, and by the double doors of the entrance were two dwarf cypresses in two huge stone jars. *Maybe,* Henry thought, *for once in my life I have had a good idea.*

'Well, go on in, then!' said Elinor. 'Go on in and parler!' Elinor only spoke French to Henry. She had avoided all contact with the natives (apart from smirking at the odd gendarme) since they docked at Calais three days ago.

Henry marched towards the front door. He could see Seebohm watching him from the car. Stifling an urge to raise two fingers to the little swine, he pushed open the door.

There was no sign of Paul or Henri. Perhaps they were playing Provençal games in the barn. All Henry could see was a bog-standard Louis Quatorze interior, complete with red plush chairs and gilt objects. It looked more like the interior of a provincial museum than anything else. There was a hand bell on a low desk to the right of the window. Henry rang it.

Finally a man appeared. He looked like a younger, more successful version of the creature in the blue overalls. He was wearing clothes he clearly imagined to be English – a blue blazer, grey trousers, a red silk cravat and highly polished black shoes. He looked English, thought Henry, the way the Martians in *They Came from Other Worlds* looked human.

'Je suis Farr!' said Henry. 'Henri Farr!'

The man shrugged. *So,* he seemed to be saying, *what do you want me to do about it?*

'J'ai reservé deux chambres,' said Henry. 'Et l'annexe!' Was there such a word in French? Shouldn't he get on with the job properly and start yelling at this little bastard in God's own dialect? 'The annexe,' he went on, 'I reserved it!'

'Quoi?' said the man.

Henry felt his temper going. 'Do you speak English?' he said.

'No!' said the man.

Henry struck the desk with the flat of his hand. 'Paul Leclerc?' he said. 'Henri Leclerc? The brothers? Or did they change their names by deed poll after some suspect New Age ceremony?'

The man looked into Henry's eyes. 'Paul Leclerc,' he said, 'est mort!'

Henry wasn't sure he had heard this right. The man seemed to be saying that Paul Leclerc was dead. Henry was looking for some internationally approved gesture that denoted death when the man drew the index finger of his right hand along his throat.

'Mort,' he said, 'et Henri aussi. Les deux!' He was well away now. The throat slitting gesture wasn't enough for him. In case the *rosbif* got the wrong idea, he started to bounce both his hands off some imaginary object, making throaty, atomic-explosion noises as he did so. Was there a war on in the Charentes Maritimes?

From a door behind him, a small, sallow woman in a black dress emerged. She went straight to a book on the desk and said: 'You are Farr?'

'I am!' said Henry.

'There 'as been an explosion!' she said. 'Many people 'ave been killed, including Paul Leclerc an' 'is friend Henri. As a result zere are a limited numbair of rheums.'

This, Henry decided, was almost certainly a joke of some kind. Henri and Paul were probably upstairs, snickering to each other. Something, however, warned him not to make his urge to join in with the laughter too obvious. Trying to look as if he had started to feel some human sympathy for these two rather shady-sounding Frenchmen, even though his acquaintance with them was limited to reading about them in the *Good Hotel Guide*, Henry said, 'Et l'annexe?'

'Eeet eez exploded also. I am sorry you must sleep in two rheums. I am vair sorry. There 'as been an explosion of gaz and Henri and Paul are . . . pouf!'

They certainly sounded as if they were pouf, thought Henry. But, although he had always been uneasy about anything like that, he found himself genuinely sorry that the two of them should have been exploded at the height of the season. *No Provençal games!* he found himself thinking. *Probably no swimming pool either!* And, worse than any of that, the fact that, unless he was prepared to let his daughter alone with a sex-crazed, fifteen-year-old lout from Cranborne School Wimbledon, he was going to have to spend his holiday sleeping with

James Seebohm. Holidays, he thought, were the final insult. Why were they here?

Without allowing himself to think about Satanism, Dr Doom or any of the other things that had brought him here, Henry looked back at Maisie, Elinor and James, who had come in to the back of the hall. Seebohm was carrying one of the cases.

'What possessed you, Henry?' Elinor was saying. 'I mean, why on earth have you dragged us here?'

Henry did not know what they were doing there. He had not really ever intended to take things this far. He should have told Elinor. But you couldn't tell her things like that. He looked at her, pursed his lips and went across to pick up Seebohm's case. Maybe Dr Doom was responsible for this. Maybe the deaths of the hotel's proprietors were just the beginning of Henry's punishment for meddling with forces he did not understand. Maybe Dr Doom was waiting for him here, in Saulieu les Trois Pigeons (Plage). It seemed as close an approximation to hell as anywhere else Henry had visited.

Henry had become involved with Satanism through a mail-order company and, like many other things he had received through the post, it had proved something of a disappointment. It hadn't brought him in touch with young, nubile girls. He was not, as yet, able to make himself invisible or to predict the future. If anything, he was hazier about it than he had been before. It hadn't, to use a favourite word of Elinor's, *empowered* him.

It was just another thing designed to screw up his life.

It had started the day he had taken Maisie to Wimbledon Year Zero. She had wanted a back number of *The Punisher* – the Punisher being one of the new breed of comic heroes who spends his time being nasty to people. In the episode Henry had looked at, he had been hiding in a dustbin, shooting at passers-by with a high-velocity rifle. Maisie liked him. She said she identified with him.

Henry wanted to identify with him.

Henry did not like going into Wimbledon Year Zero. He had never really liked comic shops. They all seemed to cater for the kind of people who might well ask you home for a spot of hand relief. And, with this in mind, he felt it to be his duty to protect Maisie from the clientele.

He stood at the back of the shop while she leafed through copies of *The Fantastic Four* in mint condition. Behind him was a reproduction of a comic he remembered from his childhood – the Illustrated Classics edition of Homer's *Iliad*. Henry picked it off the shelf, wondering once again at the Trojans' mauve armour. To his surprise there was a comic inside it. Someone must have left it there while browsing. It was called *Hades* and it had been printed, designed and distributed by someone called Tad Brewster from Portland, Oregon. It looked as if he had written it and drawn it as well.

Hades was all about a man called Hades. He looked, talked and walked exactly like the Punisher. Instead of a high-velocity rifle he had a kind of scythe.

But what caught Henry's eye wasn't the comic's hero. It was the page of adverts at the back. One advertized a box number in New York City where you could, for only four dollars fifty, get hold of a tape of women wrestling. Underneath that a woman called Marian Romescu offered to teach you how to draw your favourite cartoon characters for only ten dollars. There was one other advert on the page. It read, simply:

GAIN POWER OVER PEOPLE AND THE HUMAN WORLD! WRITE TO DOCTOR DOOM BOX 119 CAREY IDAHO. NO ONE UNDER SIX MAY APPLY FOR THIS COURSE. FIRST FOUR LESSONS ARE COMPLETELY FREE!!!!!!!!!

OTHER SECRETS OF DR DOOM'S POWER WILL BE REVEALED FOR ONLY THIRTY-FIVE DOLLARS FORTY. US CURRENCY ONLY. DARE YOU DO THIS?

Henry picked the comic off the shelf, and when Maisie was ready to go he added it to her pile. She didn't seem very excited about it. All she said was: 'Do you really want this?'

'Yes,' said Henry.

Later, when they got home she said: 'Do you want your comic?'

With that simple phrase Henry lost over thirty years. He went, alone, to his study, got down an atlas and tried to find Carey, Idaho. He could only just find Idaho, a blank space somewhere near the Yellowstone National Park.

Then he took a blank sheet of paper, and, in a clear, round, childish hand, he wrote:

Dear Sir,

I would like to gain power over people and the human world and request the first four free lessons from Dr Doom. I am twelve years of age. I anticipate that I will need extra lessons and wonder whether I should enclose cash. I am English and do not have dollars.

Yours sincerely,

Brad Porter
Wimbledon
England

The look of it was fine, but, after some thought, Henry decided that 'anticipated' was too grown-up. He inked it out – which gave the letter an extra dash of authenticity – and wrote 'think' instead. Then he put it into an envelope, on which he had stuck the entire contents of a book of stamps, and wrote:

DR DOOM
BOX 119
CAREY, IDAHO, USA

At the last minute his nerve failed him. There was something just a little scary about the wording of Dr Doom's advertisement. Henry left the envelope on the table in the front hall and, if Angelica hadn't picked it up off the floor three days later, it might have made its way, like many other bits of paper in the Farr household, quietly into the dustbin. But its recovery seemed to Henry to show the hand of fate. He had an urge to send it as far away from Wimbledon as possible. So he walked up the road to the post-box that afternoon and sent it to Carey, Idaho. He thought, as he slipped it through the gaping red mouth, that its chances of reaching Dr Doom were minimal.

How wrong I was, Henry said to himself as he carried the suitcase into a dark, dusty room, that looked out over the hotel's ragged garden. How wrong I was.

'Shall we go to the beach?' said Henry.

Elinor looked at him.

It was now 17 August. They had not had sex since April Fool's Day, when Elinor had allowed herself to be tied to the bedpost of the Lakeland View Hotel, Keswick, and be penetrated from the rear for thirty-five minutes. She had seemed to enjoy it at the time, but had shown no signs of wishing to repeat the experience. Maybe her orgasm – a prolonged scream that, even now, gave Henry a sense of quiet pride – had been an April Fool's trick.

He had gone a little over the top afterwards. He shouldn't have tried to –

He had hoped the holiday might do it. But the Hôtel des Beaux Arts and the Atlantic coast of France were not a winning combination. One night when Seebohm was asleep, Henry had crept next door and into her bed but she had pushed him, roughly, out on to the floor. 'Go back next door with your friend!' she had said.

His friend! Henry had shared rooms with some pretty unpleasant people in his life. He still recalled, with a shudder, two weeks with his brother Nigel in a cottage in Wales. But Seebohm!

He suspected him of self-abuse. Even when Henry was in the room. Perhaps especially when Henry was in the room. There had been sinister rustlings from underneath the man's duvet. Once, Henry had put out a few sham snores to see if the little bastard would get carried away, but Seebohm obviously suspected some plot.

They were sitting by the swimming pool, although there was no water in it. The green mould – as featured in the *Good Hotel Guide* – seemed to be making its way out of the deep end and towards the car park. Opposite them was the remains of the annexe, where, if things had gone according to plan, Seebohm would now be confined. If they had arrived three days earlier, he might well have been tucked up under his duvet when the gas main exploded. Nothing, thought Henry, as he shifted on his Li-lo, was going according to plan.

This was supposed to be the year when he got a grip on his life. Instead, it seemed to be slipping away from him at a faster rate than usual. And, with that, came that worryingly pleasant symptom of advancing age: the suspicion that he didn't really care.

The sky was grey and there was a nasty wind sidling around the lawn behind them. Somewhere in this godforsaken place was Dr Doom. But where? Henry propped himself upon his elbow to see if he could see a cloaked figure in the trees beyond the hotel. It was possible, of course, that Dr Doom had taken another form. He could be the guy in the dungarees, or the man in the blazer or the weird woman in the black dress.

If he was anything like as all-powerful as he sounded, moving continents would not have presented him with too many problems. However, he did not begin their relationship by communicating with Henry through any medium more sinister than the post. His reply to Henry's first letter had arrived plastered with American stamps and practically blotted out with ink stains. It looked as if it had been kicked all the way from the Rockies.

Dear Brad,
Is that really your name? You sound . . . well . . . *older*.

I am not sure that it is, you know. And Dr Doom does not like deceit. He is an enemy of lies. Lies are an instrument of THE PRINCE OF DARKNESS. (See booklet twenty-four, not available to non-subscribers.) I can see into the hearts of those who write to me and I know their secret thoughts.

Here is the first lesson in how to gain control of the human world.

The rest of the page was blank. Henry's first thought was that this whole thing was a practical joke. Perhaps devised by some deranged cable addict out there in the Mid-West. There was, however, another sheet of paper in the envelope. It read: $<D/3.457=^{\wedge}LC/45\%(*P\{I\}$ X25349. And underneath this: EAT RAW CARROTS.

Henry copied out the equation, and, when he was sure they were unobserved, showed it to Bulldike White, Maisie's maths teacher. At first she said she had never seen anything like it before. Then she became strangely agitated, muttered something about Maxwell's Unified Field Theory and started writing things on the back of an envelope. Then she said, in an accusatory manner, 'Where did you get this?'

Henry didn't like to say. The letter was signed Dr E. Doom (Human Scientist). Miss White walked away with the equation, muttering to herself, and for weeks afterwards glared at Henry suspiciously whenever she saw him near the school.

Henry was intrigued by his American correspondent. He really felt as if this curious, unidentified creature from an obscure corner of a country he had never visited had some clue to his character. Although he resisted the temptation to write to him again for some days, he soon found himself up in his room once more, framing the effortful letters of a boy of twelve.

Dear Dr Doom,
Thank you for your letter!

I am afraid I did not understand the equations. But I am not on to GCSE maths yet!

I want to gain power over the human world because my parents argue all the time and never have sex like other people's mummies and daddies. I want them to be happy! How can I do this? Even from the free lessons I would like to learn about these things. My daddy is very fat and very angry. So is my mummy. Why do they not love each other?

I love *The Punisher* because he shoots people!

Brad Porter.

As Henry turned over on his stomach he once again regretted this letter. He had, of course, revealed himself to the man. If it was a man. That was how these Satanists got hold of you. You gave away one little secret and from that they were able to expose a whole system of lies and weaknesses.

He had let Dr Doom get close to him. That was the fact of the matter. This unknown stranger in Carey, Idaho, had somehow found a line to whatever it was – loss, anger, frustration, self-pity – that was at the messy centre of Henry Farr.

'I am going to la plage!' said Elinor. 'It's so depressing here. I keep thinking about those poor young men!'

She had absolutely no proof, thought Henry, that either Henri or Paul Leclerc was young. You would think, from the way she carried on, that she had recently lost her virginity to the pair of them.

The management of the Beaux Arts did not seem in a hurry to repair the damage to the place. Occasionally men in blue dungarees would come, in vans that looked as if they were made of corrugated iron. They would stand on the lawn, their arms folded, talking seriously, and then drive away at speed. Occasionally the man in the blue blazer would smirk at Henry and ask him if his room was comfortable.

Do you think I like sleeping with a fifteen-year-old boy? Who do you think I am? Jean Genet?

'I'll come, Mrs Farr!' squeaked Seebohm.

'Me too!' said Maisie.

He had better go with them. If left alone, even for five minutes, Seebohm was quite capable of dragging Maisie off into the dunes and trying to penetrate her body in disgusting ways.

When they were changed, they set off down the sandy track towards the beach. They spent most of their time on or near the beach.

Saulieu les Trois Pigeons (Ville) had, after nearly ten days, displayed almost all it had to offer. What had seemed, at first, a frightening metropolis, now turned out to be four streets, a few shops, two banks, and some apartment blocks that looked as if they belonged in another, larger town. Saulieu les Trois Pigeons (Plage) had the caravans, the car-breakers' yard, two fluttering flags that told you when it was safe to bathe (it was hardly ever safe to bathe) and two enormous French lifeguards. It also had an apartment block that looked as if it had wandered off from Saulieu les Trois Pigeons (Ville) in a vain attempt to reach the sea.

'Est'ce-que nous allons au bar?' said Seebohm.

Henry gave him a sharp look. He had not realized the boy had an alcohol problem as well.

'I think,' he said, 'we'll just soak up the atmosphere!'

'What atmosphere?' said Elinor.

Maisie was behaving very oddly. She had fallen a little way behind the rest of them and was looking over towards the apartment block. Around it was a neat arrangement of lawns and shrubs. At the main entrance, whose doors were of smoked glass, was a canopy to shield the façade from the sun. Henry had never seen anyone go in or out of the place, although there were two long lines of entry-phones to the right of the door. Like the hotel, like everything in this place, there was something cloaked and mysterious about it.

There was an edge to Henry's voice as he said, 'What are you looking at?'

'Nothing!' said Maisie.

She, too, Henry thought, sounded nervous. 'I thought you were looking at something!'

Maisie shook her head, a little too forcefully. Henry moved back towards her and, when the other two were a safe distance away, he said, 'Something's worrying you. Isn't it?'

Maisie turned her face towards him. 'He looked . . . weird!'

'What kind of weird?'

She glanced quickly up towards her mother. Then she said, in a quiet voice, 'He was wearing . . . funny clothes.'

'What kind of funny clothes?' Henry had grabbed her arm.

'A sort of . . . cloak. And a hat. Black. A black coat and a black hat.'

143

Henry gulped. *Something about the way I'm dressed will tell you who I am!*

The response to Henry's second letter was alarmingly swift. Perhaps no other people wrote to Dr Doom out there in Carey, Idaho.

It was even spookier than the first letter. It was printed on very different paper and, although it had been handwritten, was a photocopy of an original. It was in capitals.

THE HUMAN WORLD IS EVIL. DO NOT ENGAGE WITH IT. BE MORE EVIL AND GAIN MORE POWER OVER IT. DO PEOPLE SEEM TO SNEER AT YOU AND LAUGH AT YOU FOR YOUR LACK OF POWER? DR DOOM'S SYSTEM IS SIMPLE. AFTER FOUR INTRODUCTORY ENTIRELY FREE LESSONS YOU WILL BE SENT THE BOOKLET AND OR MACHINE AS REQUESTED.

LESSON ONE

SIT CROSS-LEGGED ON THE FLOOR. LET EVIL SEX THOUGHTS OVERWHELM YOU AND I WILL APPEAR. YOU MAY NOT WANT TO SEND THE NEXT LETTER BUT YOU WILL AND IT WILL FIND ITS WAY TO ME. ONE DAY I WILL FIND YOU. YOU MUST ANSWER THIS SO THAT YOU MAY RECEIVE LESSONS 2, 3 AND 4 AND AFTER HANDING OVER ONLY $35 US CURRENCY YOU WILL RECEIVE MACHINE AND BOOKLET AND GAIN DOOM-LIKE POWER OVER THE HUMAN WORLD. IF YOU DO NOT REPLY I WILL FIND YOU AND YOU WILL BE PUNISHED.

WE WILL NOT BE CONTACTABLE AT THIS BOX NUMBER AFTER 12 AUGUST. WE WILL TRAVEL THE WORLD CHASTISING UNBELIEVERS!

Maisie came into the room while he was reading this letter. Henry hid it under a cushion. He felt as if he had been surprised while reading pornography. When she asked him who the letter was from, he told her it was from the office, and made a mental note to be first up in the morning so that he could get to the mail before anyone else.

'It's something kinky, I bet!' said Maisie.

Henry went up to his study to write his third letter to Dr Doom. He was involved with the man now. It was, as Dr Doom had suggested, too late to turn back. If he did, something nasty might pop out of the dustbin waving a high-velocity rifle. And, he found, writing the letter was a kind of release.

Dear Dr Doom,

Thank you for your second letter. I have only two more free lessons I suppose!

Although I am only twelve, evil sex thoughts are no problem for me. I have them all the time. My problem is I don't know what the point of it all is. Why do people bother?

My father is a horrible man called Henry. Why did God make him? He is completely pointless. I don't understand why he is like this. He hates so many things! I have a sister, for example, who –

When he got to this point he screwed up the letter into a small ball and threw it in the waste-bin. He had been about to write down what he felt about Maisie. Pretending to be a twelve-year-old boy had brought him to a horrible truthfulness. He couldn't tell the truth about his feelings for Maisie. What he felt about her was too complicated. It was love, of course, but it was also a lot of other things – tiredness, fear, despair, jealousy, anger – and, in starting to write about it, he found he was beginning to describe what he felt about Elinor.

That was not a good idea. It was never a good idea to think too closely about what you felt about anyone – especially if you had been married to them for twenty-five years. Did he love her? Had he ever loved her? Could he go on for the rest of his life without really knowing the answers to such questions? He put his pen down, walked to the window and looked down at the summer garden.

There was a knock at the door. It was Maisie. In her hand she held the photocopied letter he had hidden in the sofa. She looked unhappy.

'What is this, Dad?' she said.

'It's nothing!' said Henry. 'Just some mad circular. That's all.'

Maisie made a face. 'It's weird!' she said. 'Let's hope he doesn't make house calls!'

'I think,' said Henry, 'he's a bit far away for house calls!'

Dr Doom, however, even if he did not appear in person, showed worrying signs of interest in the Wimbledon end of his operation. Even though Henry hadn't sent the third letter, he received another communication from Idaho only two days after he had thrown it away. Doom had gone back to his handwritten style for this one but his prose still had the same crazy cunning to it. Henry put it on one side at first, but found he was unable to throw it away, as he had done his own letter.

Dear Brad,

I am sure that is not your name! I am sure of it. Something about the way you write suggests a much older man. Middle-aged maybe?

Why are you doing this? Are you sick or what? And why are you writing to me? Is there something the matter with you?

YOU MUST LEARN TO BE BETTER!

I think you have a family. I smell it. And I think you have to LEARN THE ART OF GIVING, OTHERWISE DOOM WILL FIND YOU AND DESTROY YOU WITH THE PLAGUE OF BOILS!

DO NOT THINK I WILL NOT FIND YOU. I WILL FIND YOU. AND YOU MUST REPENT AND CLEANSE YOURSELF. SOMETHING ABOUT THE WAY I'M DRESSED WILL TELL YOU WHO I AM!

Doom (Dr E., Human Scientist)

VENGEANCE IS MINE! I MAY APPEAR AT ANY MOMENT! ALWAYS BE ON YOUR GUARD! I KNOW NOW WHERE YOU LIVE!

Henry thought over the third letter as he, Elinor, James and Maisie headed for the Café de la Plage. It was the sort of place he would never have dreamed of going to in England. Or in France for that matter. But it was the *only* place in Saulieu les Trois Pigeons (Plage) so it was where they went. And the longer he stayed there the more convinced he became it was just the place Dr Doom might be found, flying around the world chastising unbelievers. Why, thought Henry, did holidays lead you to do these things? Why was he about to sit at a dirty tin table looking at a dirty stretch of the Atlantic, a sewage outfall and two intolerably vain lifeguards?

'Je veux absinthe!' said Maisie.

'Et moi!' said Seebohm.

The waiter looked at them uncomprehendingly.

'They will have Coca-Cola,' said Henry. 'And I will have a beer.' He pointed at Elinor who had the hunted look she often acquired in public places. 'She will have le white wine!' said Henry.

'Fair enough!' said the waiter.

Maisie looked at him. 'You should practise your French!' she said.

'But,' said Henry, 'he's English!'

The waiter at the Café de la Plage was a theological student from Durham called Derek. He slouched off across the bar while Maisie looked around for someone else on whom she could practise her, literally, schoolgirl French.

'Je veux un condom!' said Seebohm, who was in playful mood.

In order to stop himself punching the little bastard in the face, Henry got up and, taking Maisie's arm, steered her towards the bar, muttering something about finding someone with whom she could *parler un peu*. As soon as they were out of earshot, he said, 'Where did you see this guy? In the cloak?'

Maisie looked unhappy. 'I'm sure it wasn't anything. I was just being – '

'There was something that spooked you about him, wasn't there?' said Henry. 'I know there was.'

Maisie looked back at Elinor and Seebohm. They were talking about something. They quite often did this, Henry had noticed, when he wasn't there. 'I – '

'What was it, Maisie?'

Maisie looked across at her mother, who was starting to take an interest in this conversation. 'I'd seen him before,' she said. 'Twice in fact. In the same place. When I was there with James. I saw him and he was . . .'

Elinor had come up to them. 'Who did you see, darling? A nasty man? Exposing himself?' she said.

It wasn't until before dinner that Henry was able to get Maisie on her own again. Even then she didn't seem to want to talk about the man in the cloak and hat. Something about him had frightened her. She wouldn't say quite what he had been doing or why she had been disturbed by the sight of him, but she did reveal she had seen him in the château beyond the old market, just outside the town. And he had been wearing a cloak and a hat.

Something about the way I'm dressed will tell you who I am!

He should never have written the fourth letter.

He certainly didn't want any more free lessons from such an obvious fruitcake as Dr Doom. Nor had he any desire to see what the machine might turn out to be.

But the man seemed to have an uncanny knack not only of divining who the real Henry might be – even when he was pretending to be a twelve-year-old boy – but also of making him think and feel and *write down* the kind of thoughts Henry usually tried to avoid.

He couldn't get rid of the idea that, from out there in Carey, Idaho, Dr Doom had somehow managed to read his mind. To anticipate his actions. And, if he were to sit down and write to the man, he might actually appear, like a genie in the *Arabian Nights*, summoned across the world by a thought, a wish. It seemed, also, impossible to write to him without being honest – as if the black magician (and Henry was almost convinced by now that the man was a black magician and a fairly dangerous one at that) could sniff out the kind of falsity that Henry had relied on to get him through life for the last forty-odd years.

Genuine emotion, he reflected, as he sat down to write the fourth letter, is a tricky commodity. And can summon up things far worse then genies.

Dear Dr Doom,
I have a confession to make.

I am a middle-aged man. I am not Brad Porter. My name is Henry. Henry Farr. I am a middle-aged English solicitor. Perhaps you have people like me in America. I am dull and scared and nobody likes me. I want people to notice me but they don't.

I think you will find me. I do. I believe you will track me down because of the kind of person I am.

I have a wife and a daughter. But I don't love either of them. I use the word occasionally but I don't know what it means. And I don't want what I think it means. I don't know what I want. Sometimes I think I'm dead inside. Like a . . .

Like a what? He looked at what he had written for a long time. *That's about the size of it*, he thought to himself. *That about sums it up. Pathetic, isn't it, really? That's about all there is as far as I'm concerned.*

He never sent the letter. But, once again, he got as far as putting it in an envelope. And, a day later, he got rid of it. This time he burnt it.

'Il faut regarder les vineyards!' said Elinor as Maisie, she and Henry trekked through the outskirts of Saulieu les Trois Pigeons (Ville). 'You can get le free wine there!'

Something about the way I'm dressed will tell you who I am!

They were on their way to the château. It was a folly, built in 1804 in the Gothic style as an imitation ruin. If Elinor had known what they might find there, she would not have sounded so cheerful, thought Henry. Presumably Dr Doom didn't hang back on this plague of boils business. The whole family might be looking for a consultant dermatologist by tea-time.

He was being ridiculous of course. Doom, whoever he was, was probably just a confidence trickster. A lunatic who started by intriguing people, then got on with the business of conning them. He knew, presumably, that anyone who wrote to him must be in need of psychiatric help. But Henry could not get rid of the feeling, which had grown with each day they had passed in this appalling hell hole, that the man was horribly near him, watching his every move, tinkering with his future . . .

'I don't want to go up here!' said Maisie, suddenly.

'Why not, darling?' said Elinor.

'It's where I saw that horrid man!'

'What horrid man?'

They were starting up the steps that led to the château. Henry was about to try to change the subject when Maisie, who had reached the top of the steps, gave a little cry.

'What's the matter?' Henry made sure he got there first. From here he could see beyond the château to a scrubby field bordered by a grove of pine trees. Beyond that were more pine trees, and beyond them, crowding in on them and the château, like darkness on an autumn evening, was the forest that ran back from the coast into the hinterland.

Just at the beginning of the field, on the side nearest to him, he could see a tall figure in a cloak and hat, moving away across the grass as quickly and lightly as a shadow. From this distance it was impossible to make out if it was a man or a woman, or, indeed, if it was human at all. The light was slanting in from the sea as the black-robed figure flitted further away from them and towards the line of trees.

'What are you doing?' squawked Elinor.

But Henry did not answer. He was running, back down the steps, back towards the town. He heard Maisie shouting something after him but he didn't turn round. He would get back to the hotel. He would pack their things. Tonight they would be on their way back to England.

Although – was England any safer than here? Wasn't it less safe?

VENGEANCE IS MINE! I MAY APPEAR AT ANY MOMENT! ALWAYS BE ON YOUR GUARD! I KNOW NOW WHERE YOU LIVE!

Henry was sobbing for lack of breath. He started to walk back towards the château and found himself, without having planned it, on the road that led round the building towards the forest. Ahead of him he could see the dark line of pine trees, yellowed by the evening sun.

He was going crazy. This place was driving him crazy. Holidays always did that to you. He came to an iron seat set into the stone wall and stopped, looking across at the trees.

The voice seemed to come from inside his head at first. It echoed, like a thought, inside him. And then he realized it wasn't inside him but there, somewhere behind him, in the warm evening.

'Henry . . . '

Henry stopped.

'Vengeance is mine, Henry. I am Dr Doom!'

Henry had got to his feet before he realized the voice was coming from behind the wall. And he had still not recognized it when James Seebohm stepped out from a door cut into the stone a few yards away from where he was sitting. Seebohm was wearing a black cloak and black hat. He seemed to find it, and Henry, amusing. Just as Henry was about to grab him by the hair, drag him back into Saulieules Trois Pigeons (Plage) and hurl him under a passing lorry, Maisie appeared on top of the wall directly above him.

'I only opened one letter,' she said, sounding genuinely apologetic. Henry did not answer, although he made a mental note for the future not to leave any letters lying around 54 Maple Drive. He was glad to hear she had not gained access to any of his genuine emotions. You didn't want too much of that in families. They were the sort of thing best left to Dr Doom.

'It was just a laugh,' she said. 'We didn't think you'd take it seriously! We never thought you'd write to him again! What did you write?'

His face must have betrayed him. He found he was still breathing heavily. When Maisie spoke again she sounded genuinely concerned, like someone who fears they may not know the person who should be closest to them in the world.

'You didn't take all that rubbish seriously, did you, Dad? The real letter from him was scary, I thought. Didn't you?'

Henry looked behind her. He could not see Elinor anywhere. 'It's all scary,' he said. 'The whole thing is scary!'

'But it was just a laugh, wasn't it?' said Maisie. 'You pretending to be a twelve-year-old boy called Brad Porter! It was just a laugh, wasn't it?'

Maisie looked behind her. A brief, almost frightened shadow passed across her face. Then, on the instant, her mother appeared beside her. She was getting older, thought Henry, there were lines round her eyes.

She stood looking down at Henry with what looked like genuine concern.

'Yes,' said Henry, 'it was just a laugh.'

Bury My Heart on Wimbledon Common

IT WAS FRIDAY, 23 September – the day of the autumn equinox. There were apples densely clustered on the two apple trees in the garden of 54 Maple Drive. Maisie, who during the summer seemed to have lost three stone and gained six inches in height, walked to school through the mists and long grasses of the Common, wearing a skirt bought for the new term that made her look more like a woman and less like a girl. All of Nature, even the small sections of it that were allowed to surface in sw19, was mellow and fruitful.

Apart from Henry.

Henry had now not had sex for five months. Not with another person anyway. He was even finding it difficult to masturbate. There always seemed to be someone in the house when he felt like it. On this particular afternoon, for example, he had returned from work early with the specific intention of having a crafty wank, only to find Elinor and five women from the Wimbledon Study Group within auditory range of all the prime locations for really satisfying self-abuse.

He was thinking about death.

Not anyone else's death. As far as he was concerned, as he drove the Volvo up towards Wimbledon Common, everyone else could go on living. He would just go ahead and die and let them get on with it.

'I'll die!' he said, aloud, to the fat labrador in the back. 'I'll die and then they'll be sorry.'

The fat labrador, which belonged to his brother Nigel, wagged his tail and farted loudly.

Henry thought about Nigel. He thought about that disastrous lunch at the Bayee Village Chinese Restaurant in Wimbledon when Nigel 'came out' to their father. 'Can't you see?' he had sobbed, as he stormed out of the place. 'I'm gay! I'm gay! I'm gay!' To which Henry's father had replied, long after his younger son had left the restaurant, 'I would have thought that was fairly obvious.' Nigel had come out to his family a total of five times between May 1984 and November 1987, most notably during a performance of Maisie's school-play. 'I'm gay!' he had screamed during one of the blackouts. 'Can't you see? I'm gay!'

Nigel, for some reason, was devoted to his dog. He had gone away to Greece for ten days with his friend Mikhail, a hairy interior designer from Newcastle, and had left it with Henry, along with four pages of closely typed instructions.

Do not come up suddenly behind Buster. He finds this alarming and may bite. If he does his business on the carpet, I usually kick him, quite hard, in the head.

There was a lot more along these lines. Henry had never liked Nigel much, but having this unscheduled access to the most intimate details of the man's relationship with his dog had almost totally disenchanted him. Buster and Nigel seemed a tortured, almost Strindbergian item. Perhaps Henry's brother had gone to Greece simply in order to get away from the clearly disturbed, black labrador.

He may try and wee on other dogs' heads. He seems to enjoy this. If he does, *clap your hands*!

Henry didn't fancy applauding while the grotesque creature behind him urinated into some dachshund's ears. He wasn't even sure he was going to be able to bring himself to pronounce the animal's name in a public place.

He likes anchovies!

For God's sake! What did the man want?

Henry turned into the car park next to the windmill and parked as far away from any of the other cars as possible. Then he went round to the back of the car, opened the boot and looked at Buster.

I know you're not a dog person, Hen, but when you're out on the hills with Buster, watching him run for a rabbit or sniff the bracing air with his adorable little nose, I know you'll feel part of the changing seasons of the year – spring, summer, autumn, winter – the great wheel of the life-cycle – birth, death and rebirth. All of that!

You're a very *urban* person, Hen (or should I say *sub*urban!), and I want you to be more integrated in things. Mikhail sends best hugs and kisses and love for you, my darling brother!

Henry looked grimly at the fat labrador. It didn't look as if it would have the energy to stagger to the nearest phone and dial out for a take-away rabbit. It didn't seem at all keen on the idea of leaving the car. And what, while we were at it, was all this about *sub*urban?

Henry shut the boot. Almost immediately the fat labrador threw itself at the window, snarling, barking and clawing. *This may be how you carry on with my little brother*, thought Henry, *but I am determined to stand absolutely no nonsense from you or any other dog!* He pushed his face close to the glass and said, 'Down!'

This was obviously the right thing to say. Because the fat labrador lowered its head and, whimpering, retreated into the boot.

Henry found this rather gratifying. 'Stay there!' he sneered through the glass. 'One peep out of you and you are a *dead* dog!'

The fat labrador looked even more impressed. Henry was beginning to enjoy himself. 'You move when I say move, scumbag!' he went on. 'And you stay when I say stay. Because, asshole, I am numero uno in this relationship. You get?'

He turned to find a small, grey-haired man looking up at him. 'How old?' he said.

It was some time before Henry realized he was talking about the dog. 'God knows!' he said. 'He doesn't look as if he has much to look forward to, does he?'

Then, when the fat labrador was obviously not expecting it, he jerked open the rear door of the car. 'Come on,' said Henry, jerking his thumb towards the grass behind him. 'Do whatever you have to do!'

The fat labrador cowered yet further into the boot of the Volvo. Henry grabbed its lead and yanked it towards him. The dog slid across the car carpet and out into the September day; it hung for a moment, its rear legs pedalling furiously, then plummeted to the ground with a yelp.

The man had gone – perhaps to telephone the RSPCA. Henry looked down at the fat labrador. It still seemed disinclined to walk. Perhaps if he took it off its lead, it would start to behave like other dogs.

On the other hand, perhaps it would hare off across the Common and start biting people. What did dogs do when you let them off the lead? Nigel hadn't bothered to tell him this. Henry got down to the fat labrador's eye level and faced up to it squarely. 'When I let you off the lead,' he said, 'I want you to remain in the seated position. You understand me?'

The fat labrador licked his face. Henry got to his feet.

'I am going to let you off the lead now,' he said, 'but you stay *right there*. Comprende?'

The fat labrador farted loudly.

Henry took off the lead. Almost immediately the dog, beating the ground with its front paws, swayed from right to left and then rose up and down rapidly. It looked as if it were trying to dance. Henry ignored it. He walked up the broad path that leads from the windmill to Roehampton Vale, past a sign that said HORSE PRIORITY. The fat labrador, its brief burst of activity over, followed him at a respectable distance. It seemed, he thought, tired. After about fifty yards, Henry moved over to the right, towards a clump of silver birches, their leaves yellow and brown and their bark bright in the pale September sun.

Henry found he was walking on clover. The soil seemed as dark as peat and as full of bounce as a mattress. The dog, who seemed to find this exciting, managed to get ahead of him. It must have seen something in the bushes because he heard the thud of paws over to his left. Then, without his really being aware of how Buster had done it, the labrador was behind him. Apparently disorientated, it ran at his legs, nearly knocking him over.

When Henry recovered, he realized he did not know where he was. He had been following the dog too closely. There was something pleasantly aimless about this. He seemed to have left the path. Ahead of him the fat labrador had reversed into a bush and was crouched over it making grunting noises. Then it scampered off.

There were trees in the distance, a stretch of bracken between him and the trees, and, over to his right, a bench. He could not recall seeing it before, or ever finding himself in this part of the Common. It had a weird, neglected feeling to it. There was no noise of distant traffic, no paths, and the bench, surrounded by trees, gave the impression that, like Henry, it had wandered away from where it was supposed to be.

The labrador was very excited by it. First of all Buster cocked his leg against one side of it. Then he smelt all the way round it. Then he suddenly decided the bench was potentially hostile. He ran round it barking. Then he charged forward and tried to nip its legs.

Eventually, exhausted by this, the dog gave up. It lay about twenty yards away, keeping one eye on the bench in case it should try anything. Henry, who, by now, was beginning to feel a little tired, walked round the thing and then sat down.

The fat labrador farted again. So, after a while, did Henry. He yawned. There was an inscription, he noticed, behind him, although he could not be bothered to read it. He knew the kind of thing. FOR DOROTHY WHO LOVED THIS PLACE. Or IN MEMORY OF MABLE AND JOHN ATTERIDGE (1904–1984).

When I am gone, he thought, *no one will put up a bench in memory of me! Elinor wouldn't even put up a frame tent in my memory. I'll just disappear. Henry Farr, not very important solicitor. They'll take me to Roehampton Vale and burn me and chuck me in the scattering area and that will be that. I won't even get a few lines in the local paper. I've never done anything or been loved or –*

He found that, without really intending to, he was checking the inscription on the bench. It wasn't, as some of these things were, carved into the wood, but a sequence of inlaid letters in what looked like white ivory. FOR JOHANN KRIEGMULLER, Henry read, WHO LOVED TO WALK ON THIS COMMON.

That was what he thought it said, anyway.

Except it didn't. When Henry looked at it again he realized that some anonymous wit had carefully altered a letter so that it read: FOR JOHANN KRIEGMULLER WHO LOVED TO WANK ON THIS COMMON.

Henry was studying the lettering carefully when he became aware that there was someone watching him.

The small, grey-haired man who had appeared behind him in the car-park was leaning over the fat labrador. 'You're beautiful!' he was saying to it.

This clearly false statement went down very well with the dog. It wagged its tail furiously. Then it farted again.

'What's your name?' the man said. He was wearing a long, shabby overcoat and a wide-brimmed hat which almost completely obscured his face. All Henry could see was the edge of one of his cheeks, which was a dull, livid grey, hinting at some disease or a long absence from the world in some closed community.

He felt, suddenly, frightened. As if this man might have been following him.

'His name,' said Henry, 'is Buster. He belongs to my brother Nigel.'

Henry caught what might have been a smile from the little man. It occurred to him that perhaps the hat was there to hide some wound or deformity. Perhaps he should get up and walk away. But there was something about the man that fascinated him.

'You're looking at the inscription!' he said. He had a light, Irish accent.

'I am!' said Henry, getting himself ready to hear a speech about vandalism. He himself was rather sympathetic to vandals. He had quite often, recently, felt the urge to sneak up to a vacant wall and write SHED WANKERS on it in large letters.

The little old man was peering at the bench. 'FOR JOHANN KRIEGMULLER,' he read, aloud, 'WHO LOVED TO WANK ON THIS COMMON.' He gave a short, dry laugh. His Irish accent seemed more pronounced. It was from the west, Henry thought, the weird, plangent vowels of the Kerryman. He still kept his face away from Henry. 'He loved to wank on this Common,' said the little man. 'And in other places in Wimbledon also from what I hear!'

Henry looked again at the inscription. It hardly seemed as if the letters had been tampered with in any way. They were not carved. The words were made up of plastic characters, set into the wood like bas relief. Some unusually conscientious graffiti artist had clearly spent hours out here on the Common getting the details exactly right. The British, thought Henry, are now really conscientious only about vandalism.

'He would wank,' said the little man, 'at the drop of a hat.'

Henry began to experience a certain amount of fellow feeling for Kriegmuller. If Elinor did not come across soon he might well find himself stimulated to perform with as little provocation.

'He would pull his pudding,' said the little man thoughtfully, 'in front of the bathroom mirror. A day wasn't fit to be in the calendar until the feller had coaxed a little semen out of himself.'

He had a high voice. That, and the Kerry accent, gave his speech the haunting rhythms of a folk-tale. When Henry spoke he felt he was playing a part for the little man's benefit. But it wasn't, for the moment anyway, an unpleasant experience.

'You knew him, then?' said Henry.

The little man gave a bitter laugh. 'It was impossible to avoid him,' he said. 'The man was something of a local landmark. He was grossly fat. He was gigantic. In Wimbledon, you might say, he loomed large.'

The fat labrador, who seemed to find the man's presence soothing, had gone to sleep.

'He weighed,' said the little man, 'eighteen stone. It was a wonder the man was able to locate his organ, let alone pull the damn thing! He was gross in the extreme. But he was married to a very difficult woman. Sexual relations between them had broken down entirely.'

'Is that right?'

'Kriegmuller,' went on the little man, 'liked to do things in bed that no decent woman would permit.'

Henry had the impression, suddenly, that the man knew something about him. That he was making this story up in order to make some point about Henry and Elinor. The idea was, of course, absurd. No one, not even Maisie, had any idea about what went on, or didn't go on, in the bedroom of 54 Maple Drive. Or, he found he was sweating at the memory, what had nearly gone on in the bedroom of the Lakeland View Hotel, Keswick, on the evening of 1 April 1994.

'I can see you don't believe me,' went on the man, 'but what I say is the truth. I knew the family well. They were in the undertaking business. But it didn't go well for them.'

Henry found this easy to believe. If you wanted to have your nearest and dearest taken down to Roehampton Vale and done to a crisp, you would not automatically reach for a firm called Kriegmuller.

'Wrong name I suppose!' said the little man.

Henry once again had the impression that the stranger was reading his thoughts. That he knew things about him that Henry had never shared with anyone.

'It did not do the sexual side of their relationship any good at all!' said the man. 'Mrs Kriegmuller took over more and more of the work. Even herself, eventually, acquiring the skills of a carpenter. She made coffins, if you understand me? With her own hands!'

Henry made sympathetic noises. The little man gave him a shrewd look. It was as if his words were a game which he and Henry had decided to play. And yet a game in which only he knew the rules.

'Are you married yourself?'

'I am,' said Henry.

'What I am saying,' said the little man, 'is that wedlock is a two-way street. You have to work at it. And those two did not. They let things slip. With her working long hours and Kriegmuller really doing very little in the business at all, she had less and less time for him. And Kriegmuller, not to put too fine a point on it, whanged off more and more and more.'

Henry coughed. The little man leaned forward, resting his elbows on his knees.

'He devoted his time and energy to the pursuit of self-abuse. Skills that properly should have been used to build up the undertaking business were wasted on the search for self-stimulation. He did not stop at beating his meat in front of the mirror. That was just the start of it.' There was something curious about the timbre of the man's voice. What was it? 'He became increasingly inventive. He took to wearing Mrs Kriegmuller's underwear during the act.'

'Did he,' said Henry, 'continue to do it in front of the bathroom mirror?'

The man gave him an odd look. Then he chuckled slightly. 'That was no longer enough for him. He sought other locations. Theirs was quite a large house. It adjoined the undertakers, which was made up of a front office and a small chapel of rest.'

In answer to Henry's unspoken question the little man continued: 'He even did it there. He used the altar candles for unspeakable purposes. Which, as you may imagine, did not do their business any good either. He looked a mess. He was haggard with it. Everything was subordinated to the man's onanistic tendencies. Eventually they were down to only a few clients. In the end they only had one prospect. Undertaking, you understand me, is a question of who you know. Contacts is everything in that business.'

Henry nodded.

'Mrs Kriegmuller had this feller's coffin already made for him. And it was a beautiful affair. It was a work of art. People who knew the couple and who knew a little about the trade used to say that it was a coffin to die for. It was in mahogany – not a cheap wood, I may say – and the sides were fluted. The handles were designed by Porters of Raynes Park, of whom you may have heard. Their funerary work is of a very high quality.'

Henry looked at his companion. He certainly seemed well up in the undertaking business himself. If he wasn't making this up – and Henry was increasingly sure that he was – how could he have heard it? Unless he was some professional rival of the unfortunate Kriegmuller, a man with whom Henry was beginning to identify. Not only because of his reported passion for self-abuse, but also because, like Henry, he sounded an out-and-out loser.

'So what happened?'

'The coffin was in the parlour. It was, you might say, their last throw of the dice. You are only as good as your last funeral and this one Mrs Kriegmuller intended to be very highly thought of indeed.'

'But he – '

'He did not,' said the little man, 'use the coffin for the purposes for which it was intended.'

Henry gulped. 'You mean – '

'He used it to stimulate himself!' This was said without rancour, but with a certain seriousness.

Henry leaned forward. 'What did he do with it? Shove it up his arse or what?'

The little man showed no trace of taking this subject anything less than seriously. 'He was capable of that. But what was not what he did with it. He lay in it. It was silk-lined and extremely comfortable. And it fitted him perfectly, since the gentleman for whom Mrs Kriegmuller had designed it was of the same dimensions as Kriegmuller himself. In fact there were those who said the undertaker's wife was drawn to him. But even if that was the case, Mrs Kriegmuller was never anything less than a lady. She was a person of sensibility and feeling. I always felt their marriage had a chance. I was one of those who wanted it to succeed. But this wasn't the way. She needed, you understand me, to be wooed. Not to be faced with an eighteen-stone fellow tossing himself off in a coffin.'

'I see that,' said Henry.

The little man put his face into his hands. He seemed distressed. Henry noticed that the light was beginning to go. He had no idea of how long he had been here listening to the man; he felt himself to be as interested in the identity of the storyteller as in the story itself. And the little man seemed as concerned with its effect on his audience as he was with the tale.

'You have to work at marriage,' he said. 'It's no good running away and yanking your John Thomas all over the place. It takes more than that to get you through twenty-five years of sharing your life with someone.'

'So what happened? Did Mrs Kriegmuller leave him?'

'How could she? They were tied together, those two. All she did when she caught him at it was to tell him that if he wanted to do that he had better go and do it somewhere else.'

'And what did he do?'

'He went and did it somewhere else. He took his coffin out on to the Common. Or so I have been reliably informed.'

Henry obliged the man with a laugh. But, like all born storytellers, the little man looked at him sharply, as if he was offended at the suggestion that this fantastic tale might not be absolutely true.

'They say that this is what the man Kriegmuller did. Believe it or not. He climbed into it and stretched his whanger until the old spermatozoa obliged. He had become, as you might say, fixated on this particular piece of wood. He was unable to reach climax unless he was lying in it. Never mind that his wife's client was intended to lay his last mortal remains inside it. Never mind that it represented a considerable investment to them.'

Henry looked over at the fat labrador. He was sitting up and looking over in their direction. Something about the stranger's voice seemed to attract him. When the little man fell silent, the dog would put its head on one side as if coaxing him to continue.

'And where did he . . . do it?'

'He came here,' said the little man. 'He came to this very spot. He would toss himself off almost exactly where you are now sitting.'

Although Henry was interested in local history, he felt he could have been spared this detail. But he composed his face into an expression of polite concern as the stranger went on with his fantastic tale.

'He would park the coffin just over there, lower the Y-fronts and point his willy at the Milky Way. It was beyond an obsession, you see. The man was tugging away at his Hampton as if it held the answer to eternal life.' The little man shook his head. 'Mind you,' he said, 'you get some very odd people on this Common.'

Not 'arf, thought Henry. And you would appear to be one of them, mate.

'Out here in the middle of the night it can get quite something. I have seen things out here in the moonlight that would make your hair stand on end.'

And probably joined in with them, thought Henry. Presumably this was how this character had run across the hand-jobbing burial expert.

'I have seen naked men and women copulating. I have seen men doing it with men. I have seen people doing things with animals that you would not believe possible.'

He looked over at the fat labrador. The labrador got up and started to pad back towards them through the trees. Henry had, once again, an uncomfortable feeling. He hoped he was not going to be asked to join in with anything.

'Well,' said the storyteller, 'things went from bad to worse between him and Mrs Kriegmuller. With him out here in the coffin in all weathers pleasuring himself, and her coping with the dwindling list of customers and the boys from the Inland Revenue and all of that. She got to feel bitter about it. Or so I have heard tell. Very bitter she was, or so they say in these parts.'

Henry, who had decided to play the stranger's game, nodded, as if he was being made to listen to a detailed and serious technical explanation rather than a folk-tale improvised by an elderly man of questionable sanity.

'Did the guy get his coffin back?'

The little man looked away. He seemed, Henry thought, embarrassed. Henry couldn't quite think why he had asked the question. Except that almost everything about this improbable group of people had started to fascinate him. He was almost sure, sometimes, as the little man talked, that they *were* real, that the stranger had known them. Storytelling, he thought to himself, however crazy or half-baked, exerts a strange power even over people as unimaginative as Henry Farr.

Elinor always said he had no soul. Perhaps he did have a soul, even if it wasn't a very attractive one, and perhaps this curious little man was conjuring it out of him, here on the bench on the deserted Common.

'Did he get his coffin back?' Henry asked again.

'He did not, in fact. In fact I have to say that the man did not oblige them by dying. It was as if the removal of his box from the scene had put him off the idea of stiffing. Since old Johann Kriegmuller was "stiffing" on a fairly regular basis, in the same casket. He got a great deal better, which was nice for him, but not very good for the undertaking crowd. You need the customers to croak in that line, I'd say.'

He looked quickly at Henry, and almost as quickly looked away again. 'It was terrible for her. Or so everyone said.'

It certainly didn't sound good. Bad as Henry's marriage was, at least he wasn't wanking in a coffin that Elinor had designed for a close friend. Or in the open air. He had confined his activities to the bedroom and his study. Masturbation hadn't, so far anyway, affected his work.

'She followed him out here one night and they had words.'

Henry tried to picture the scene. It wasn't easy.

'She was kicking away at the old box and telling him to face up to the world. *Get out of it*, she said, *and do something with your life!* Not Johann. He lies there in the now rather unsavoury funerary item giving himself hand relief while she howls and screams like a banshee. Imagine it! Right here under the stars! Imagine it!'

'It seems,' said Henry carefully, 'quite incredible!'

The little man nodded. 'I am telling it,' he said, 'as it was told to me. No more or less.'

The fat labrador had returned to a position close to the bench. It was looking up at the little man appreciatively, as if this was a story it had heard before and was able to dip into or out of at leisure.

'He struck her hard on the side of her face. Wounded the poor woman terribly. And she grabbed one of the carpentry tools she had brought with her, some kind of mallet, and she struck him hard on the side of the head. Kriegmuller died instantly.'

Henry gave a low whistle. The fat labrador, too, seemed impressed.

'She was full of remorse,' went on the man. 'She did not love him. It is possible to lose all love for someone if they no longer deserve your love. But she did not want to kill him. Their relationship was bad, but not that bad.'

Once again, Henry had the uncanny impression that the little man knew something about him and Elinor. He was looking at him from under that all-enveloping hat. Was this man someone he knew, perhaps?

'But he was dead all right. Johann had literally fastened his fingers round his sexual organ for the last time. I am told he went out with an erection many men would lay down their lives for. He lay there with Percy in his paws, since even during their battle he had not taken his fingers off it. Mrs Kriegmuller realized she had not a hope in hell of getting rid of the body. It weighed over eighteen stone and, as I think I said, she was not a big woman.'

Henry looked around at the browned grass, the silver birches and the peaceful Common, empty of people.

'She had her tools with her. She buried him right here. Right in the very spot where you are sitting.'

Henry looked down between his feet. The bench seemed set into the earth. The grass had grown up around it. But if you looked closely you could see that it was different to the vegetation around it.

'And then she broke up that coffin and from it she built the very seat on which you are sitting. And wrote on it FOR JOHANN KRIEGMULLER WHO LOVED TO WANK ON THIS COMMON. Because my God he did! There never was a truer word said. The seat concealed the freshly dug earth, you understand.'

The storyteller chuckled and Henry, aware that it was now safe to laugh, chuckled with him. 'Made it non-controversial, I suppose,' said Henry.

The little man looked at him sharply. It was clear that no one else but him was supposed to be telling this story.

Henry went back to the role of totally credulous listener. 'Didn't anyone – '

'My dear man,' said the stranger, 'if they were looking for a grave, the last place they'd look for it is under a memorial seat. Have you not read "The Purloined Letter" by Edgar Allan Poe? And anyway, Kriegmuller was not missed. By anyone. Thousands of people like him disappear off the face of the earth every day. Not all of them have as appropriate a tomb as the one on which you are now sitting! Or so, at any rate, I have heard!'

The little man got up to go. The story was at an end. The light had almost gone and a grey mist was rising through the trees. Over to Henry's left a single leaf fell slowly through the darkening air.

'And Mrs Kriegmuller?'

It was not possible to see but Henry felt that the man was smiling.

'She married the man for whom the coffin had been intended. And they are very happy indeed, I am glad to say.'

Henry was about to ask him whether he was that man, because he was sure that that was what he was supposed to ask. But before he could do so, the storyteller turned to pat the fat labrador and as he lowered his face to the animal Henry saw that on one cheek there was a long, livid scar.

He realized something else as well. The little old man wasn't a man at all. He had been listening to a woman. Her hands were thick and muscular, the kind of hands that might have graced a woman who did some manual labour. Carpentry, he found himself thinking, so completely had he fallen under the spell of her tale. There were cuts all along the outside of her fingers. She looked him full in the face.

'Was Mrs Kriegmuller,' said Henry, 'by any chance an Irish lady?'

The woman smiled as her eyes met Henry's. She seemed pleased with the question and answered him with a crazy playfulness.

'She was from the County Kerry of course,' said the little old woman, 'and she'd many stories about her. She had the magic of tongues, that one. And could say true things to a person. She could conjure a world out of a few well chosen phrases, I'd say. That's how I see her anyway.'

She smiled, as if to banish her tale to the same shadowy region as the mist that was now creeping up round them. It was the very hour of the day and the month when light and the season seemed to be dying together. She put her head on one side. 'There's something sad about you,' she said. 'You're too much with yourself. You're looking in. I can see it. You have to look out, my friend. It's a beautiful world and it is all we have,' And she smiled broadly.

Before Henry had time to think that this was not an original or a very well-expressed remark, the little old woman had vanished into the trees as if she were part of the dusk, and her words no more than an echo in Henry's mind. He sat for some time, listening to the rustle of leaves falling and letting the darkness come in across the damp grass.

When he looked again at the inscription he could see quite clearly that it was a very clever piece of work by some unknown graffiti artist. If you looked closely, you could see where the 'L' had been altered. He smiled to himself in the dusk, and when he got up to begin the walk homeward he said out loud to the fat labrador, 'I might as well love Elinor. She's all I've got.'

The fat labrador wagged its tail and farted. Elinor was all right really, thought Henry. At least she was the only person he could think of who was almost as awful as he was. And six months wasn't so long to do without sex. Lots of married people only had it about twice a year.

He would buy her some flowers. Women liked that. She might even give him a shag. He didn't know why he hadn't thought of that before. Sheer laziness probably. But he had better stop wanking in the fairly near future. You could take that sort of thing too far.

The Hallowe'en Murderer

YOU HAD TO *use it to kill them. It wasn't the same otherwise. Oh, there was a kind of pleasure when they opened the door to you and you saw their stupid old women's faces – the wrinkles and the grey hair and the solicitous smiles when they saw it was you and they thought they had nothing to fear. The fear came later, after you had hit them with it once. You never hit them with it too hard the first time. Not because you were worried about them screaming. In fact the screaming was part of the pleasure. There was so much noise in the street – so many yells of mock terror – that one old lady shouting blended with the whoops of children as they ran up the street, bent on terrifying their neighbours.*

After you had hit them once, the blood started. That was when you started to enjoy it. You always hit them in the same place so that the blood started where it had started all those years ago. And you felt an unimaginable pleasure. The pleasure of sex. Because this blood was blood that would ransom us, heal us, forgive us and keep us from evil.

Old women have to die some time. Why not now?

'He always kills at Hallowe'en!' said Elinor's mother, brightly.

She was wearing a witch's hat and black cloak and carrying a broomstick. She looked, Henry thought, rather less like a witch than usual. In her brown skirt, red cardigan and pill-box hat she quite often made him cast around for a crucifix or send out for a few extra cloves of garlic. If that was what you used to ward off witches.

Except that there was no warding off Elinor's mother. Like Terminator Two, she kept coming. Even if you were to blast off her head with an automatic rifle (something Henry had quite often thought of doing), she would probably carry right on through the hall of 54 Maple Drive, headed for the washing machine, the sink or some other corner of the house where she might conceivably be of use.

'She's only trying to help!' Elinor would scream, as her headless mother, bloodied arms out in front of her like a blind person, clumped robotically towards Henry's underpants. 'She's only trying to help!'

'If we all stay together,' said Mrs Gross, 'we'll be fine!'

Elinor's mother pursed her lips. 'He always kills women of over pensionable age!' she said. There were five women over pensionable age in the room: Mrs Gross, Mrs Duckett, Mrs Lampbeare, Mrs Jeans and Elinor's mother.

When the Hallowe'en killer first struck four years ago, Inspector Dixon of Wimbledon CID had said, on nationwide television, 'This, in our view, was a burglary that went tragically wrong!' 'What are they saying?' Henry had asked Elinor. 'That it would have been better for all concerned if the lads got away with some swag? Why this sudden concern for burglaries to be well executed?' It wasn't until a year later, when he struck once again on 31 October, that the killer got his title. And as he only struck once a year, it was well into his fifth year of operations before people caught on to the fact that he was a serial killer.

All the victims were over sixty-five. All lived in Maple Drive. All were female and all had been battered with what looked like the same blunt instrument. Not only that. On every occasion he began by striking his prey in precisely the same spot – on the upper right temple – and, burned into bone and skin (the first blow in all cases had not proved fatal), were two marks like those of a doll's feet. The first blow was followed by a savage and fatal battering with what looked like a heavier object, a club or loaded sock.

Some of the papers were calling him the Doll Killer. The *Wimbledon Courier*, the downmarket free-sheet, called him the Hallowe'en Puppet Slayer, and its rival, the *Express*, not to be outdone, came up with the Maple Drive Hallowe'en Puppet Pensioner Batterer.

'Who'll be next?' said Elinor's mother, who had rented a basement flat at number 43a (only, as Henry pointed out, a hundred yards from his bedroom) two weeks ago. All the other women, who seemed to find her as unnerving as Henry, looked round. Elinor's mother patted her iron-grey curls. 'Bash, bash, he goes!' she said. 'And you're a gonner!'

Elinor's mother had been a receptionist in what she still insisted on calling 'civilian life' and long hours of sitting in deserted lobbies with an anticipatory smile on her face had given her a very special quality. She bestowed a provisional quality on almost every social occasion at which she was present. She had for quite a long period worked for MI5 and still gave the impression that she was screening even quite casual acquaintances. 'They think the milkman is not all he's cracked up to be,' she said, as she applied lipstick to her mouth and pressed her lips together in a still expressive bow. '*I* don't like the look of him!'

Elinor got to her feet. Since their holiday, Henry had noticed, she had abandoned the elegant coats and jackets from Valentina of Wimbledon and now slumped around the place in garments that seemed designed to hide her ever-increasing bulk. Today she was wearing a kind of loose woollen tube and a pair of old carpet slippers.

Henry did not mind this. In many ways he found it reassuring. Since the incident on the Common last month, he had been paying rather more attention to Elinor and rather less to his own organ. The results had been spectacular. In the first week of October they had had it nine times. On one occasion she had allowed him to –

'It may not be a *he!*' said Elinor, giving Henry a knowing look. 'Women are capable of amazingly bestial things!'

Henry smirked. 'Absolutely right, love!' he said, and glared round at the rest of the room in case of any of them tried to disagree with her.

At this moment the doorbell rang. Henry looked out of the front window and saw a woman in her sixties standing looking back at the street. She had a handbag looped over the crook of her elbow.

'Wham!' said Elinor's mother. 'Out he comes at you from some dark alley and before you know where you are your brain is being pounded to jelly with . . . ' she shuddered dramatically – ' . . . a doll! I was always rather fond of my dollies!'

Elinor started to grind her teeth. The doorbell rang again. Henry went out to answer it.

Mrs Malpas had only been in the street for nine months. And everyone agreed there was something very peculiar about her. She was recently widowed – or so she said – and had moved to Wimbledon from the country. She had involved herself in almost every local activity on offer. She had made dough mermaids for the craft fair, attended dog obedience classes with Bulstrode, her Norfolk terrier, and, like several other elderly ladies in the street, she was active in the church. Mrs Gross, the retired architect's wife, described her as 'a poppet', 'a tower of strength' and 'a really useful alto'.

But her stories did not always seem quite consistent. She had told Norah Joyce that she had two brothers, but later the same week she had declared to Mrs Gross that she only had one sibling, a sister who was 'the light of her life'. There was also the question of her frequent absences and the mysterious car sometimes parked outside her flat late at night.

She was, thought Henry, as he opened the door to her, surprisingly physically powerful. She was almost as heavily built as Angelica. Angelica had become increasingly devoted to Henry during the course of the year. In July she had offered to work for nothing. At least Henry thought that that was what she had said. Her English seemed to be getting worse.

Could Angelica be the culprit? Had she worked for any of the murdered women? Her cleaning was getting increasingly eccentric. Last week she had had tried to throw away Henry's shoes, Elinor's radio and Maisie's collection of compact discs.

'I've come to reclaim the night!' said Mrs Malpas.

'Come on in!' said Henry. At least she was wearing the correct clothes – sensible tweeds, flat shoes, cardigan and winter coat.

When Mrs Gross had proposed holding a non-denominational exorcism in Maple Drive on 31 October, there were many people who assumed she was giving a Hallowe'en party. With the result that the groups of people now gathering at different houses all along the street wore a weird blend of pagan and Christian garments. Dr Lewis from number 93, who had taken over Donald Templeton's practice, was wearing a top hat, an evening suit and a pair of bloody fangs; Jamrags Pleckett was got out like a vestal virgin; and the local Anglo-Catholic vicar – a man who insisted on being called Father Dupont even thought he was supposed to be in the Church of England – had climbed into a set of purple and gold vestments that made many people even more dubious about the man's sexual tendencies.

Dupont had rather forced himself on the exorcism committee. As Norbert DuCane, Man Who Loves Shopping, had pointed out, the purpose of the evening was to discourage perversity. Gary Fraser, the wholesale butcher, described Dupont as an 'out and out shirt-lifter' and even Mrs Gross was rendered speechless when she caught sight of his exorcism kit – incense with silver salver, stoup of holy water that took two men to carry and a crucifix on a thirty-foot pole that looked like something straight out of a National Theatre production.

'I think, Mother,' Elinor was saying as Mrs Malpas came into the room, 'that you should change!'

Elinor's mother smirked round at the room to let them know that she knew what a difficult daughter she had. Then she tucked her broomstick under her arm. 'I don't know,' she said, 'it's the spirit of the thing, isn't it? Apparently he wallops them twice! Once with the doll and then he finishes them off with a bloody great hammer!'

Over in the corner Mrs Duckett had gone pale. Mrs Gross was comforting her. The retired architect's wife got to her feet and in her familiar braying voice said, 'Now! Over sixty-fives stick together!'

Henry looked across at Elinor and Maisie. They were both up to something. Maisie and James Seebohm (who was wearing an amazingly realistic axe in his head) were taking heavy petting to places where it had never been before. Full intercourse – if it hadn't arrived already – was going to seem like an anticlimax after what Henry suspected them of getting up to in the garden last Friday night. And Elinor, he had decided, had probably been having an affair with Esmond Brice for the last six months.

He had only just managed to save his marriage in time. If he hadn't started paying her a bit of attention after that strange encounter with the old woman on the Common, she might well even now be getting up to something with Brice. And if Henry knew anything about the psychotherapist, it would be a bit more basic than early music. You had to be constantly on your guard in a marriage, Henry told himself. There was no time for slacking.

He took a quick sideways look at Brice, who was over in the corner clutching his tenor recorder. He had definitely been giving her a lot more than tips on how to phrase Monteverdi, thought Henry. But he couldn't be bothered to feel jealous. The man was clearly on the way out. Why, only last night she had bent over the washbasin, wearing only a pair of wellingtons, and he had –

Henry sneered openly at his rival. Then, feeling generous again, he turned the sneer into a smile. He was a sophisticated man of the world. He felt suddenly clever and witty and distinguished. Soon he would be mingling with sophisticated people. He would be quaffing champagne with Harold Pinter. Sharing a joke with Melvyn Bragg. One minute your wife was having affairs; the next she was back in style, allowing you to lash her with your brother's dog lead and offering you oral sex on the Aga.

If anyone was going to solve the mystery of the Hallowe'en Murderer, it was probably him.

Henry parted the curtains. He could not have said why, but he was almost certain the killer came from Maple Drive. The person most likely to have a grudge against ladies of over sixty-five from this street was someone with direct experience of the old bastards. And that person was most likely to be a neighbour.

'The police think,' said Elinor's mother, as the party started to drift towards the street, 'that it might be an adolescent!'

Maisie prodded Seebohm in the shoulder. 'He isn't organized enough to be a serial killer!' she said. 'You need certain basic organizational skills!'

Seebohm laughed gloomily. He had got only one pass at GCSE, but he would not say in which subject. His ambition, he had told Henry, was to be 'a sort of gardener or something'.

Henry sighed to himself as the group moved out into the street, where 'Father' Dupont was already pacing up and down trying out a few basic moves with his crucifix. It had been specially designed for him by Ebenezer Jarvis, a Roman Catholic priest who had reversed the career progress of the founder of his religion and left the church to go into carpentry. Henry tried to get close to Elinor, even perhaps to hold her hand in the darkness, but Brice was pestering her. She shot him a quick, sympathetic glance as Esmond started to bore for England on the subject of a concerto for violas by some long-dead loser called Lugmuller.

If you knew, thought Henry, *that only last Wednesday as she gripped the mantelpiece with both hands, I –*

To his surprise, over to his left, he saw the milkman. What was he doing here?

It was impossible to tell whether he was dressed for Hallowe'en or a church service. His outfit – funereal black suit, white shirt, black tie and black shoes – was a model of propriety, but his face, pinched, dead white, and his big, grey eyes that searched the crowd restlessly belonged to a music-hall version of Burke and Hare.

Even as a milkman Mr Norris was pretty scary. Something about the way he put down your bottles on the doorstep, and then tiptoed back to his float as if they were about to explode, made some women stifle a scream as they looked out at him from behind the curtains. But after dark! Without his apron! The man had *serial killer* written all over him.

He appeared to be grinning at Mrs Malpas. Was she going to be next?

Henry scanned the faces of the crowd to see if Norris was anywhere near Elinor's mother. He was not. Henry reflected on the unfairness of life. If any woman over sixty-five deserved to be pounded to pulp by a psychopath, it was his mother-in-law. But serial killers never got the right people. Some innocent old granny was going to get the treatment before the night was out and Mrs Meaulnes was going to be there bright and cheerful tomorrow morning, talking through the precise damage to the poor old trout's occipital region with anyone who would listen.

Brice had taken out his recorder. A couple of drummers had started up and the core members of Doublet and Hose went into one of their star numbers. It might have wowed the odd monk in 1187, but even in the open air it didn't do a lot for Henry.

The music made it worse somehow.

When the music started and I was among them, I knew I was going to have to do it again. And do it by the end of the night. Because the souls of the dead wander at night. There were so many souls, hovering in the air above us, mocking our pathetic show of faith.

Farr, the fat one, was at the back, smirking round at the world. His wife has made a monkey of him with the Brice boy. They make no secret of the fact. Brice is doing it with her. The Farrs will be divorced by the end of the year. They are so typical of this street. So narrow! So soulless!

There is no one here with any breadth of vision. No one who can see as I can see that all this pathetic attempt at surburban order, the gardens laid out like dresses for someone's wedding, and the houses standing as stiff as soldiers in the autumn night – this is all a temporary arrangement. It won't last. It can't.

As they marched up the road chanting, none of them knew, as I knew, that by the end of the night there would be one lady the less. One old lady more would have been kicked in the head by my friend. I like that. That he's a vandal. That he flaunts the blood of his victims, puts it on show where all can see. See, see where Granny's blood streams on my toecaps!

I sometimes think I might be going mad. I don't know why this should be. But I am finding it hard to remember even the simplest telephone numbers. And the other day I got lost in Cannizaro Park, a place with which I ought to be totally familiar. I sometimes get the urge to remove my clothes in public places. To exhibit my private parts to them. I would like to see their faces if I were to pull down my pants and show them my arse!

This is not normal, is it?

Soon, soon, I will choose my old lady. And even though they are all here, she will die. He will fly down from the air like a bat and swoop out of the dark at her when she least expects it. You cannot keep Him out. He comes and goes as He pleases!

When he got to the top of the street, Father Dupont, handing over his crucifix and his salver (which he had been swinging round his head at considerable risk to those around him) to Morgan 'Going Over to Rome' Ferrers, knelt ostentatiously outside number 114.

'O Lord,' he said, 'hear our prayer!'

Mrs Gross, whose husband was, as ever, watching events in the street from an upper window, replied, 'And let our cry come unto Thee!' A few other people responded but none with the panache of Mrs Gross. Her returns of service were quite famous in the local religious community. She had ruined the nerves of at least three vicars.

'Lord have mercy upon us!' said Dupont.

'*Christ* have mercy upon us!' boomed Mrs Gross.

She said this in a manner that seemed to imply that Dupont had got the words wrong. But Dupont, who knew how to deal with difficult parishioners, came back well. While maintaining the kneeling position he started to sway to and fro and cross himself wildly. Gross, who was shaping up for 'And let our cry come unto thee!', was badly thrown.

Dupont moved to consolidate his advantage by switching to Latin. '. . . vobiscum Deum at aeternum sacula, saeculorum . . . '

Gross, who had had enough of this, cut him short. 'Amen!' she boomed.

This more or less made it clear who was boss. Norbet DuCane, The Man Who Loves Shopping, cried 'Amen' as well. Several other people followed suit. Dupont paid no attention. He was still crossing himself violently and had started to improvise more Latin. Henry thought he vaguely recognized what the man was saying as a chunk of Livy that Maisie had had to learn for her GCSE earlier in the year. All of the group were now crossing themselves and muttering 'Amen!' Some were looking up at the sky as if they expected the Hallowe'en Killer to swoop down at them through the darkness.

Henry had his eye on the milkman. Norris had sidled up close to Mrs Malpas and was whispering something to her. When he saw Henry looking at him he edged away through the crowd. Henry came up to Mrs Malpas. 'Was Norris bothering you?' he said.

Mrs Malpas looked at him. 'Oh no,' she said. 'No, no, no! Not at all!'

There was something so insistent about the way she said this that Henry suspected she might not be telling the truth. All around him the more devout members of Maple Drive and a few non-believers who happened to be female and over the age of sixty-five were commending themselves to the Almighty's care.

He felt a pressure on his arm. It was Elinor's mother. 'He'll get someone before the night is out!' she said, patting the back of her hat. Then she grabbed hold of her broomstick with both hands and started to beat the ground with the end of the handle. 'It'll be bash, bash, bash! I tell you! And one more old lady won't be touting her pension book up to the post office in the morning.' She turned to Henry. 'I think,' she said, 'that he has supernatural powers!'

After the stupid chanting and the praying was over – it's funny how people think that God might actually have an interest in human beastliness – the good folk of Maple Drive all retired in small groups to each other's houses.

That was about ten.

I only had an hour. And I knew that they had their people among the crowd to watch me. The police are so stupid! They imagine that a killer doesn't notice anything! Every time I pass one of them, their hats like black nipples and their ridiculous boots, beating time like a clock, I want to do something outrageous. I want to say, 'Can I piss in your mouth?' But instead I say, 'Can you tell me the time?'

Because I am so respectable! And he is so respectable. He helps me off. He does! He helps me to do it. He helps me to get rid of them with their sagging breasts and their false teeth and their absurd conviction that they matter! That they are, in some way, attractive!

I am sick. I need help. I need counselling.

But where can I get it? There is nothing for people like me. No help or solace. I go it alone. And I will still go it alone. As I did that night, knowing I had to kill before the night was out!

It was ten-thirty. Henry was sitting in the front room. James Seebohm had announced that he wanted to do some apple-bobbing. He and Maisie were spraying each other with water and giggling hysterically. Elinor, who had been backed into a corner by Brice, who was giving a long and not very coherent speech about flugelhorns, was looking across at Henry, signalling desperation with her eyes.

Henry heard a noise. Someone out there in the street was clearing their throat. And yet after the service was over the area had been emptied of people. 'Father' Dupont, before lugging his equipment back to Mr and Mrs Gross's house, had recommended everyone to stay together and to keep indoors.

Elinor broke away from Brice and came over to Henry by the window. Once again he marvelled at the unbearable contradictions of marriage. A few weeks ago he had been seriously contemplating divorce. Now he was secure in the knowledge that, in only a few hours, Elinor would be getting on her black leather patent shoes and a red fur boa and he would be –

'It's Norris!' said Elinor, looking out at the street. 'Skulking around in the dark! It's Norris!'

Several people in their group joined them at the window. 'I knew he was a nasty piece of work!' Mrs Jeans was saying. 'He never leaves you full cream when you ask for it!'

Mrs Dutton looked even paler than usual. 'Take him, Henry!' she said. 'Sort him!'

Henry turned to face the group. 'I don't think – '

'He won't bite, Henry! He's a coward!'

Out on the street, Norris appeared to be making every effort to behave like a serial killer. He was creeping from doorway to doorway, looking over his shoulder as if he were frightened of being observed.

'Let's all go!' said Elinor.

'I'll deal with it!' said Henry, who had not felt as macho as this since he had managed – admittedly by accident – to lead his family off a mountain in thick fog earlier in the year. 'You never know how he may react. I'll get out there and sort him out, though. Never fear. You all – ' here he gave Brice a significant look – 'Just stay here where it's safe!'

Elinor's mother took off her hat. Her hair, dyed an improbable shade of black, gave her an evil, intense air. 'Mind he doesn't whip round and clock you with his dolly!' she said.

Henry smiled in a superior manner. 'He only goes for ladies over sixty-five!' he said.

'In the dark,' said Elinor's mother with a wicked grin, 'you could easily be mistaken for one.'

She cackled at her own joke. Henry, with as much dignity as he could manage, went through to the front door. He went right, back up Maple Drive, and after about thirty yards saw Norris.

The milkman had stopped in front of Mrs Gross's house. But he wasn't looking in at the ex-architect's wife. He was by the front gate, looking down into the basement flat. Where Mrs Malpas lived. Henry ran up the street towards him. As he ran he was aware that doors and windows were opening, and that neighbours he recognized were coming out on to the street.

'Norris!'

The milkman was so absorbed in looking down into the basement flat that he started with shock at the sound of Henry's voice. He whipped round, grabbing at the railings in front of Mrs Gross's garden as he did so.

'What are you doing? We're all supposed to be inside!' said Henry.

Norris's face darkened. He seemed angry about something.

'You had better tell me,' said Henry, marvelling at his own boldness, 'or the police will want to know about it!'

Norris shrugged wearily. 'I am the police,' he said, reaching into his pocket and producing a plastic identity card which he waved at Henry. 'And I was, until a few moments ago, what we like to call "under-cover".' He said this with an elaborate sarcasm that Henry found offensive. He had not been a great success as a milkman. As a police-man, Henry thought, he was an unmitigated disaster.

'You know?' Norris went on, the same unpleasant sneer in his voice, '*Undercover*. Like in the movies. Deep, deep, deep cover. OK? When you get into civilian clothes and penetrate the local community. Heard of that one?'

Henry peered at the man's identity card. It looked, he thought, pretty suspect.

'It sounds rather unlikely to me!' he said. Norris's face looked even meaner. If he was an imitation policeman, he was a good one. He had precisely the touch of weary arrogance Henry had noted among members of the force, especially when carrying out their duties.

'Does it?' said Norris. 'Of course I am only an inspector in Wimble-don CID, but I should have thought it was rather a sensible idea to keep a watchful eye on Maple Drive.'

'By peering into an old lady's flat?' said Henry. 'Who just happens to be exactly the right age to be a target for our friend?'

At which the door of the flat opened and Mrs Malpas emerged. Although she still had on the clothes she had been wearing earlier, she seemed different. There was a mannish, no-nonsense tone about the way she spoke that Henry had never heard before. 'I think,' she said to Norris, 'there are certain advantages in going public at this stage.'

Norris assumed the cringing air Henry had noticed among policemen talking to their superiors. 'If you say so, ma'am!' he said.

Mrs Malpas looked at Henry with contempt. 'We'd have given this out over a public-address system anyway,' she said, 'but as you have poked your nose in . . . '

Henry looked behind him. Almost the whole street seemed to have gathered outside Mrs Gross's house. Elinor was there. The Dussmayers. The people from number 24 and Mrs Jeans and Mrs Dutton and 'Father' Dupont and Norbert DuCane and Is the Mitsubishi Scratched Yet? and the Nazi Who Escaped Justice at Nuremberg and Maisie and –

Mrs Malpas looked along the line of faces. 'And in this case,' she went on, 'it doesn't much matter if I tell you the truth. Though you probably know it already.'

She took a pack of cigarettes from her left-hand pocket and lit one in a frighteningly professional manner. 'Superintendent Jenny Malpas, retired!' she said. 'Someone had to go in and get the confidence of all of you. And let me tell you it hasn't always been a pleasant experience. I sometimes wished I had been undercover somewhere a bit easier, like in a Mafia community in the Lower East Side or among a group of Glasgow football hooligans!'

She inhaled deeply and shook her head. Then she gave a brief, mannish laugh to show that this was a joke. 'The English suburbs,' she said, 'would make a strong man quake. What you lot get up to is *nobody's* business.'

A few more neighbours were coming up from behind. But the silence that greeted her words was complete. Apart from Derek Husson, the company director, who could be heard asking his wife whether she had discussed VAT with either Malpas or the milkman, the only sound in Maple Drive was the October wind rattling the windows and pulling the tall trees in Mrs Gross's garden to and fro against the pale, ragged sky.

'He's one of you!' she said. 'We know that. Don't ask me how I know, but we know no one from outside the street came into Maple Drive last year. Which was when I entered the picture. And we know the kind of person our killer is. We think we know what excites him, what turns him on and how and why he does the things he does!'

Norris was looking worried. 'Jenny – ' he said, but Superintendent Malpas (retired) cut him short with a wave of her hand. Then she looked up at the assembled population of Maple Drive. 'He's one of you!' she said. 'And after nine months of listening to you I cannot say that that fact surprises me.'

She started to single out individuals, addressing her remarks first to one then another of the crowd above her. 'You like a challenge, don't you?' she said. 'And it has to be tonight doesn't it, eh? Well . . . ' She spread her arms wide. 'Come and get me! I'll be here. Every other old lady in the street will be surrounded by protectors. I won't. I'll be right here. You only have an hour. And I'll be waiting for you.'

Norris started to protest but Malpas waved her hand at him. She looked like a woman, thought Henry, finding the thought mildly erotic, who was accustomed to being obeyed. 'Get our people at both ends of the street,' she said, 'and watch every front and back entrance! But let him come. Don't stop him before he gets to my door. Because I will be ready.' Her eyes were bright with righteous anger. 'You won't be dealing with an amateur this time,' she said, 'but that'll make it all the more exciting, won't it? And you won't be able to resist, will you? You . . . *animal*!'

And with these words she turned and, slamming the door after her, retreated into her flat. It was only after Norris had gone in after her that he re-emerged to confirm that these were the orders of the night. A police car went up and down the street repeating them from a public-address system.

As Maisie, Elinor, James Seebohm, Henry and Elinor's mother went back to number 54, Henry said, 'She's a brave woman!'

'She's an idiot!' said Elinor's mother. 'Like all the police force. He'll get her before the night is out. It'll be thwack, thwack, thwack and bysey bye to Superintendent Malpas (retired).'

Henry said he thought the Hallowe'en murderer might not strike that evening. He indicated the large numbers of policemen hiding all over the street.

'He'll probably just change his angle!' said Elinor's mother. 'It'll be the Guy Fawkes Murderer next. Or the Ascension Day – '

'*Shut up!*' screamed Elinor. 'For God's sake, shut up!'

Elinor's mother smiled round at the company and patted her witch's hat. 'She's overwrought, poor darling!' she said. 'It's all been too much for her!'

Somewhere in the darkness a child set up a banshee wail. A police car started to move up the street, and an amplified voice repeated the order for residents to return to their houses. In silence, the group went in to number 54 Maple Drive.

They don't know I can fly. When I am after blood I can fly. I fly in out of the darkness. I come down like Dracula in the shape of a bat. But I don't suck, I strike. I'm Him anyway. I'm in Him. And people come to My house and bow down to Me and when they kneel to kiss the blood away they don't know what it is they're kissing.

I knew I had to do it before twelve. And I knew I would do it. No matter how many stupid policemen they set in the street. Because I go where I want to go and kill whom I wish to kill. I am a God and the world is quite literally at my feet. Get it? Get it? Get it?

It was ten minutes after twelve before Norris sent his men into Mrs Gross's basement. Everyone said he should have done it earlier. They said, too, that he should have used more than twenty men. He should have put more of them on the roofs. He should have had more of them in the gardens. He should have ordered helicopters. The Hallowe'en Murderer, people said, was clever enough to have slipped past the men on the ground. He could have moved from garden to garden, he could have tunnelled his way from a neighbour's or perhaps, some people said, he had supernatural powers.

He certainly had something. Because there were no footprints on the path going up to Superintendent Malpas's door. There was no sign of anyone having gone anywhere near the garden or even the frontage of the house. None of Norris's men had seen anything.

The closed-circuit camera installed in Superintendent Malpas's front hall had the best view of what had happened, Mr and Mrs Gross and 'Father' Dupont having been ordered to stay at the back of the house by the police.

The videogram recorded a long peal of the bell at the front door. Then it showed Malpas, who was armed, moving cautiously towards the front door. She opened it. There was no one there. The camera showed her moving out into the garden and calling, 'Is there anyone there?'

There was no response. Malpas walked back into the house, then out again. She appeared to be looking at the sky. Then she closed the front door, walked back through the hall and off to the left, towards the front room. After this there was no record of what had happened, although certain things were clear. She had opened the window of the front room (or someone had already opened it from the outside) and someone or something had struck her on the upper right temple. The first blow bore the marks of all such wounds inflicted by the Hallowe'en Killer – 'As if,' Norris told his superiors, 'a doll had flown in at the window and kicked her, hard.' But the second blow, the one that had killed her, had come from something like a stick or a truncheon, wielded with supernatural force. The pathologist, 'Mucky' Duck of the Wimbledon CID, reported that the force used was greater than that in the case of the Kingston Strong Man Murder of 1987. 'It was,' he said, 'the kind of thing that I would not like to ascribe to a merely human agent.'

Mrs Gross's evidence was the most decisive.

At nearly twelve o'clock she had heard a noise that she thought was coming from the street. Going to the front window and looking out she said she thought she had seen a figure 'like a doll'. Not usually a fanciful woman, Mrs Gross went on to say that it seemed to have a 'grinning face – like some tribal idol'.

'I thought at first,' she told Norris, 'that it was a bat. It was dark and it was swooping down very swiftly. I only saw it for a moment when it was near to the lamp opposite and I am sure I didn't see what I *thought* I saw. But it looked like a doll, flying by itself, out in the darkness.'

When Norris questioned her more closely she said it looked like 'a puppet', but she wouldn't be more specific than that. It had clearly frightened her, he thought. She told WPC Habib, who had been sent to sit with her in the early hours of 1 November, that it was making 'a whistling noise'.

The *Wimbledon Mercury* carried the headline HALLOWE'EN REMOTE-CONTROL PUPPET SLAYER BATTERS UNDERCOVER POLICEWOMAN. Which was not only their longest, but some said their most effective, headline in forty years of newspaper publishing.

But nobody apart from the media took the remote-control puppet theory seriously. People in the street said that Mrs Gross was only trying to draw attention to herself. Anyway, they muttered to themselves, how could a puppet deliver a blow with the force of the one that had smashed Ms Malpas's skull, delivered, according to 'Mucky' Duck, 'with the force of a steam hammer'.

It was, as Henry pointed out to Elinor, 'a locked street mystery'. How had the murderer managed to get to her front door? And how had he managed to escape?

The most obvious theory was that he had come from one of the houses immediately adjoining Mrs Gross's house and crept from garden to garden, returning by the same route. There were three neighbours whose movements were unaccounted for by their families, including Luigi 'Bumhole' Cappezzana, but even though he was questioned for four hours by Norris, the fact of the matter was that there were no traces of any animal or human passing through any of the gardens that adjoined the space above Superintendent Malpas's flat.

What perturbed the residents of Maple Drive the most was the fact that the events of the night of Hallowe'en seemed to prove Norris and Malpas's theory beyond any doubt. The murderer was, as Elinor said, 'one of us' or, as Henry put it, 'one of them'.

'We pass him every day in the street!' said Elinor's mother. 'He sits at our table! He walks our children to school! He is me! He is you! And *why should he stop at old ladies*?'

It was 'Father' Dupont who hit on the idea of a memorial service for Superintendent Malpas at his church. The unkind said that this was simply a way of filling it, since hardly anyone went there apart from Mrs Gross who, when she was feeling depressed, deviated from the Presbyterian Church and, to use her own words, 'went for the vestments'. But the police agreed to turn out in force. And after a while so did most of the rest of the street. Henry and Elinor were placed in the front pew, even though Henry had asked to go at the back so that he would watch people and work out when to kneel.

He and Elinor had become obsessed with the details of the case. They spent hours every evening going over possible suspects among the neighbours and, as the organ music started for the service, Henry was looking round the congregation going over his list of suspects.

His favourite candidate at the moment was Elinor's mother. Although he hadn't yet quite worked out her motive, apart from the desire to create an issue worth talking about, he found himself fantasizing about her arrest and trial quite frequently.

I laughed to see them in the House of God. The way they bow and kneel and scrape makes me laugh. Always makes me laugh. Because I can do as well as they can. I gave, I thought, one of my better performances. And I thought about how I swooped down out of the darkness and how I was there for all of them to see. How I was the most obvious thing in front of them and so, of course, could not be seen.

They trust me. It's funny. I am thought of as reliable. They have no idea of what I really do. Of what I really think and feel.

'It's staring you in the face!' I wanted to shout. 'Can't you see it, you fools?' Now I am alone here, all alone. Now they watch me through the door, waiting for me to come alive again, I go over and over and plan my next killing. Because I will kill again. They can't hold me back. I shall kill Farr's mother-in-law next year. I will go to her door the way I did last Hallowe'en and she will gasp as I swing in out of the darkness and leave the marks of my feet on her temple!

'Father' Dupont had spared no expense. He may have been a little out of his depth at the exorcism but he knew his way round a memorial service.

He was a great one, Henry thought, for processions. At the least excuse he and his choirboys would be out from the altar and roaming round the church swinging incense at the punters. His lead sidesman, Gabriel Matheson, dressed in a mouth-watering surplice designed by Hubert Prynne, the ecclesiastical tailor from Leatherhead, was hardly ever still. Even during Edmond Brice's 'Lament for Mrs Malpas', scored for flute, harp, organ and boy soprano, Matheson was jigging round in his seat as if someone had slipped itching powder down his back – which in fact one of the choirboys had.

Henry, even when the praying had started, did not move from his seat, his eyes lifted up above the altar. Elinor, who had fallen ostentatiously to her knees, peered at him and hissed, 'What's the matter?'

Henry did not answer. Maisie, who had remained equally ostentatiously standing when she was supposed to be sitting, sitting when she was supposed to be kneeling and, to the horror of Mrs Gross, deep in a copy of *The Punisher* during the Lord's Prayer, said, 'He has a right to his beliefs!'

'Not a question of beliefs!' was all Henry said.

'He's thinking about You-Know-Who!' said Elinor's mother. 'Our Henry quite fancies himself as a detective. Don't you, Henry? Not that it'll do much good, my dear. I fear he's too clever for you. In eleven months he'll be walloping some other poor old trout over the bonce!'

Elinor followed the direction of her husband's gaze. He seemed, she thought, to be looking at Ebenezer Garvey's crucifix.

Above the waist it was a fairly conventional representation of Jesus. He was gazing soulfully off to the right, each arm flung out behind him. There was a crown of thorns on his head. But Henry wasn't looking at his head or his upper body. He was looking at Christ's elegantly carved, slender legs and at the elaborately carved feet. They were not pointing daintily downwards, but jutting out. And the right foot was slightly in advance of the left, as if Christ was about to deliver a penalty kick. Each one marked with an alarmingly realistic trail of blood.

Henry looked from the crucifix to the pole that stood next to it, leaning against a pillar. The pole Father Dupont had used on the night of Mrs Malpas's murder. Then he looked at the front line of the congregation. He took in Mrs Gross, noticing her head uplifted in song and her surprisingly broad and muscular shoulders. Her wrists, too, were as thick as a manual labourer's. For a woman of her age she was surprisingly strong.

Henry closed his eyes and thought about the night of the exorcism ceremony in Maple Drive.

Then, although the service was still in progress and although 'Father' Dupont gave him two or three un-Christian glances, he got up from the pew and made his way along the front of the congregation to where DI Norris, in full dress uniform, was sitting. Henry squeezed himself in next to the policeman and whispered, 'Tell me. This time, was there anything odd about the marks of the feet on Malpas's head?'

Norris gave him a worried look. 'How did you know that?' he said. 'They were – '

'Don't tell me.' said Henry with a faint smile. 'Usually the big toe of the right foot is to the left of the temple. Yes?'

'How did you – '

'And this time it was the other way round. To the left. Yes?'

Norris's jaw dropped open. He looked as if he was about to send out for back-up. Henry did not lower his voice, in spite of an almost audible clucking from the priest, as he said, 'It was the other way round because the figure was upside down.'

The two men looked up at the cross. Henry saw once again how bold Garvey had been with the feet. How the right foot was slightly forward, as if poised for a kick. As they watched, Dupont lifted the Christ from its resting place and prepared to make another sortie into the congregation.

'Look at the right foot!' said Henry. When you looked closely at it, the blood that streamed from the right foot of Jesus was suspiciously dark. As if it had dried naturally. It had none of the brightness of paint. Then, as Henry watched, it picked up the light from the silver candlesticks and from the silver plate, caught it and winked it back at the stained-glass windows as if it were suddenly alive, the fresh blood of slaughtered women, fresh as paint. Henry looked across at Mrs Gross.

'She swung the crucifix from the front-room window,' he said. 'She rang the bell with it, then tapped on the window to lure Malpas away from the door. That was why the second blow was harder than usual. The pole she was swinging was twenty-foot long. It's a wonder she didn't take the head clean off.'

Mrs Gross started to cross herself.

'I think,' said Henry, 'that she'd always used a figure of JC. Those were the marks of Christ's feet on the foreheads of the old ladies of Maple Drive. She left the blood on the cross where it was safe to do so. So that people could see.'

Norris was looking puzzled. The music started for the last hymn of the service. Low and solemn, the organ growled through the church as the congregation struggled to their feet for the last time.

'Why kill old ladies over sixty-five?' said the inspector.

'She's around that age!' said Henry.

Mrs Gross started to bellow out the opening verse of the hymn.

> Drop, drop, slow tears
> And bathe those beauteous feet . . .

'And,' said Henry, 'she is a very competitive old lady!'

I sang extra loud during 'Drop, Drop, Slow Tears'. I could see that idiot Farr looking at me and whispering with the stupid policeman. That was when I knew that he suspected me. Afterwards, when they took me to the station and I told them everything, he came with them. He looked proud and conceited. And his stupid wife looked almost pleased with him. Perhaps I have brought them together. People are never happier than when discussing someone else's suffering or someone else's evil. And of course Farr would be bound to suspect me because, inside, he is as evil and twisted as I am. He knows it. I can see it in his eyes. I didn't care. I just kept looking at the blood on His feet. And thinking it was real blood just like the blood He gave to ransom all these stupid, vulgar, narrow-minded people. Christ died for everyone apart from the population of Wimbledon. That's what I say. As I looked up at Malpas's blood, still fresh on Our Lord's feet, all I could think about was how . . . was how . . .

I'm still prettier than any of them. I may be sixty-five. I may be sixty-seven, for all you know. But I'm still the prettiest girl on the street.

Guy Fawkes Had It Coming

EVERYONE SAID the guy looked a lot like Henry.

There were those – Elinor, for example – who said it was a great improvement on Henry.

It had been made out of one of Henry's old suits, stuffed with copies of the *Independent on Sunday* (the only newspaper Elinor would have in the house). It had been given a pair of Henry's most comfortable cast-off shoes.

It had, thought Henry morosely as he humped it into the wheel-barrow, been given a rather better deal than Henry all round. It had got a fairly clean white shirt, a rather daring tie (that Elinor had said did not suit Henry) and on top of its muslin head packed with straw was Henry's father's Homburg hat.

Henry had kept his father's hat and his father's glasses after Mr Farr Senior had been stabbed to death by one of the staff at the school of which he was headmaster.

He had, in the first flush of grief, often taken out Norman's spectacles and twisted them between his fingers. They were in those days still marked with his father's sweat – on one of the lenses was the clear mark of a thumb.

'You never liked the old toad!' Elinor had said, when she came in one day to find Henry sobbing over his masculine parent's bifocals.

'That,' Henry had replied, 'is not the point.'

Mr Farr had, since his demise, acquired a number of qualities that no one had ever perceived in him when alive. He was suddenly, according to Henry's mother, no longer 'the old bastard', but 'wise, courteous, every inch a gentleman!' At his funeral, a glum humanist affair in South Wimbledon, the assistant headmaster of the school had suggested that Norman was 'a man of immense and tender sweetness who was now in Arthur's bosom'.

Henry, who was, according to Elinor, deeply homophobic, found this an offensive remark. 'Arthur's bosom!' he had growled on their way home. 'Immense and tender sweetness! Per-lease!'

But now, after his death, there was something tender and sweet about Norman. Secure in the knowledge that he was not about to leap out at you from behind the bathroom door, shouting at you to finish your homework, you could, Henry decided as he bumped the guy down the garden path, start to mourn the person he ought to have been rather than the person he actually was. He would never make an anti-Semitic remark again. He would never again come out with one of those brief, enigmatic phrases for which he was, in a small way, cele-brated in the Wimbledon area.

'Coons away!' for example, was the way he had greeted the news of the creation of the Independent Republic of Malawi.

'Micks ahoy!' was his response to the Sinn Fein electoral victories of the eighties. And perhaps most famously of all, shortly before his death, Mr Farr had registered Derek Walcott's winning of the Nobel Prize with the words, 'Wugga wugga wugga!' But he was dead now.

Now you could remember his good qualities. Or at least begin the arduous task of trying to work out what they were.

Maisie was waiting at the bottom of the garden. She was smiling beatifically. *Her period has started*, Henry thought. Maisie had, for as long as Henry had known her, been a bad-tempered girl. There were times when Henry thought the first fifteen years of her life had been nothing more than a decade and a half of pre-menstrual tension. Cer-tainly when she first started to perform, Elinor's joy was of the kind observable in newsreels of people celebrating the end of a major war.

'The woman's blood is flowing!' she had croaked as she thrust Maisie's undergarments in Henry's face. 'She is all woman now!'

And fifty per cent crocodile! muttered Henry to himself as he trudged upstairs.

During her periods, Maisie was, if anything, even more difficult to live with than she had been during the long slow crescendo to what Elinor called 'her womanly nature'. She sat on the most comfortable chair in the house, looking as if she were sitting on a clutch of eggs rather than bleeding quietly into a Tampax.

The brand names of possible varieties of sanitary towel were almost the only topic of conversation at the dinner table. Was it to be the ones you were supposed to wear because you didn't want to even know you were wearing them? Was it to be the more in-your-face style of sanitary towel, the no-nonsense chunk of absorbent material that reminded Henry of a nappy? In the end Maisie settled for the latest high-tech device – a thin strip of fabric in a modish plastic box called, simply, Paradise. It was, the advertisements claimed, more than just a towel. According to the box of instructions, once it was between your legs it allowed you to do almost anything up to and including defecation while playing squash, running through long grass and dictating memos to your secretary. It also made you good at tennis, swimming and horse-riding, and increased your attractiveness to the opposite sex three-hundredfold.

'It's a horrid looking guy!' said Maisie. 'It looks like you!'

'It has a slight touch of Mother about the eyes, don't you think?' said Henry, as he lowered the wheelbarrow to the ground.

Father and daughter looked at the bonfire. It was already about twenty feet in height. It looked, Henry thought, as if he were about to set light to the whole of Maple Drive rather than one measly old suit stuffed with newspaper.

'Your need to build up the fire high,' Elinor had said, 'is simply another way of saying *admire my penis*!'

'Admire my penis!' Henry had muttered to himself as he dragged more brushwood up the lawn, damp with the autumn rains.

He was not looking for a full scale *auto-da-fé* – although if a few of the neighbours were to fall into the flames during the course of the evening, Henry for one would not shed too many tears. But he hoped, at least, to inflict some mild damage to Elinor's garden. Since their brief sexual renaissance in September and October she had been neglecting him for several large-scale projects she had begun in the back garden. Every time he made a grab for her she would dodge, snicker and head for the builder's merchants in South Wimbledon to buy white sand, cement, bricks and other things that Henry was required to hump instead of Elinor.

As Maisie and he pulled the guy out of the wheelbarrow, Henry told himself not for the first time that his marriage was a bit like a badly run army. It could never consolidate any of its gains. One minute there you were thinking you were the marital equivalent of Samson Agonistes and were likely to be in calm of mind, all passion spent for the foreseeable future. Then she was back to throwing items of domestic equipment at you and telling you how you were crude, unfeeling and lacking in the things she needed for her womanly essence.

Henry spat glumly on what his wife of twenty-five years described as 'the patio'.

She had taken fifty or sixty bricks and buried them headfirst in the lawn underneath the apple tree. It reminded Henry of the kind of thing planted by the Germany army on Normandy beaches in 1944 in order to make life difficult for the Allied invaders. It had certainly stopped Henry in his tracks several times. He had once fallen headlong after tripping over it, and once he had hurt his thumb when trying to break bits of the thing off with a hammer. No one, so far, had sat on it.

'We should send it to your office,' said Maisie, as the two of them carried the guy towards the bonfire. 'No one would notice the difference!'

They had reached the outer fringes of the patio, where the bricks were so widely scattered and so deeply buried that the project that had deprived him of Elinor's attention for nearly four weeks resembled a fragment of a Roman road. Henry, who was walking backwards, caught his foot on one of the bricks and fell sideways. Maisie, who was holding the guy by the neck, was left clutching its severed head. She held it aloft. 'Behold!' she said. 'The head of Farr the traitor! So die all enemies of the Queen!'

'Shut up!' said Henry. 'Shut up!'

Maisie held the head close to hers. She shot out her lips like a shubunkin. 'Did 'oo lose 'ore head?' she said. 'Did 'oo have it chopped off?'

'We'll take him into the shed,' said Henry, 'and do a bit of facial surgery. I don't think I can take any more jokes about me being burned alive.'

He wasn't quite sure what to do about the guy's resemblance to its creator. He decided to go and look for some props. Maybe a moustache would do the trick.

Mrs Farr did not like to surprise her son.

She had always considered Henry to be a stolid, unimaginative boy. Unlike his younger brother, Nigel, who was always so vivacious (although she wished he would find a nice girl and settle down), Henry from a very early age made his preference for routine very clear. 'I like only red biscuits!' he said to Mrs de la Tour on his first morning at her day nursery. 'And only red drinks!'

He liked to be told what his birthday and Christmas presents were about six months in advance. He had never, even at the age of six months, shown any enthusiasm for peekaboo. Hide and seek reduced him rapidly to tears.

Mrs Farr's unscheduled arrival at Maple Drive was not deliberate. She had simply forgotten to tell Henry she was coming. The way she had forgotten the name of that thing with cherries in it that you ate out of pots. Yoghurt, that was the stuff. Yoghurt.

There were other things she had forgotten. She had not forgotten her age. She was eighty-seven and sound in wind and limb. But she had forgotten what you did when the Queen was introduced to you – from the waist or was it the knees? Curtsey, that was it. She had also forgotten, although she did not know this as she drove at speed up Wimbledon Hill towards Henry's house, to turn off the gas fire in her front room, to turn off the tap in the bathroom and to wear any tights or knickers.

'Bastard!' she growled at a motorist, who was like so many of them these days, driving straight at her on her side of the road. 'Bloody, bloody, buggering bastard!'

She had never sworn when her husband was alive, although often after he had had a hard day at South Wimbledon Grammar she had overheard him muttering words that she did not even like to acknowledge that she knew. But recently she had taken to profane language when talking to herself. She talked mainly to herself these days. There was no one else to talk to. Even that nice man, whatever his name was, who had taken her to the place where they show plants and you queue once a year near the King's Road, had died. Sylvester, that was it. He had such a lot of hair for a man of seventy-three.

There was another stupid policeman waving at her as she turned right off Wimbledon Hill into what she thought was Bracken Drive (although wasn't that in Wolverhampton?) but turned out to be someone's front garden. There was a man having tea on a small plastic table before she knocked it over and although she was hardly there for a moment, he seemed to be screaming something at her as she reversed into some rather badly kept geraniums and out into the path of a double-decker bus.

It was just as well it was still light. In the dark – and that would be coming soon – she couldn't see a thing. She might as well be driving blindfold. Perhaps she was.

The war seemed to have started again. Over on the Ridgway was an enormous explosion, very like the one that had ruined her and Norman's wedding reception in 1941. It was only when she struck off right, down something that turned out to be a road rather than anything else, that she remembered it was 5 November. What did you do on 5 November? Make resolutions, that was it. Or put out boxes or something. Whatever you did, it was unlikely that Henry would be doing it. He didn't like doing whatever it was you did on 5 November or on any of the other days, for that matter. He was a miserable bastard really, was Henry. Just like Norman.

Oh well, she thought, as she bounced off the kerb and found herself once again in that horrid little road they insisted on living in, at least she had brought those ginger biscuits that Henry liked and she didn't.

Mrs Farr looked up at the windows of her son's house. She could not see Elinor but the curtains twitched once or twice, reminding her that her daughter-in law might well be peering out from behind them. She would not put that past her. Hideous curtains, like knickers. Probably they were her knickers, she thought to herself, and then guffawed at the idea of Elinor walking around with her bottom wrapped in curtain material – it was big enough, God alone knew. Mrs Farr had always had a very small bottom. Even after she had had Henry, the doctor had said her bottom was her best feature – or something along those lines, anyway.

She would creep round and see what Elinor was doing in the garden. She might be able to steal a few cuttings.

The woman didn't know an acanthus from a cyenola, but she was trying. She bought it all, of course, from garden centres and then put it in pots and called that gardening. That wasn't gardening. Gardening was getting down on your hands and knees and weeding, weeding, weeding, until the blood came, but that wasn't good enough for them these days, it was out for the Italian meals and heigh ho for the videos, and the things they gave that child were disgusting – you could finance a small South American republic out of the clothes and compact discs she left all over her room that the Spanish woman whisked round for forty pounds a week. But she was trying. *Very* trying, said Mrs Farr to herself and cackled at her own joke.

The old lady levered herself out of the car. She put both feet on the ground, grasped her stick between both hands and, uttering a short prayer, made a shallow dive for the road. Somehow or other she ended up vertical. Well, almost vertical. Semi-circular, let us say. Her head was between her arthritic knees and her hands, without her really intending that they should do so, seemed to be trying to touch her swollen toes. She looked, she said to herself, like one of the witches in *Macbeth*.

She shook with laughter at this thought and nearly threw herself off balance.

'I can help you, madam?' said the German from up the road. The war was obviously over before it had even started. They had smashed our sea defences and were getting on with the job of digging out the quislings from the local population.

'No!' barked Mrs Farr.

They would have to complete the work of Nazification without her. There was another loud explosion from further down the road. It was getting dark, too – the sad, damp twilight of an English November. She would hardly be able to see the plants. If there were any plants. Of course, *Ancilla teneborosa* flowered in November (or was that a disease?), as did *Thurifer ingens*, which might well be a town in Dorset, except Mrs Klopstock had got her something like that as a present before she got cancer. Not that there was much chance that a woman as fat, ignorant and complacent as Elinor would have heard of *Thurifer ingens*, let alone have the gumption to grow it or spend the night in it or whatever you did to whatever it was. All she did was go to garden centres and buy plants in pots and call that gardening, when real gardening was getting down on your hands and knees and weeding, weeding, weeding, until the blood came.

She must learn to like her daughter-in-law. She wasn't all bad. At least she let her near the grandchildren. Mind you, that could be considered an act of hostility. There was only one of them, anyway, even if the girl could have been quite happily divided into three and still leave change. How did they let her get so fat?

She closed the gate carefully behind her and lurched off down the little path that led to the garden. To her right was a miserable bit of *Clarex populus* that she had given to Henry on his fortieth birthday and up ahead was a shape she could not recognize, although it turned out to be a door. Doors, doors, doors, she cackled to herself as, winching one leg after the other, she moved crabwise down the side passage.

At the end of the passage was a little wooden house. Sweet really, like the woodcutter's house in the fairy story. Her mother had told her a fairy story or two. But she had ended up, as had Angela de Freitas, who had been *stunning* at teacher training college, looking like one of Henry's early attempts at carpentry. Gnarled, as Norman used to say, wasn't in it.

She would go into the shed and have a little lie down. It had all been a bit much. She would have been much better off staying at home tucked up in those things that you slept in that Norman never made. Her Mummy would come and read a story about the pig who was eaten by the wolf. She was fond of pork.

Slowly, Mrs Farr put her hand up to the door. She noticed, with a surprise that was becoming usual, that her knuckles were the size of golf balls and her veins the size and consistency of telephone cables. Then, very cautiously and slowly – because in fairy stories, or that book Mr Baldwin liked, there were nasty things in woodsheds – she raised her hand to the thing whose name she had only just forgotten on the door and turned it in the direction opposite to which the hands of a clock go, although of course they don't, because you forgot to wind them.

The door swung open.

There, in the gloom of Henry's garden shed, sitting on the lawn-mower in *exactly* the way he used to do when he was alive (if you could call it living), was her husband. He seemed to be reading a copy of *The Times*, or rather sneering at it, which was absolutely typical of him.

He was doing several other very Norman-like things. He was wearing his hat indoors. That was very Norman. His moustache, as it had always done, looked as if he had just bought it from a joke-shop. He looked as if he had been stuffed with wet newspaper rather than created in the image of God the Father. He was also – and this was the thing that made her absolutely certain it was Norman, even though he had been carved up by that mad maths master at South Wimbledon Grammar School nearly ten years ago – ignoring her.

If the figure had leaped up and said, 'Hullo, my dear!' or 'I live on!' she might have suspected some trick but, as she often said to Henry, there was not much chance that death would have improved Norman's temper. This was him all right. Grumpy, almost totally silent, annoyed about something he refused to own up to that was probably sex, which they couldn't have in a shed anyway and even if they did was almost bound to be something of a disappointment, and generally looking like those things you put out for birds in fields. Scarecrows.

'Norman,' she said cautiously. Norman still did not look up.

'Norman, is that you?' His head seemed to turn slightly. Or perhaps it was just sagging.

'Norman!' It was absolutely typical of him to come back in a garden shed.

He had probably not died anyway, she decided as she peered into the gloom. She couldn't remember putting him into one of those expensive boxes with handles and trundling it up to be burned, which was another waste of money – leave me out for the vultures; there are plenty of them in Wimbledon.

People pretended to be dead all the time anyway, for tax purposes. You paid less tax when you were dead. You left your clothes on the beach and then hid under a name like Stonehouse. Or there was probably another woman, like Lord Lucan.

He was having an affair with someone, that was it. In the garden shed. Perfect. He was never a romantic person. Doing it in the garden shed was probably his idea of a good time and as it was usually over before it started, it probably gave you something to look at, all those folding chairs. Angry now, she slammed the door shut and looked round for Elinor.

Elinor knew about this. She probably engineered it. He was probably Humperdincking her. She wouldn't put it past the bastard.

'Bugger,' she grumbled to herself, as she walked away from the shed. 'Bugger, bugger, bugger!'

She would have to find a way of telling Henry what was going on. He was a pathetic creature really, but that was no reason to let Elinor walk all over him with those boots with little round things on the sole. Unless she wasn't having an affair with him but hiding him from her husband's mother. On balance, Mrs Farr decided that that was more probable and less forgivable than her bonking him.

It was as well, she decided, she had got there when she did. She hobbled off to see if Elinor had made any basic mistakes in the herb garden.

Elinor saw her mother-in-law talking to herself at the bottom of the garden.

Mothers, she knew from reading *Mothers Not Fathers* by Julia Kreitzmann, Eleanor Stiffens and Julie Weinberger of the University of Southern California, were good. If we had had less fathers and more mothers, we would be a lot further ahead.

Mrs Farr was a mother. She was mother to Henry. She was also (God help her) mother to Nigel Farr. When they were dishing out medals in the motherhood department, Mrs Farr should qualify for the equivalent of the Victoria Cross.

Why, then, every time she opened Elinor's fridge, did Elinor feel the desire to brain her with a frying pan? Why, every time Mrs Farr hobbled over to the sink, rolled up her sleeves in that offensively public manner and said 'Righty ho! I'll wash!' did Elinor dream of flipping open the kitchen scissors and burying one arm of them in the old bat's neck?

Mrs Farr was bending over one of her flowers. She seemed to be prodding it with her stick. How long had she been here? How long did she intend staying? Surely Henry hadn't invited her?

Didn't Eleanor Stiffens have something to say about this?

Deformed by patriarchy, women of our mothers' generation slaved for men. They wore their names, carried their children and dreamed their dreams rather than their own. They became men.

Mrs Farr was what she might have become. Back there in 1940, with no therapy, no women's groups to speak of and hardly enough feminist texts to go round, British women had been so twisted out of shape that it was impossible for them to ever grasp their potential for change. They were almost totally unaware of their video-spatial abilities. They were –

'Hullo, dear!' called Mrs Farr, as she hobbled back down the garden. 'Am I too late for lunch?'

It was nearly five o'clock, thought Elinor grimly. Where did the old rat think she was – on a transatlantic flight?

It was comforting to think, however, that none of this was her fault. It was patriarchy – or, to be more specific, Norman Ferdinand Farr, who had produced this monster, this half woman, this gnarled, bearded monstrosity, who was even now heaving herself up the steps from the lawn and, with the grim determination of an experienced sailor tacking into a gale, bearing down on Elinor's french windows.

'Or,' said Mrs Farr, as Elinor opened the doors and her mother-in-law lurched into the dining area, 'did you ask me for tea? I forget things, you know.'

Elinor knew. Not that the old cow forgot things like the fact that no one had cleaned the bath at 54 Maple Drive, or that Henry never had enough clean shirts. She forgot things like Maisie's birthday or Elinor's mother's name.

'It's bonfire night!' said Elinor. 'We're going to have a bonfire!'

'Why are you going to do that?' said Mrs Farr.

'Because it's bonfire night!' said Elinor, slowly and clearly. It was best, she had decided, to treat the old dragon as if she was still in primary school. Her mother-in-law snorted contemptuously.

'We're going to let off fireworks and have a bonfire,' said Elinor, even more slowly and clearly, 'because of Guy Fawkes!'

'Who's he?' said Mrs Farr.

'He tried to blow up the Houses of Parliament in 1606. I think it was 1606. Anyway I *think* he tried to blow up the Houses of Parliament. There is some doubt about it.'

Mrs Farr was looking puzzled. For once, Elinor thought, this was a not unreasonable reaction. The more she tried to explain what they were about to do in the back garden, the more ludicrous it sounded.

'And so we make a guy out of straw and burn it every year on a bonfire. To celebrate the fact that we're not Catholics. On 5 November.'

Mrs Farr lowered her chin and looked at her daughter-in-law suspiciously. *Are you*, her expression seemed to say, *taking the piss?*

'I don't agree with it,' said Elinor, 'but it's nice for the children.'

'Burning someone? Nice for the children?'

Elinor decided to abandon this conversation. 'You can watch it from inside,' said Elinor. 'It can be upsetting. When we put him on the bonfire we've put bangers in his head so that his head will explode. He's in the shed at the moment.'

A look of sheer terror crossed Mrs Farr's face as her daughter-in-law said this. 'Poor Norman,' she said, 'Poor, poor Norman!'

Why was she dragging Henry's father into this? The best thing to do was to get the senile old cow into a chair with a cup of tea. 'Norman – ' began Elinor, but mention of the man's name set her mother-in-law off again. She started to pluck at Elinor's sleeve pathetically.

'Why do you want to make his head explode?' she said. 'What has he ever done to you?'

'He tried to blow up the Houses of Parliament!' said Elinor.

'Norman would never do a thing like that!' said Mrs Farr. 'He was a very law-abiding man.'

Elinor pushed Henry's mother towards the sofa. 'I'll get you a gin and tonic!' she said.

The best thing to do was to make her drunk. Elinor might well have a large one at the same time. The thought of Mr Farr Senior was bringing back a great many unpleasant memories. The day she first went into his sitting room and he barked at her, 'Stand in the light, girl! Let's have a look at you!' Really, there was no wonder that poor Henry was as inadequate as he was with a father like that.

She reached into the cupboard and thought about Norman Farr. She thought about the afternoon he stood under the window of the hotel bedroom she was sharing with Henry in the South of France and yelled at his youngest son Nigel, 'He is fucking the bloody woman in there! He is fucking her!' She was thinking about that afternoon as she poured two gin and tonics. And at the same moment, Henry emerged from the garden shed with Norman under his arm.

Except that it wasn't Norman, of course. It was the guy, now wearing not only Norman's hat but also his glasses and a fair imitation of his moustache. Its head was over Henry's left shoulder. Someone had also given it a rubber nose that was the living image of the stabbed headmaster's. Presumably this was what the old bat was on about. It had flashes of Henry in its chin (or lack of one) and in the slight look of smugness around the eyes, but now it was more or less one hundred per cent Norman Farr, BA Oxon, the man who had once referred to Elinor, again in her hearing, as 'that slut'.

Some devil took hold of Elinor as, three or four feet to her left, Mrs Farr started to have some kind of seizure.

'He's taking him down the garden!' she said.

'Yes,' said Elinor with undisguised pleasure. 'And soon he'll be burning away nicely on the bonfire!'

Mrs Farr started to whimper.

'Bang, he'll go!' said Elinor as Henry, in the gloom of the garden, started to haul the guy on to the brushwood. 'Bang, bang, bang, bang, bang!'

She handed her mother-in-law her drink. Mrs Farr was pressing her nose to the glass, trying to see into the shadows. Elinor heard the doorbell ring.

'And when he's all burned up there'll be absolutely nothing left of him!' said Elinor with malicious glee. 'It'll be spread all over the garden! You'll be lucky if you get a piece of his shoes!'

Something was wrong with the bonfire.

'It's because it's green wood!' said Roland Devereux, the youth who had the dubious distinction of being James Seebohm's best friend.

'I've soaked it in kerosene!' said Henry. He hadn't really been allowed to soak it. Every time he got near it with the can, Elinor grabbed his arm and started muttering about the fire brigade. As a result the guy, still deep in his copy of *The Times*, was sitting just above head height in billowing clouds of whitish smoke. Which gave him an even more eerily human appearance.

Each time the smoke cleared he seemed to be in a new attitude, possibly because Henry's intensive work on him in the shed had made him bend and buckle in too many places to keep him stable. At one moment he seemed to be gargling. At the next he was leaning to his left. Then he appeared to be saluting. At one point Henry could have sworn he was masturbating vigorously.

'Great party, Mr Farr!' said James Seebohm. He was drinking Strongbow cider out of a can. He looked as if he was going to be sick at any moment. Mandy Makepeace had already been sick over by the clematis. Maisie did not look too healthy.

'Good, James!' said Henry. 'What time are you leaving?'

Seebohm laughed. 'You're so *funny*, Mr Farr!' he said, in a newly acquired working-class accent. 'All of Mazza's friends think you're *such* a laugh!'

His friend Roland seemed to find this remark amusing. He, too, held a can of Strongbow about six inches above his face and allowed the liquid to trickle down towards his mouth. All of Maisie's friends seemed to find glasses effeminate.

'Nutter!' said Devereux.

'We'll soon get a good fire blazing,' said Henry, 'and then we can set light to Roland's hair!'

A little away from the firelight, Henry's mother had one hand leaning on her stick and was staring into the smoke. Something about the guy seemed to bother her. Henry couldn't think what it might be. It didn't look like him any more. It looked like someone he vaguely remembered, but he couldn't have said who. Best to get on with things.

When Elinor wasn't looking, Henry tipped some more kerosene on to the brushwood and fresh tongues of flame licked up through the dark sticks around the guy. When she saw this Mrs Farr started to weave her way towards the bonfire. 'Norman!' she called, 'Norman! Norman!'

Elinor started to laugh crazily. She seemed rather drunk. 'She thinks it's Norm!' she said. 'She thinks we're burning the old bastard!'

Henry looked at his creation again. He saw with sudden, awful clarity what she meant. The thing didn't just look like Norman. It *was* Norman. And he hadn't seen it. Not only did you turn into your old man without being aware of the fact, it would seem that even your first attempts at figurative art were doomed to bear his features. There was no escape. Now he saw it, he couldn't understand why it hadn't been clear earlier. That nose! That moustache!

Henry's mother, who had never been a religious woman, seemed keen on committing suttee. She was headed for the flames, now writhing up at the darkened sky. Elinor seemed to be trying to stop her.

'Leave me alone!' yelled Mrs Farr, belabouring her daughter-in-law with her stick. 'Murder! Murderer! You've put bangers in his poor old head!'

It was clearly time for Henry to do something. Over towards the Common a rocket climbed into the sky, brushing the night with a comma of sparks. Further towards the town another one burst into a shower of what looked like coloured sweets.

Henry went to the back of the fire and, putting one hand up to the platform on which the guy was resting, pulled it from behind. It fell back into his arms. The straw was warm and the figure felt as if it was quick with life. Its left foot was smoking. Henry started to beat it out savagely.

'We must burn him!' Elinor was yelling.

'Run!' shouted his mother. 'Run with Daddy!'

Henry looked down at the cradled image of Norman Farr. Perhaps this was what had fucked him up. Norman Ferdinand Farr. Fucked him up and loved him at the same time. That was the really low trick, wasn't it? Because as he walked round the side of the fire, the guy in his arms, Henry found himself thinking about his father and not every thought was a grotesque or a comic one.

He seemed to be standing next to Elinor. His left hand was under the head. He readjusted Norman's Homburg which had slipped down over his eyes. 'I loved my father very much!' he found himself saying.

'My arse you did!' said Elinor.

Henry was thinking about walking to Cranborne School with his hand in his father's. For some reason, as they crossed Wimbledon Hill, his dad would always start singing, 'Hold my hand . . . I'm a stranger in paradise . . .' *I am like I am because of him. He has still got something to say to me.*

Mr Farr Senior had never said much to his family when he was alive. On one occasion the only remark he had uttered between three o'clock on 13 December and the morning of 1 January was, 'I don't like Christmas.' Once on a six-hour journey to the Lake District in the family car, the only thing he had said was, 'Wordsworth was basically a homosexual.'

But there was something he had said. Once. On a night like this, with darkness almost palpable in the suburban gardens and the rockets climbing youthfully into the sky. On a 5 November a long, long time ago. *If I could understand what it was between me and him, maybe I could make a start on things with Elinor.*

'Norman!' called Mrs Farr. 'Norman! Don't go, Norman!'

Maisie, who had collapsed on to the wet lawn with Seebohm, climbed wearily to her feet. 'Granny's gone mad!' she said.

Henry started off down the lawn towards the house.

'Where are you taking him?' shouted Elinor.

'To a place of safety, you wicked, wicked woman!' yelled Mrs Farr.

Elinor started after him. So, after a while, did Maisie. And so, after an even longer while, did Mrs Farr. And Henry was thinking about other things his father had done and said, and looking for that one remark (there is always one) that promised to explain everything.

It wasn't 'You're not made of sugar, boy!', which Mr Farr had growled one night when he was drying Henry after his bath. It wasn't 'There is going to be a war!', which he had come out with in the kitchen on the day the Berlin Wall went up. Neither was it 'I have put the skids under the pandit!', which was how he announced to his family that he was about to dismiss the incompetent Indian mathematics master who later stabbed him to death. It was . . .

What was it?

Elinor was running now, as Henry carried the guy up Maple Drive. So was Maisie. And Henry was running too, the way he had run when a schoolboy, his feet slapping the pavement, his heart banging against his ribs, all of him flushed with the simple, animal joy of being alive.

He ran out on to the hill and towards the Common. He didn't stop until there was no one following him. Until there was just him and the smouldering guy, alone on the wet grass. *Alone with Norman*, he said to himself and giggled. It was only as he laughed he realized that, when he did so, he made a sound just like his father. The rockets were still going up into the blackness. In front of one of the large gardens of the large houses on Parkside he could see a huge Catherine wheel spinning insanely on what appeared to be an untenanted gate.

Henry sat Norman on the rough grass. Miraculously, Mr Farr's hat, although at a rakish angle, was still on his head. Henry still had the can of kerosene in his right hand.

He could burn him. Burn him again. The poor old bastard had been burned once. Why not again? No one had given a stuff about him when he was alive and no one gave a stuff about him now he was dead. *My story, Dad*, thought Henry.

Henry, who was, he now realized, rather drunk, felt a sudden urge to burst into tears. Instead he sprinkled kerosene on his father's legs and chest and lit the right toe. The fire gobbled up Mr Farr's calf thirstily, as if it had been waiting for this, then rose swiftly into his chest and rose through his shoulders towards his head, where lay the twelve firecrackers, the fifteen bangers and the three sticks of Java rain left over from last year. It was not until the flames were almost to his father's chin that Henry remembered what Norman had said to him, one 5 November, a long, long time ago. And it seemed to him – he could not have said why – to explain just about everything: 'Guy Fawkes had it coming.'

That was it. *Guy Fawkes had it coming*. And, as he found his way to the phrase, the head of something that was very like his father exploded outwards into the darkness. Henry, who had dropped to the ground like a soldier under bombardment, reached out and found he was holding something he thought he recognized. His father's glasses. He put them on the bridge of his nose, rolled over on to his back and looked through them at the November sky to see if, by any chance, the stars should look any clearer.

Lay Down Your Sweet Head but Not Here

EVEN THOUGH there was light, of a kind, visible through the curtains, Henry had a nasty feeling that there was quite a lot of Christmas morning left. Down below he could hear Elinor shouting at the turkey. Henry turned over on his side and closed his eyes.

The year had not really given him any serious grounds for optimism. So why should he imagine he was going to get out of sitting down to lunch with his daughter, his wife, her mother, *his* mother, his brother, his brother's lover and their dog? And why should he or anyone else imagine that being blind drunk and wearing paper hats was going to make the occasion any more bearable?

He opened one eye. Elinor stopped shouting at the turkey and shouted up at him.

'They'll be here any minute! Henry!'

'Coming!'

He rolled over on to his back. Julia Lewis, the podiatrist from the next road, had sent out a chain letter telling all those who were interested what she and her family had been up to during the year.

The children are blooming! Gilbert has attained a place at the University of Central Lancashire, while our two eldest daughters, Terry and Juliet, continue to run a Vegan Centre in East Sheen!

He shuddered slightly as he tried to imagine what a chain letter detailing the Farr family's exploits would look like.

Henry has sunk lower and lower in all our estimations and his frequent moods of self-pity have often made it hard for Maisie and me to conceal our disgust. Maisie herself has been rejected by the one boy in the whole of South West London who was small enough, ugly enough and insecure enough to allow himself to be seen in public with her.

He thought bitterly of Seebohm's letter to his daughter, a document that two weeks ago Elinor had steamed open and read, hours before Maisie was awake.

I just can't hack it, Mais! You are just too *big* for me to handle. Your demands swamp me. I want to see other people. And I want you to see other people. But not necessarily the same people, if you see what I mean . . .

The tone of the letter was, in the main, cravenly submissive but, from time to time, there were flashes of pure sadistic pleasure observable in Seebohm's prose.

I need someone glorious, someone free and bright and special and you are just not that person, amazing though you are in many ways . . .

As Henry struggled into his trousers he thought about Mr and Mrs Seebohm. They would hardly be able to wipe the look of pleasure off their faces. They had never thought Henry's daughter was good enough for their son and, though he had a sneaking feeling they might be right, he would have preferred Maisie to have made the first move.

He lurched suddenly to the right and his foot encountered a small glass ball. Downstairs Elinor had started to shout at the potatoes. Scrooge, he decided, as he pulled on his ugliest jersey, was a much maligned man.

'Henry!' yelled Elinor from the kitchen. 'Come down here! We're going to open a present!'

Henry was giving Elinor a face flannel. He had still not decided whether to wrap it or to leave it around the washbasin for a few days and not make the transfer of ownership formally until the thing had been broken in. He was particularly pleased with his present for Nigel, a paperback edition of *Our Lady of the Flowers*, which he had taken off the shelves in Elinor's room and wrapped in brown paper late last night.

Henry hated buying presents. As he was fond of telling his family, no one should give presents to anyone, especially not at Christmas. Every year, right up until the day itself, he maintained the fiction that he had not bought presents for anyone and that he expected none himself.

He always gave in, of course. And after he had bought the damned things, he hated them even more. When the time came to pass them over, inexpertly wrapped in paper stolen from Elinor, he hated them so much that there ought to have been some pleasure in having the things taken off one's hands. But then there were the awful false smiles and elaborate phoney surprise that your victim really *hadn't* expected you to get them the things they had written down on some stupid piece of paper three weeks previously. And, almost immediately after that, was the more or less public acknowledgement that they didn't, of course, *need* the ivory backscratcher or the horrible silk scarf or the amazingly expensive personal organizer because, if we were truthful about it, everybody in Wimbledon had more than enough of everything.

He went through to the front bedroom and looked over Maple Drive. The houses had that abandoned look familiar from other public holidays. There were hardly any cars in the street. It was a pity that Mr and Mrs Is the Mitsubishi Scratched Yet? hadn't taken their Mitsubishi to the country where, with any luck, some local yokel would be even now reversing his tractor into it. With the meek and poor and lowly, eh? Fat bloody chance, mate.

'I'm going to have a glass of champagne!' Elinor, who hardly touched alcohol during the rest of the year, seemed to think it was necessary to start drinking early on Christmas Day. By eleven she would have become quarrelsome. Just in time for brother Nigel and his new Turkish boyfriend, Jondon.

'I hate Christmas!' said Henry to the empty street. 'I fucking hate it!'

Slightly comforted by speaking his thoughts aloud, he went down the stairs. Elinor had put some Christmas carols on the CD player and the son of some over-protective stockbroker was warbling on about how the infant child had come to save the world. Oh yeah? muttered Henry to himself as he headed for the kitchen. Well, if he did come to save the world, he is taking his fucking time about it.

Elinor turned on him immediately he came into the kitchen. She said something long, involved and hostile about sprouts and then held a large plastic bag out at him. 'Take that out the front, anyway!' she said. 'If you think you can manage it. If your mother sees it, we shall have the oh dear, oh dear, it's a *plastic bag* speech, and we never had *plastic bags*. We ate all the rubbish and licked the floor clean and we – '

Henry left the room in the middle of this speech. She was peaking early this year.

There was something calming about the thought that in less than a minute he would be outside, rather than inside, 54 Maple Drive. Outside wasn't the Caribbean or the Swiss Alps or the south of France, but it was a step in the right direction. Henry pulled back the door.

The first thing he noticed was that it was beginning to snow. It had started with the surprising shyness of all snow. There was no wind and the white flakes seemed to hang in the grey day, sewn into the gloom like jewels.

The second thing he noticed was that there was a tortoise walking down the middle of the road.

It wasn't a very big tortoise. But it obviously had a clear idea of where it was going. It moved each gnarled, rubbery stump of a leg and twisted its neck to left and right with what, in a tortoise anyway, looked dangerously like urgency. Perhaps it was trying to get back to its box. Weren't tortoises supposed to go to sleep from September to April?

As Henry walked out into the street to pick it up he remembered that, asleep or awake, tortoises were now not supposed to be in England at all. Wasn't there a world shortage of tortoises? Hadn't they all been so abused by the English that, for their own good, they had been told to stay on Mauritius or Honolulu or wherever they usually dragged out their long and uneventful lives?

He bent over the little creature, and its head snaked round in his direction. It stopped, gave him one appraising glance from its beady eyes and then slowly withdrew its head and feet into its shell. It lay quite still in the middle of the road.

'I know just how you feel, mate!' said Henry.

Mrs Farr had not got Henry a present. There was no point in buying him anything. He just grunted like a pig when you gave him things. She had thought of getting him a face flannel as a joke and then she had thought of getting him a bottle of wine, but what was the point of buying him wine? He would only drink it. He didn't take care of things. One year she had bought him Stilton cheese and port in a beautiful box and he had just yanked the thing open and stuffed it all down his face right in front of her, like a Goth or a Vandal or something.

Elinor and that ridiculous mother of hers had rung her and they had all agreed not to give Henry anything. Mrs Farr Senior could no longer remember who had suggested the idea, but if it had been her, she was prepared to stand by her decision. He was such a misery these days it would serve him right. Nigel and that queer he hung around with for some reason had agreed not to give him anything either. Maisie had resisted the idea at first but, as she had pointed out to her paternal grandmother, 'He moans so much at Christmas he has it coming!' The trouble was, of course, that Elinor had not had the guts to tell him yet. And the mother was a pathetic specimen, who never told anyone anything apart from what she had done in the War Office or wherever she had worked – she hadn't done anything with her life, whereas Mrs Farr had been president of something. If she concentrated hard she might be able to remember what it was. Townswomen's Guild. Something like that although, if she was truthful about it, it had been a complete waste of time and she only went for the cakes which were delicious. Like mother like daughter. Elinor had never known how to manage him. She shouted at him, which was stupid because when you shouted at him he just drew in his head like a tortoise and –

Mrs Farr put her foot suddenly on the brake and felt herself being propelled quite fast towards the windscreen. Something which she thought might be a mugger in the back but turned out to be a seatbelt slammed her back into the upholstery as she realized she was looking at Henry and he was holding up a tortoise. Talk of the devil and he appears. What was he doing with a tortoise? She had given him a tortoise when he was ten and he had only cried!

Had he cried? Something had happened with the tortoise, if only she could remember what it was! And now here it was again. It was cruel to give tortoises, really. They didn't like people. They weren't, as far as she could tell, wild about other tortoises.

Elinor had probably cheated and given it to him. That was entirely typical of the woman. She was sly beyond belief. Not that she knew how to look after him. She couldn't wash a dish as far as Mrs Farr could see, but she made enough fuss about it and it would just suit her to bring out a tortoise when Granny the Bad turned up with bugger all for him so they could all agree how mean she was. The mother had probably bought him a train set although he was a bit old for train sets, not that that would stop her with her lipstick like a tart's.

'Mum!' Henry was saying in the sort of way she could remember talking to her mother when the poor old trout was senile. 'Mum! Look what I've found!'

Still not sure what Elinor and her mother might be up to, Mrs Farr did not respond to this. Instead she drove at speed towards what looked like a safe patch of kerb, mounted the pavement and found herself in the garden of that ridiculous man who lived opposite but was, thanks be to God, in Zimbabwe on some conference, not that his front lawn was anything to write home about and might well be improved by a few tyre marks.

Christmas was a time for settling old scores and she was going to have a word or two to say to her daughter-in-law and her apology of a mother. No one knows about Henry apart from me, she said to herself as, tortoise in hand, her eldest son came over towards the car. Before the day is over we are going to have some home truths some of us would rather not face with our nice little trips to garden centres and our bottle of wine and our daughters who are clearly on the pill or whatever they use these days when they do it, if they do it.

Henry was looking in at her window. He looked just the way he did when he first went to primary school. As if he was going to burst into tears at any moment. Christmas always made him feel like that. Suddenly he looked like her father, who had been dead for over fifty years and she smiled up at him like a little girl, the way she had smiled at Dr Lewis (and he had been a *marvellous* surgeon, everyone agreed), as she said, 'Happy Christmas, darling!'

Henry put the tortoise in a box in the kitchen. It did not remove any part of itself from its shell, even when he held it up at eye level and, peering into the dark hole that contained its saurian head, remarked, 'Come on, boy! Tell us your troubles!'

Maisie said she thought it had probably died of fright immediately it had caught sight of Henry. 'Put the box on its side!' said Maisie. 'In case it wants to get out and run around!'

Henry pointed out that tortoises did not run around, especially in the middle of December. 'The best thing we can hope for,' he said, 'is that it gets off to sleep. Then we can ring the RSPCA.'

Maisie said she had never seen Henry be so concerned about any living creature before. She suggested they call the tortoise Henry. 'You could keep it!' she said, in an openly satirical manner. 'It would be something to love!'

Elinor looked rapidly at her daughter, who, as always, seemed to sense the criticism almost as it rose through her mother's conscious-ness. As soon as Elinor had seen Henry bring the little creature in, as pleased and proud as a small boy with a new puppy, she had regretted that that witch-like mother of his had talked her into forgetting his present. It hadn't always been an easy year. There had been times, as there always were with Henry, when she had seriously thought of running him through with a carving knife, or at very least getting a tough lawyer on to him as soon as possible; but now, only a week away from the end of another year, she wanted to end the twelve months on a note of optimism.

Things could get better next year.

As she thought this, as if in mockery of such a vain hope, the door-bell rang. Through the glass panel of the front door she saw the unmistakable shapes of Nigel Farr, her mother and a gigantic, muscular figure that could only be Henry's brother's new Turkish lover, Jondon. Something behind them that could only be Buster barked twice.

'I wonder what he's dragged in this time!' said Nigel's mother, peering suspiciously at her younger son and his newly acquired, twenty-nine-year-old physical-training instructor. The happy couple, heads held high and wearing what looked like identical clothes, marched into Henry's living room.

Elinor's mother gave Henry a broad wink. 'The boys are here!' she said in an offensively suggestive tone. Buster made for the sofa, leaped up on to it, looked proudly round at the assembled company and farted loudly.

'Good boy!' said Nigel.

It was twelve o'clock. Some time between now and the end of the afternoon, Nigel would almost certainly get to his feet and tell anyone who was listening that he was glad to be gay. He might, as he had done at a wine and cheese party in 1991, go on to describe in great detail exactly what he and his lovers got up to. The question facing Henry was whether to use some carefully placed homophobic remark in order to provoke him into going through this routine before the neighbours arrived, or whether to hope that he could hang on until after they had left. The thought of Is the Mitsubishi Scratched Yet?, Mr Gross, the retired architect (whom Elinor had asked in because 'Ever since his wife has been in Broadmoor he looks so lost'), not to mention Gunther, Nazi Who Escaped Justice at Nuremberg, having to listen to a detailed, slightly complacent description of the joys of fellatio did not, to Henry, seem to promise an easy Christmas morning.

'We're not giving you presents this year, Hen,' said his brother, 'because you're such a miserable bastard! So we hope you haven't given us any!'

Henry looked up at Elinor. She looked away. Mrs Farr Senior, too, looked suddenly guilty. Maisie shifted from foot to foot and started to say something about how Christmas was too commercialized and she for one thought that what Henry had maintained for the last three Decembers was perfectly correct. Scrooge had a lot going for him, she said. It was clear that Nigel was speaking for everyone in the room. Henry felt suddenly as if he was going to burst into tears. It was not unsatisfying playing Scrooge, but it rather lost its charm when other people started to do it to you.

And what about the face flannel, for God's sake! Or the copy of *Your Garden through the Year* he had bought for his mother at a cost of nearly twelve pounds! Or the half bottle of gin he had bought for Maisie or the gift-wrapped paperback edition of *Our Lady of the Flowers* he had bothered to lift off the shelves for that selfish little shirt-lifting brother of his!

Henry tried to look as if this was what he had wanted to happen. If they wanted Scrooge, they would get Scrooge. He opened the bottle of champagne and at the bottom of his glass placed two fingers of brandy. By the end of the afternoon, if he drank as much as he planned to drink as fast as he intended to drink it, he was going to make Scrooge look like Mary Poppins.

The front door bell rang again. Out in the hall, as he poured glasses of champagne, Henry heard Is the Mitsubishi Scratched Yet? apologizing for bringing Norbert DuCane, the Man Who Loves Shopping. Behind him he heard Mr Gross, the retired architect.

'I saw Gwendolen last week!' he said. 'She was in fine form. She talks of returning to the community very soon. She wants to help people!'

There was a muttering from Elinor, then the psychopath's husband added, 'Broadmoor is a wonderful place in many ways!'

Indeed, thought Henry, and if today goes on the way it has started, I may find myself doing something that earns me a place there sooner than any of you think.

It was five o'clock. The Farr family were halfway through lunch. Elinor had gone out to the kitchen to fetch the Christmas pudding. The neighbours had left only at three, having drunk ten bottles of champagne between them. Mr Gross had burst into tears and had had to be taken home by Norbert DuCane. Nazi Who Escaped Justice at Nuremberg had reminded everyone in the room that he was only nine when Hitler came to power ('Not that that means he had clean hands,' as Henry had observed to Elinor's mother.) Esmond Brice had dropped round with Lingalonga Boccherini, the relict of Jungian Analyst Beyond the Reach of Winebox, and had handed Elinor a large sheet of brown paper on which someone had stuck several ears of corn. 'It's a collage for you, Elinor!' Lingalonga had said, gazing at Brice in a way that suggested that the therapist was once again engaged in intimacy with a local mother.

It was dark outside. Henry was very, very drunk. Buster had defecated in the hall and had been sent out to sit in the car. Nigel and Jondon seemed to have left the table and were kissing on the sofa. Every so often Henry's mother would look over at them, snort to herself and mutter, 'Showing off,' as she had done when Nigel had come out to Gunther, Norbert DuCane, Man Who Loves Shopping, and to Brice (who had left him his business card).

The floor was piled high with wrapping paper. Everyone had given everyone else presents. Maisie had given her mother a scarf. Each granny had given the other granny something from the Body Shop. Neither granny seemed very pleased with the exchange. Elinor had given Maisie a blouse, some jewellery and a copy of the collected works of Gerard Manley Hopkins. There were other presents – Jondon had given Nigel a book about the SAS and Elinor's mother had given her daughter a plant, which Elinor had described in tones of amazing insincerity as 'lovely'. So many things had been exchanged between so many different people that Henry had lost track of the afternoon's transactions. The act of giving had created brief, weird flashes of coupledom in the room, as when Nigel presented Maisie with a torch or Maisie gave Jondon a pair of socks.

But no one had given Henry anything.

No one loves me, he thought to himself, everyone hates me. I'm on my own. It would serve them right if I died right here, over the Christmas lunch. It would mark a fitting end to a year in which once again I have failed, failed utterly. I am in the wrong place at the wrong time. If I had been born in another place or at another time I might have been Louis Pasteur or Goethe or Chopin. But what chance did I stand being born in Wimbledon and being called (here he looked at his mother bitterly) Henry Farr?

Elinor came round the door carrying an object about the size of a cannonball. It was decorated with currants, holly and icing-sugar, and as the group applauded his wife set light to it and placed it triumphantly in the middle of the table.

'Merry Christmas!' said Nigel, picking some of the hairs from Jondon's moustache out of his teeth.

'Merry Christmas!' said Mrs Farr Senior darkly, as she glared over in their direction. She reached out for a glass of white wine. 'I miss Norman!' she said.

Henry put his head in his hands. 'I miss Norman!' he said.

Then he remembered the tortoise. He would go and talk to the tortoise. Like him, the tortoise was alone in the world. Like him, the tortoise was in the wrong place at the wrong time. He, too, should have been in Lanzarote or Tunis or wherever tortoises came from. Like him, the tortoise had retreated from the world and, like him, the tortoise had been despised and put in a box with straw, along with the baby Jesus and the ox and the ass and all the rest of the no-hopers.

He really was amazingly pissed. He would be lucky if he made it through the pudding and the mince pies and the chocolates and coffee and brandy. Oh my Christ, thought Henry, this is all I need – to be sick all over the Christmas lunch. Although it would serve the bastards right. No presents. Serve the bastards right. If you think you're getting a face flannel out of me, you have another think coming, sunshine. I'm going to talk to the tortoise.

He seemed to be crawling on his hands and knees across the floor towards the box in which the little creature lay. Just as the Wise Men had knelt before the tortoise all those years ago in Bethlehem, now he would kneel before it and ask it why the world was such a horrible place and why no one had given him anything. And, come to that, what the little bastard was doing crawling down the middle of Maple Drive on 25 December.

'Henry!' said Elinor sharply. 'What are you doing?'

'Tortoise . . .' said Henry. 'Tortoise!'

He heard Mrs Farr Senior snort with irritation. 'He's only showing off,' she said, 'pay no attention. And you two boys stop messing about in the sofa and come and have pudding. She's made a lovely pudding!'

'She has,' said Elinor's mother. 'She's made a lovely pudding!' She patted her curls and stared round at the rest of the dinner table as if daring them to contradict her opinion of her daughter's cooking. 'She makes a wonderful pudding,' she said. 'I don't know why, but she does!'

Normally a remark of this kind would have provoked her daughter into at very least a bark of displeasure, but clearly Elinor, like everyone else around the table apart from Henry, was yielding to the spirit of Christmas. 'It's only a pudding!' she said. 'I try!'

Mrs Farr Senior gulped more wine. 'You do,' she said with what to the superficial observer looked like generosity. 'You're marvellous with your puddings. And your garden. Even if it isn't my way to buy so much, I think you're marvellous!'

Elinor poured champagne down her throat as if in an attempt to quench an unseen fire within her. 'You're marvellous too, Jenny!' she said, through an only-just-achieved smile. Henry, now on his knees in front of the tortoise's box, felt the familiar chill he always experienced when his wife called his mother by her Christian name.

'You're . . .' Elinor searched desperately for one of her mother-in-law's positive qualities, as Jondon and Nigel, hand in hand, returned to the table and pushed their plates forward for pudding. 'You're still here!' she concluded.

Everyone, apart from Henry, laughed uproariously.

He was looking into the tortoise's box. It had buried itself so deeply in the straw that he could no longer see it. Hesitantly he put his right hand in after it. Did tortoises bite? *I don't care*, thought Henry, *I don't care if it gnaws me to death! I hate my life!*

'Come along, Henry!' said his mother. 'Jondon and Nigel are eating up. You come to the table and eat up the way they're eating up!'

Henry put his hand further into the box. As far as he could tell, it appeared to be empty. He looked back up at the table. Maisie was forking a mouthful of pudding into her face. How could she, he thought, how could any of them have done what they had done? How could they have forgotten that Christmas is a time for reconciliation and peace and love and Christian charity? How could they not give him any presents? 'You're all bastards!' he said.

'There's no call for that, Henry!' said his mother. Nigel looked smug.

'I hate you all!' said Henry. 'The only one I like is the tortoise. And now he's gone. And I don't blame him. He's gone!'

So saying, he up-ended the box. Elinor squawked but nothing fell out apart from straw. Henry turned on his family, all of whom were gulping wine and stuffing their faces with pudding. 'What about the spirit of Christmas?' he went on. 'What about peace and love? I've got a copy of *Our Lady of the Flowers* upstairs, Nigel, which I looked out especially for you. I got a lovely . . .' – he judged it best not to actually use the words 'face flannel' – '. . . piece of bathroom equipment for you, Elinor, and for you, Maisie, I . . .'

What had he got for Maisie? Had he managed to get her anything? 'I feel that Christmas is a time when we should make up our differences and try and start afresh. This year hasn't been easy. Why can't we all try and start the new one in the spirit of giving and sharing and forgiveness?' His voice was breaking. He was, he realized with horror, going to cry. 'I expect that poor little bastard has taken his shell back where he came from. And I can't be bothered to take any more. I'm going.'

He heard his mother say something about getting above himself. He noticed Maisie and Elinor, their faces suddenly alive with concern, get to their feet. He noticed, too, a worryingly concerned look on Jondon's face. Before the physical-training instructor could take him in his arms and croon tender things to him, Henry blundered through the hall and into the street where thick white flakes of snow were driving through the darkness.

Somewhere out here, he said to himself, is the tortoise. The tortoise understands. I had a tortoise once and that tortoise understood. No one else understands. I am alone. Now and for ever. Come to me, tortoise. Come to me. As he slammed the door behind him he realized he had drunk three bottles of champagne and half a bottle of cognac. Come to me, tortoise! Silent tortoise! Holy tortoise! Born the King of Tortoises! Oh come, let us adore him. To-ortoise! Behind him he could hear voices but he did not listen. He went on up the icy street, drawing his head deep downward into the hideous jersey that armoured him as seriously as a reptile's skin.

After Henry had gone everyone was quiet for quite a long time. 'Well,' said his mother, in the end, 'he was always saying we shouldn't bother with presents. Every year he says it.'

'He does,' said Elinor's mother, 'I get sick of hearing it!'

Mrs Farr Senior looked narrowly at her opposite granny. 'That's no reason, of course,' she said, 'to be horrible to him.'

'I thought,' said the ex-receptionist, whom Maisie always referred to as Granny Two, 'that it was your idea not to give him any presents!'

'It was, Mummy!' said Nigel.

'I can't remember whose it was!' said Mrs Farr Senior, in a tone that suggested that the idea could not have possibly come from her. She smiled crookedly round at the table and added, 'I love all my children equally. They are all marvellous!'

Maisie looked as if she was going to weep. Elinor put her elbows on the table and stared at the pudding in blank despair. She had been cooking since seven-thirty that morning. Why did she bother? Just so as they could sit round her table and bitch about each other? Why? Why did families have to include other people? Why couldn't she and Henry and Maisie have gone away to a health farm or to Crisis at Christmas or somewhere where they could have done something useful. She reached for the white wine.

'When Henry was little I gave him a tortoise!' said Granny One, who was the only person round the table still visibly unmoved by Henry's display. 'And he was devoted to it. He used to give it bits of tomato which it used to chew off. It ate lettuce too and he put it in a crate for the winter. It was called John. He was never a very imaginative child. He had a rat called Paul. I said, "Can't you think of a more original name than Paul?" and he said he couldn't!'

Maisie was now sobbing openly.

'In the end,' said Henry's mother calmly, 'the tortoise was eaten by rats!'

Jondon seemed to find this interesting. 'By Paul?' he said, keenly.

'Paul? What do you mean, Paul?' said Henry's mother, giving her younger son's lover a sulky look.

'Paul,' said Jondon patiently, 'was a rat!'

Mrs Farr snorted. 'He wasn't a bad bloke!' she said. 'He was no great shakes, but he wasn't a rat. For God's sake!'

Maisie leaned across the table. She was wearing a low-cut blouse and since her transformation over the summer had shaved off most of her hair. 'We've been horrible to him,' she said, 'and he's not a horrible man. He's sweet and good and kind and deep down he really cares for us all!'

A respectful silence greeted this remark. Elinor's mother said in a low voice that if there were real human feelings in Henry, they were very deep down *indeed*.

'He may be awful sometimes,' went on Maisie, 'but he's trying. He really is. He really wants to be like other people and give presents and be nice to people!'

Elinor, too, wiped a tear away from her eye. 'What he said about giving and Christmas,' she said, 'is so true, isn't it?'

Nigel said that it was, adding that it was especially surprising to hear it from his brother's lips. He went on to say that he always felt that Henry had never liked him. He too started to cry. He had never felt easy, he said, about his gayness in Henry's presence. Mrs Farr Senior asked him what he meant by that, at which Jondon, who was by now also in tears, started to try to explain.

Then Elinor said, 'We must go out and bring him back. We must go out and get him a present!'

Maisie pointed out that six o' clock on Christmas day was not the ideal time to buy a present. She wasn't criticizing anyone, she said, glaring at Granny One, but she had always been against the plan of not giving Henry anything.

It was at this point that from under the sink a small grey object emerged and started to walk towards the dining table. The tortoise seemed cheerful. Its four feet clicked noisily against the kitchen tiles as its scaly head snaked this way and that. When it got to Mrs Farr Senior it stopped and looked up at her. It put its head on one side and watched her carefully with its beady little eyes. In its mouth was a wisp of straw.

'I know,' said Maisie, 'we could give Henry the tortoise. We could tell him that we bought it for him only it escaped in the night and that's why we pretended that we hadn't bought him a present.'

Her mother was watching her carefully. The tortoise, bored with Mrs Farr Senior, started off in the direction of the fridge. 'That wouldn't be the truth though, would it?' said Henry's mother.

Nigel laughed. When he laughed he looked suddenly like his mother. 'Who cares about the truth?' he said. 'It's Christmas!'

Maisie was getting increasingly excited. She said, 'We could say it was an amazingly expensive tortoise. That's why it's from all of us. To replace the tortoise he had when he was small. And we could all say we're sorry. And then he could give us our presents.'

Nigel started to say something which seemed to suggest that he personally wasn't crazy about *Our Lady of the Flowers* and that in his opinion Jean Genet was homophobic. Elinor said, 'Would he believe it, though?'

Mrs Farr Senior looked at her daughter-in-law. 'Henry,' she said, 'believes only what he wants to believe. Anyway, he's always wanted a tortoise.'

The tortoise had reached the fridge and seemed to be trying to walk through it.

'We'll have to wrap it up,' said Elinor's mother, 'or put a bow round its neck or something. Not that Henry cares about things like that!'

Out on the street, sobered by the cold wind and the snow in his face, Henry was on his way home. He had been unable to find the tortoise. It was probably dead by now anyway. It was all his fault. If he hadn't been such a mean-spirited, narrow, bitter little *worm*, none of this would have happened. Tortoises were sensitive creatures. They could probably spot when someone was a hundred-carat arsehole. 'And that's what I am,' said Henry, 'a hundred-carat arsehole. That's all I am.'

Everything that had gone wrong with last year had been his fault, he decided. *There is no such thing as unhappiness in personal relationships. There are only failures of character.*

He knew where his failure lay. Like so many Englishmen, he seemed unable to understand what he actually felt. And even when he had worked out what it was he felt, he was incapable of doing anything about it. *Maybe that's why I always identified with tortoises,* he said to himself as he turned into the front garden of 54 Maple Drive. *I'm slow on the uptake, out of date, cold-blooded and have a tendency to retreat into my shell whenever anyone comes near me.*

How could he make the next year any better? By discovering his feelings and acting on them. By being true to whatever turned out to be his real self, his real feelings.

So what did he feel about them? About Maisie and Elinor and about everyone else now waiting for him inside the house, with the possible exception of the Turkish physical-training instructor. He didn't think he would ever know what he felt about Jondon except that it was not unlike what he had felt for Mikhail, Saul, Damien, Randy and Lee.

As he came to the front door he decided he thought he knew what he felt about his family, even if it had taken him twelve months to find it. He knew what he felt. If he was honest. And why, while we were at it, was he so ashamed of his feelings? Why was he frightened to dignify what he sometimes felt for Maisie and Elinor with that word they used all the time in the magazines? If it was only the *word* love he was afraid of, perhaps that was because, unlike some people, he was determined to take it seriously. 'I'm just an average guy,' he said out loud to the empty street, 'with slightly lower than average feelings. But I'm here. And I won't go away. OK?'

With the heavy sense that the rest of his life was just about to begin, he took the last few steps towards his own home and his own people. And as he did so the door opened, and there in the light and warmth of his suburban house were the ones he cared most about in the world. If you excepted the twenty-nine-year-old physical-training instructor.

In the middle of the group were Maisie and Elinor, and Elinor was holding up a small tortoise with a large red bow round its neck. She put her arms round him and said, 'Happy Christmas, Henry!'

Henry blinked. So did the tortoise. Both of them looked more than usually lively.

'Happy Christmas, Henry!' said everyone else. Henry picked up the tortoise and, very gently and slowly, began to stroke its shell.